There the ships go to and fro, and Leviathan, which you formed to frolic there.

—PSALM 104:26 (NIV)

Can you pull in Leviathan with a fishhook or tie down its tongue with a rope?
Can you put a cord through its nose or pierce its jaw with a hook?

—JOB 41:1-2 (NIV)

MYSTERIES & WONDERS *of the* BIBLE

MYSTERIES & WONDERS *of the* BIBLE

SEEKING LEVIATHAN
MILKAH'S STORY

Virginia Wise

 Guideposts

A Gift from Guideposts

Thank you for your purchase! We want to express our gratitude for your support with a special gift just for you.

Dive into **Spirit Lifters**, a complimentary e-book that will fortify your faith, offering solace during challenging moments. Its 31 carefully selected scripture verses will soothe and uplift your soul.

Please use the QR code or go to **guideposts.org/ spiritlifters** to download.

Mysteries & Wonders of the Bible is a trademark of Guideposts.

Published by Guideposts
100 Reserve Road, Suite E200, Danbury, CT 06810
Guideposts.org

Scripture references are from the following sources: *The Holy Bible, King James Version* (KJV). *The Holy Bible, New International Version* (NIV). Copyright © 1973, 1978, 1984, 2011 by Biblica, Inc. Used by permission of Zondervan. All rights reserved worldwide. www.zondervan.com.

Cover and interior design by Müllerhaus
Cover illustration by Brian Call represented by Illustration Online LLC.
Typeset by Aptara, Inc.

ISBN 978-1-961251-80-9 (hardcover)
ISBN 978-1-961251-81-6 (softcover)
ISBN 978-1-961251-82-3 (epub)

Printed and bound in the United States of America

SEEKING LEVIATHAN

MILKAH'S STORY

CAST OF CHARACTERS

Amarsin • Ninsun's and Urshanabi's oldest daughter

Javen • a trader who sails on Peleg's boat

Jubal • Milkah's neighbor and small-time trader; married to Shiptu

Kalumtum • a trader who sails with her husband, Peleg

Kubaba • Javen's mother

Kushim • Javen's cousin

Milkah • a young Sumerian woman

Nahor • Milkah's betrothed

Ninsun • wealthy Sumerian woman; married to Urshanabi

Peleg • a trader who owns a reed sailboat; married to Kalumtum

Shiptu • Milkah's neighbor and small-time trader; married to Jubal

Urshanabi • a wealthy trader; married to Ninsun

Uruk • Jubal's and Shiptu's donkey; ancient Mesopotamian city founded c. 4500 BC

Zimu • Javen's youngest sister

GLOSSARY OF TERMS

abba • father

Dilmun • located on the coast of the Arabian Peninsula; mentioned in ancient Sumerian literature as a commercial center as well as the mythical land of the gods; much of its history remains a mystery

einkorn • an ancient variety of wheat

emmer • an ancient variety of wheat

imma • mother

kelek • round boat made of animal hides stretched over a frame of branches

mangar (Luciobarbus esocinus) • large species of fish living in the Tigris-Euphrates River system that can grow to over 300 pounds

Nanna • Sumerian god of the moon

onager • Asian wild ass

Sippar • ancient Sumerian, and later Babylonian, city located on the Euphrates River

CHAPTER ONE

Milkah sat stunned and silent in the doorway of her mud-brick house. A warm breeze swept up from the barley fields, carrying the scent of wet dirt. Sunlight fell across her bare feet and bathed the hard-packed, earthen courtyard in a golden yellow glow. She pulled her feet closer to her body, into the shade of the house, and wrapped her arms around her knees. The jangle of her copper bracelets seemed too loud in the solemn quiet.

This house had never been silent before. There had always been the laughter of her younger sisters, the low murmuring of her *imma* and sister-in-law as they lit smoky fires and stirred a pot of lentils, or the good-natured shouts of her *abba* and older brother as they jostled for the last piece of flatbread at dinnertime.

Milkah had not bothered to light a fire today. She had not soaked the lentils or ground the barley into flour. The morning's goat milk sat untouched beside the hearth, beneath a circling fly. She had no appetite. How could she, when everything she had known and loved was gone?

The funeral rites were over, the dirt floor smoothed flat over the graves where her family would lie together forever, beneath the home they had loved. Now she did not know what to do but sit and wait. Wait for what, she did not know. "Show me what to do, God," she whispered. "Show me that You are still here, with me."

A shadow blocked the sun, and Milkah looked up. Her neighbor, Shiptu, stood in front of her, a serious expression on her face. "I did not hear you coming," Milkah said then looked down again.

"Your thoughts are elsewhere, I imagine." Shiptu adjusted the coarse fabric of her single-sleeved tunic that covered one shoulder and left the other bare, squatted on the ground near Milkah, and sighed. A donkey brayed in the distance. "You cannot stay here, you know."

"Yes," Milkah said without looking up. "I know." She turned the bangle on her wrist in a slow circle. The metal felt familiar and comforting against her skin. "I have never been farther than a half day's walk from the village."

Shiptu hesitated. "No one here will marry you now. They do not want any part of this."

Milkah's eyes flashed as they shot up to Shiptu. "Part of what?"

Shiptu frowned and made a vague motion with her hand. "This..."

"Just come out and say it, Shiptu."

Shiptu grunted. "That is no way to talk to a woman who has known you all your life. I have been a friend to your mother since she first arrived from the coast—"

"Please, just say what you are thinking," Milkah said in a softer voice.

Shiptu lifted her hands in a gesture of helplessness. "Since you insist. You know how people are. With the gods turned against you—"

"Not 'gods.' My family still worshiped the One True God." Not many people did anymore. Memory of the old times faded with each generation, blotted out by the lure of new gods that could be seen and touched and understood. The great cities had glorious ziggurats soaring toward the heavens so the gods could come down the pyramid steps to their people. The educated men living behind the glistening city walls understood that the new ways were better, more advanced, and felt sorry for the country folk who clung to their myths of a lost garden, remembered a righteous ancestor they called Noah, and taught their children there was only one God.

"Either way. There is not so much difference between them all, is there? They all need to be placated. Whatever you have done to offend them..." Shiptu shook her head. The blue beads and copper ornaments in her headdress rattled with the movement. "Well, no man will risk a god's curse coming on his house."

"My abba always sacrificed burnt offerings for all of us on the family altar. We welcomed every guest who came our way. We never turned anyone away. My abba—my entire family—feared God and did right. We followed the old ways."

Shiptu reached out and patted Milkah's arm. "Even so, dear. Even so." She shifted her weight. "Sometimes we offend a god without knowing it."

"I only serve the One True God."

"Then you must have offended Him. Offer a better sacrifice. Promise your firstborn child."

"Never. My God does not ask that."

"How can you expect the favor of any god when you refuse to do what they require? When we offend them, we must pay. Then they will turn away their anger, and all will be well. It is not complicated."

"We did not offend Him."

Shiptu pinched the bridge of her nose between her thumb and forefinger. "Milkah, you are not making this easy."

"Please. I just want to be left alone." Milkah moved her gaze beyond the small courtyard, to the fields and the long, narrow irrigation ditch lined with date palms. Their green fronds swayed in the breeze. Sunlight sparkled against the muddy water. Milkah had looked at those fields, those trees, those waters every day of her nineteen years on earth. She could not imagine a life anywhere else. This land was in her blood. Her abba had been born here, and his abba before him. And they had all faithfully worshiped the One True God.

"You know I cannot do that."

"I need more time."

"You do not have time. You have no father, no husband, no brother. You cannot stay here alone."

"I will go to Nahor's family. They might take me in."

Shiptu did not respond.

"I waited all those years for them to afford the bride-price my abba set. We should have already been married when he was killed."

"'Should have' counts for nothing in times like these."

Milkah stood up so fast it made her feel woozy. She remembered she had not eaten that day, and she pressed a hand against the cool mud wall for support. "I will go talk to them now."

"Come with us, Milkah," Shiptu said quietly. "We have a place for you in our boat. We pass right through your mother's hometown. We will find her people there."

"We cannot be sure they are still there. My imma left there to marry my abba twenty-five years ago, and she never went back."

"No, no, they are still there. You have a few cousins, at least. We pass through there every year, so I would know. And anyway, I would never steer you wrong. You know that, do you not? You can trust us. Your mother always did. The entire village does. We always come back with a fair trade for their goods, do we not?" Shiptu caught Milkah's eye. "Your father trusted us to trade for him." She let the statement hang in the air.

Milkah turned away. Her bare feet pounded the earth as she hurried across the courtyard. "I have to try," she said without looking back. The path to Nahor's house was as familiar as her own body. Her feet knew every stone, every curve, every palm tree along the way. His family worshiped the One God too, so her abba and Nahor's abba had arranged their marriage from a young age. It grew harder every year to find like-minded families to marry into. Milkah had been especially fortunate because she had liked Nahor. He had been quick to joke, and his smile lit up his entire face. He never raised his voice to her. He was kind to animals. He was a good man who had offered the promise of a good life for both of them.

Milkah's future had died with him.

Three women stood chatting beside the dirt path as Milkah hurried past. One of the women held a baby in a sling, his big dark eyes following Milkah's movements. She knew these women, had grown up alongside them, gone hungry with them when the crops failed, celebrated with them when there was a marriage or birth in the village. Milkah and her sisters had brought figs and honey when the baby was born. They had sat with his mother in the cool of the evening, whispering and giggling as they admired his tiny hands and feet. Now the women fell silent as she passed, and the young mother made a sign against the evil eye.

Milkah pretended not to notice. Nothing they did could be worse than what had already happened. Her life had ended even though she still walked through the village alongside the living. Before the Terrible Day, she had walked in peace with the One God, trusting that life would go on as it always had, following the predictable rhythms of village life. Good begot good, and evil begot evil. This was the way the world worked. Life might not always be easy, but it would be good, and it would be secure with the One God—the just God—watching over them all. Milkah had kept that knowledge deep inside her since childhood, and it had filled her with a quiet, steady warmth.

Now, fearful questions that she had never before thought to ask boiled within her. Did the One God really have power over her life? And if so, did He actually care enough to intervene? Ever since the Terrible Day, she had become consumed by a growing, gnawing terror that life was nothing but a series of random events.

It had all started on an ordinary morning, with shouting in the fields. Her abba's panicked voice had pierced the still, dry air, followed by the growl of a dog. More shouting. Milkah, her imma, sister-in-law, and two younger sisters had flown from the house, leaving a pot of lentils to burn. It was only when they drew closer that they understood her abba's words. "Do not leave the house!" he had screamed. "Stay away!"

The women had stared, confused. The men were shouting as they tore through the barley toward them, trampling the stalks as if it didn't matter. And in the end, it hadn't. There was no one left to eat the harvest now.

"Get back in the house!" Milkah's older brother had shouted, his face locked in an expression of shock and fear. "They are mad! All of them, mad!" His wife had stood for a moment, watching, before she turned and ran, mud splattering up from her bare feet. Then three dogs had erupted from the barley field, eyes wild, mouths foaming, and chased Milkah's sister-in-law as she fled. Milkah had stood frozen, watching but feeling as if she were not really there—that none of this could really be happening—then closed her eyes and covered her ears when the dogs reached the woman.

And then the dogs had wheeled around and descended on the rest of them.

Somehow, in the chaos, Milkah had not been bitten. She, her abba, and her four-year-old sister were the only ones of her family spared. Nahor and Milkah's sister-in-law had not survived the attack. As for the others, they all knew that nothing but a miracle could save a person from the bite of a mad dog. Milkah's abba had offered their finest goats as burnt offerings to the One God as they had pleaded with Him to intervene. After that, the ones who had been bitten could do nothing but wait, day after day, huddled on the reed mats in the stifling heat of their one-room house, watching each other for the first sign of the sickness to come. Eventually, the madness that brings death took each of them.

Afterward, Milkah and her abba tried to make sense of it all. He offered another burnt offering at the family altar, seeking the One God's protection and restoration. The three survivors had prayed and held each other and had tried to remember how to go through the motions of normal life. During the night, Milkah's little sister would scoot onto Milkah's sleeping mat, snuggling close in the stillness, and Milkah would feel that she could go on because she was still needed and loved.

Then, less than a week after her family had been buried, Milkah's abba had offered to take her little sister down to the river to play. "Rest," he said to Milkah. "You do not sleep anymore. Your sorrow is too heavy. Lie down and forget for a while."

Milkah had nodded, numb with grief, as she settled onto her sleeping mat. She watched her sister smile for the first time in days as their abba lifted her to his shoulders and strode through the courtyard, toward the muddy riverbank beyond the fields and date palms.

Milkah did not know how long she had slept, but when she awoke, groggy and disoriented, she wandered outside in time to see her abba and sister in the middle of the distant river, splashing and laughing. Milkah shaded her eyes from the sun and smiled. Perhaps life would go on after all, and those who were left of her family could find their way back to happiness. But then her abba's hand jerked to his chest and his expression changed to one of confusion then pain. He fell down, dropping his small daughter alongside him. Both of them disappeared beneath the muddy water. By the time Milkah reached them, it was too late.

Now she had no one left.

Ever since then, the villagers had kept their distance. An entire family attacked by a pack of mad dogs? Then the survivors drown in the river? Bad things happened sometimes—that was life—but this was too random, too senseless. It sent a ripple of fear through the village that was best soothed by the reminder that this couldn't happen to them. This kind of thing only happened to those who deserved it somehow.

Even Nahor's family had retreated, despite the ties that had bound them to Milkah's family for as long as Milkah could remember. Her stomach churned as she approached their house. She straightened the fabric of her tunic where it draped from her shoulder and whispered a prayer to the One God that Nahor's family would take her in. The prayer had escaped automatically, and she wondered if she meant it. Her eyes cut to the muddy river that had swallowed her abba and sister. How powerful could her God really be? She wanted to believe in His power and love—with all her heart she wanted to—but a pang of doubt gripped her like the iron jaws of the mad dogs. Perhaps they had bitten her after all, in a strange sort of way that could not be seen by human eyes but left her wounded nonetheless.

The front door opened before Milkah reached it. Nahor's mother stood in the cool shadow of the interior. Her eyes were red and swollen, and she wasn't wearing any kohl or jewelry, as she normally did. "Stop."

Milkah froze.

"Have you come to bring more death to our house?"

Milkah opened her mouth then closed it again without answering.

"Who is there?" A deep voice boomed from behind Nahor's mother. His father appeared in the doorway. The man's face hardened when he saw Milkah and he stepped protectively in front of his wife. "We trusted your abba," he said. "With our son. Our only son." The last sentence carried so much quiet rage that Milkah took a step back.

"It was not our fault. The dogs came out of nowhere—"

"And killed no one else in the village."

"If my son had not been betrothed to you, he would have been spared. God's wrath fell on him only because he was bound to your house."

Milkah shook her head. "No."

"God does not punish the innocent."

"This was not punishment."

"Then what was it?"

Milkah took a step back. She didn't have an answer for that.

"Leave us," Nahor's mother said from behind her husband. She made the sign against the evil eye.

"But what will I do?" Milkah held up her hands to them. "Where will I go? I have no one."

"Would you have God strike us too? We cannot help one that He has seen fit to cast out. You are on your own."

CHAPTER TWO

Milkah saw that Shiptu was waiting beside the path that led to Nahor's house, beneath the shade of a date palm. With one hand raised to her forehead to block the sun's glare, she watched Milkah approach. Milkah knew what Shiptu would say and tried to walk past her, eyes set on the distant horizon. But Shiptu reached out and grabbed Milkah's wrist, her copper bracelets jangling in the silence. "It is bad news. I can see it in your face."

Milkah shook Shiptu's hand away. She didn't want to respond. She wanted to run back to the little mud-brick house that had sheltered her all her life, lie down on her sleeping mat above her family's graves, cover her eyes, and wait until somehow, miraculously, the world righted itself again.

"Milkah. Listen to reason."

"There is no reason. Nothing makes sense anymore."

Shiptu sighed. "There is only one thing that makes sense for you now. Come with us. We leave today." She swept her hand through the air. "There is nothing for you here anymore and no one to help you. You have no choice."

"I have lived here my whole life."

"And now you will live somewhere else. Go pack what you can carry. We will wait for you, but we have to leave soon."

Milkah stood without speaking for a moment. She looked past Shiptu, to a cluster of women standing in the entrance of a mud-brick courtyard, staring at her and whispering to one another. Beyond them, her house lay empty and silent. Milkah released a long, deep breath. "All right. I will go with you."

"Good. You know we are doing this because we care about you. I wish there was another way, but no one will help you here anymore."

"I know." The realization lay like a stone in her belly, although she was almost too numb to feel it. Nothing felt real anymore.

"Hurry. We need to get going."

Milkah started to turn away, but Shiptu reached out and put her hands on her shoulders. Her touch felt warm and reassuring after the long days and nights spent alone. Shiptu looked Milkah in the eyes with a firm, steady gaze. "You are doing the right thing. We will take care of you. I promise."

Milkah felt herself letting go inside. She wanted so desperately to feel safe again. Maybe God had a new plan for her, one that would take her far away, to a better place. "Thank you. No one else will help me."

"I know." Shiptu squeezed Milkah's shoulders before dropping her hands. "But we will. You will always have us."

The ground felt unsteady beneath Milkah's feet as she hurried to her house. She drank in the sight of the familiar row of date palms, the old crack in the wall surrounding her courtyard, the way the sunlight reflected off the whitewash to create patterns of shadow and light. Inside, the open-air hearth lay still and silent, waiting for a fire that she would never light again. Her bare feet slapped the beaten earth as she crossed the courtyard and ducked into the dim interior of her home. She worked quickly, trying not to think or feel as she folded her sleeping mat, then gathered everything she could carry. She put on her leather sandals and slipped on the copper arm-band, hoop earrings, and beaded headband that she had inherited from her mother. A strand of black hair had fallen from her braided bun, and she tucked it beneath the headband.

Then she stopped, crouched down, and pressed the palm of her hand against the dirt floor, where her family rested below. There was too much to say, so she said nothing at all. She just remembered for a moment. Then she stood back up, adjusted her tunic, and walked away without looking back.

"What will happen to my house?" Milkah asked Shiptu as soon as she reached her.

"Do not worry. We have made arrangements for you. We have sold it and will keep the money safe for you."

"Sold it? To who?"

"Your neighbors. It is a good house, and they need more room now that their son is getting married. They will have children soon. It will be good for them to add your house to theirs."

Milkah hesitated. Another family would sit beside her hearth and sleep above the graves of her parents and siblings. She imagined the footsteps of her neighbors' children in her courtyard, their laughter echoing off the mud-brick walls. She imagined her neighbors' new daughter-in-law cooking in the courtyard where Milkah and her mother had cooked, churning goat butter where they had, grinding grain where they had. "I cannot…"

Shiptu took Milkah by the hand and pulled her toward the river's edge, where Shiptu's husband waited. "You can and you will. I know it is hard. But remember, nothing lasts here. The Euphrates floods every year, does it not? Everything washes away in the end. And your house will not stand forever. It will wash away eventually, like everything else here."

"But we repair it every year. As long as someone is here, rebuilding after the rains, it will last."

Shiptu stopped walking and looked Milkah in the eye. "Someone will be here to repair it. It just will not be you."

The words sank into Milkah like a dark, storm-filled cloud. But there was no other choice. A woman couldn't live alone in a village that did not want her.

"Is she coming?" Shiptu's husband, Jubal, asked as soon as they were in earshot.

"Yes," Shiptu said. She turned back to Milkah and motioned for her to hurry. "Yes, of course she is."

Jubal stood beside their *kelek*, a round boat made of animal hides stretched over a frame of branches. The Euphrates flowed southward, so when they reached the Great Water, Jubal and Shiptu would take the boat apart and walk back, against the current. Their donkey, Uruk, would carry the disassembled pieces on his back. Now, the beast of burden waited alongside Jubal, his skin twitching every time a fly landed. On the way down, he would help steady their path as the kelek floated with the current.

Uruk leaned forward and brayed at Milkah as she approached. His long yellow teeth glistened in the late morning sun. "Easy now, Uruk," Jubal murmured and scratched behind the animal's ears. "We are late," he said as he turned back toward Milkah. "Let us go." Milkah felt a strange uneasiness at his tone of voice. And there was a distance behind his eyes that unnerved her. But the unease was as vague as the whisper of the wings of a bird that flies in the night. Then Jubal smiled, and Milkah realized that she had been looking for danger that wasn't there. She recognized the familiar crinkles around the corners of his eyes that she had seen since childhood, the endearing, crooked front tooth, and she relaxed. "I am sorry." Milkah walked faster. "It was not easy to leave."

"No, I suppose not." Jubal scratched his jawline. "Well, in you go." He reached out a large, workworn hand and steadied Milkah as she stepped into the boat. It bobbed under her weight, and Jubal chuckled as he tightened his grip on her arm. "Watch it."

Milkah dropped to a crouch as the boat dipped and began to spin. Jubal let go of her arm to grab the rope attached to the kelek. He pulled it toward him until the spinning stopped and the vessel bobbed gently on the current. Milkah felt queasy, and she wanted to hop back onto good, stable land. She had ridden in a kelek before—it was the common way to travel—but her body knew this trip would be like no other. She twisted to look back at the village, but it set the boat in motion again, so she had to keep her attention forward, away from everything she had ever known.

Shiptu stepped lightly into the kelek and settled into place beside Milkah. Parcels of barley, *emmer* wheat, sesame seeds, and dates filled the rest of the boat. There was no shelter, just the round, open kelek, exposed to the sky and sun. Jubal pushed the vessel out into the current, then tugged Uruk's lead. The donkey brayed, stomped a hoof, and plodded forward. A moment passed before the rope went taut, jerking the kelek. Milkah grabbed the side to steady herself as the boat rocked then settled into a steady, forward motion.

Milkah watched the familiar row of date palms as they sailed past, followed by long rows of irrigation ditches and barley fields. The sun caught on the water and the grain, turning everything golden in the yellow light. A child ran alongside the water and waved. Milkah recognized him and shouted goodbye, but her words were lost in the humid air as the boat bobbed past the child and glided downriver.

They began to pass fields and mud-brick homes that were less familiar, until suddenly Milkah realized she was passing a village she had never seen before. The houses were constructed just like hers had been, the fields surrounding them grew the same crops, but they all looked different somehow. And when the people stooping in those fields turned to look at her, the faces were those of strangers. "I have never been here before," she murmured.

"You will see a city before we reach the sea," Shiptu said. Her eyes were closed against the glare of the sun. "And the ziggurat."

Milkah felt a strange excitement at the thought. There was a world beyond her village that she had not seen. "I never thought I would go this far from home." She watched as another boy ran alongside the riverbank, shouting words she couldn't quite make out. He flashed a smile, and she waved.

"This is your home now." Shiptu waved across the water in front of them without opening her eyes.

"And then what?" Milkah asked. The endlessness of the river made her feel small inside. It went on and on, farther than she could imagine. She wanted to believe there was a safe place waiting for her, somewhere. Otherwise, she felt as if the endlessness would swallow her.

"Your mother's people." Shiptu shifted her weight and sighed. She tilted her head back so that her face caught the sun. "I could go to sleep," she murmured.

"But how will we find them?"

"You worry too much. We should not have trouble finding them."

"But what if they will not take me in?"

"They will."

"How can you know?"

Shiptu opened her eyes. "Who knows what will happen in life? What can we do but try to placate the gods and hope for the best?"

Milkah stared ahead, to where the ribbon of muddy water met the distant horizon. "You think things might be okay for me now?"

Shiptu hesitated. "Well, who can say? That depends on your God, does it not? You refused to offer your firstborn, so I do not know." She dipped her hand in the water and let the current flow around her fingers. "I have never failed to offer what the gods demand. They have never punished me like they have punished you."

Milkah turned away. "We have already been over this. My God is not punishing me."

Shiptu laughed. "Say what you will, the evidence is still there."

Milkah swiveled to look at Shiptu. "Then why have you invited someone who is cursed to travel with you? Why are you helping me?"

Shiptu paused. The water swirled around her fingers and formed little dips in the smooth, sparkling surface. "I am doing what is best. You will understand someday." Shiptu pulled her hand from the water and wiped it across the front of her tunic. "It will be all right. We can show you how to leave a sacrifice at the ziggurat. The gods will hear you then. That is where they come down to listen to us."

"No, that is not where my God lives."

"Then where is He?"

Milkah waved her hand in a broad arc. "Everywhere."

Shiptu grunted. "Well, where was He when the mad dogs attacked? Or when your father and sister disappeared into the Euphrates?" She shook her head. "No god can be everywhere. It is not possible."

"With my God, all things are possible." Milkah said the words so quietly that Shiptu couldn't hear. For the first time in her life, the statement felt hollow. Never before had she felt the pull to find God in a place that could be seen or touched. But now... Milkah pushed the thought away.

She tried not to think about anything after that. Instead, she watched the farmers in the fields alongside the river. They stooped and straightened, stooped and straightened, as though locked in an exhausting, repetitive dance. Then they passed a small village where all the houses were made of reeds. Each home was taller than Milkah's had been, and the roofs were rounded like a barrel, instead of flat. She studied a group of women sitting on the riverbank, weaving reed mats, until the boat whisked past and the village disappeared.

Jubal and Uruk trudged alongside the river, heads down, feet moving in a soft, steady beat against the mud. The afternoon sun hovered over the water and pressed against Milkah like warm hands. Its rays beat down on her bare shoulder and face, until she closed her eyes and drifted into the soft haze of sleep. The boat rocked gently beneath her as she huddled against a sack of barley, forgetting everything for a moment.

Something woke Milkah with a start. She straightened up, alarmed but unsure why. The fog of sleep still clung to her. And then the boat lurched violently to the side. She gasped and scrambled to regain her balance. "What is happening?"

Shiptu's face twitched, and Milkah caught the flash of fear on it. Her eyes flicked to the water, searching.

"Steady now!" Jubal shouted from the bank and began to pull the lead rope, hand over hand. His eyes darted from side to side, studying the river as he strained to reel them in.

Something bumped the boat again. Milkah grasped the sides and stared into the muddy current. She could see nothing. "What is it?" she asked in a low voice, afraid that whatever lay hidden underwater might hear her.

Shiptu shook her head.

Milkah's heart pounded inside her throat. She wished that she had never gotten into the kelek. She belonged on the good, solid land where she had been born. The water stilled. Milkah twisted around, desperate to see beneath the river's flat brown surface. There was no movement except for the eddies that swirled around the boat as Jubal pulled them to the riverbank. She exhaled, and her body began to relax.

Then there was a splash right beside the boat. A flash of silver. Wet, slick scales slid past and disappeared beneath them. The smooth, shining body was bigger than the boat, bigger than a grown man. Milkah's heart rocketed into her throat again.

But Shiptu's expression eased, and she laughed. "It is nothing. It is fine."

"No," Milkah said. "There is something there."

"It is just a *mangar*," Shiptu shouted to Jubal. He nodded and let the lead rope slacken until they were drifting freely again. Shiptu turned back to Milkah. "You have seen mangar before. You know they have no teeth. They cannot bite. There is nothing to be afraid of."

Milkah felt a flush of embarrassment. Everyone who lived alongside the Euphrates ate mangar. She should have known better than to be afraid. "I have never seen one that big before."

"Have you not heard that the priests in the cities wear their skins as cloaks? A priest could climb right inside a mangar, if he wanted to, and have room left over."

Jubal laughed from the riverbank. "They look like fish, when you see them in their temples, walking around in those funny-looking skins."

"Quiet!" Shiptu hissed. "Do you want to bring a curse down on us?"

"Their gods are not here. We are too far from their ziggurats. There are other things to fear in the water."

Shiptu frowned.

"What things?" Milkah asked. "Do you mean the annual floods?" The Euphrates brought destructive floods, but it also brought life to the crops. They knew and expected the cycle—death and life, then death again, in an endless march that the villagers were powerless against.

Jubal chuckled, but his eyes were not smiling. "No." He nodded toward Shiptu. "She knows, and she was afraid. She is pretending otherwise now, but do not let her fool you."

Shiptu's head snapped toward Jubal. "And so were you. You reeled us in fast enough, did you not?"

"Of course I was afraid. There is no shame in it. A smart man knows what to fear."

"Stop." Shiptu shook her head at her husband. "Do not speak its name while we are on the water."

"What?" Milkah's head turned from Jubal to Shiptu, then back again. "Do not speak whose name?"

Jubal's eyes roved over the water, then met Milkah's. "I will tell you when we are on land. Shiptu is right. It is better not to speak of these things while on the water. Who knows if it might hear?"

"I do not believe in the new gods."

"This is not a god. Not one of ours, anyway."

Milkah frowned. She had a lot to think about while she waited for the sun to set.

Jubal hauled the boat to the river's edge as orange rays of sun spread across the water in a warm glow. The entire world felt soft and golden in the gentle evening light. They hit the bank with a thud and a splash. Milkah stumbled onto land, and her leather sandals sank into the soft mud. Her legs felt weak and rubbery from sitting too long. Shiptu grabbed her arm and steadied her. "You will get used to it," she said with a smile. "Tomorrow will be a better day."

Milkah looked around. "There is nothing here." Flat plains stretched along both sides of the wide brown river. A white ibis stood on one leg, watching them. Milkah saw no other life, although she knew there must be animals slithering through the wild grass or beneath the water that she could not see. "Would it not be better to stop at a village for the night?"

Jubal scratched his jaw and shrugged. "You cannot always trust strangers."

"But…" Milkah looked toward the horizon. The sun was a sliver of orange against the earth, and darkness was seeping toward them.

"It is better this way," Shiptu said and patted Milkah on the shoulder. "When we reach the city, you will not be able to avoid the people. You will wish for this place then."

Milkah felt small against the vast sky and flat, humid plain. She had never slept in a place without people before. There had always been the low murmur of voices from other houses, the shouts and cries of children, the bleating of goats, and laughter in the distance. Here, the quiet settled into her bones and felt wrong.

Jubal unpacked a fishing net from the bundles on Uruk's back. The donkey brayed and swung his head around to nip at Jubal's hand.

"I will take care of him," Shiptu told Jubal. "Go on and see what you can catch for us." She clucked her tongue and patted Uruk on the flank. "Calm down now, little one. Supper is coming." Shiptu glanced over to Milkah. "Have you even met a stranger before?"

"Of course. People come down the river sometimes." Milkah frowned, trying to remember. But, hard as she tried, she could not think of a time that her familiar, steady life had been disrupted by a stranger. Every year had been the same—the floods, the planting, the harvest, and then the floods again. And always, there had been the knowledge that she would marry Nahor one day, fill their house with children, and repeat the lives of their parents. Life was supposed to go on like that, forever.

Milkah didn't want to think about it. "I will take care of the fuel." She turned toward the date palms in the distance.

"Do not wander out of earshot," Shiptu said as she unfastened the lead rope from Uruk's neck. "You do not know what you might find. Or what might find you."

Milkah kept glancing behind her as she loped along the riverbank. Jubal stood knee deep in the water as he flung his fishing net, just as her abba had done back home. She made sure not to leave his sight as she collected palm fronds for the fire. By the time she returned to camp, Shiptu had unpacked dates, figs, and unleavened barley bread. Uruk stood quietly, flicking his tail against the bugs that rose from the riverbank and buzzed in the still, night air.

Jubal trotted back from the water's edge, a handful of carp wriggling in his net. A short while later they were lounging by the fire, snacking on dates as the fish sizzled in the flames. The smoke rose into the night sky, toward the stars that spilled above them in a great dome. The sound of water slapping the riverbank was the only noise beyond their camp. "What were you talking about today?" Milkah asked. "What is in the water that you did not want to speak of?"

"Ah." Jubal leaned forward and turned one of the fish. "Have you not heard of the water beast?"

Milkah drew her knees to her chin and wrapped her arms around them. "The fish from the Great Water that sometimes swim up the Euphrates? The ones that grow big enough to eat a man whole?"

"The shark?" Jubal shrugged. "Some say so."

"And what do others say?"

"That there is a beast that roams the deep. They call it Leviathan."

Shiptu made a sign against the evil eye.

"You do not think it is the same as a shark?"

Jubal thought for a moment. "No. I have talked to enough boatmen about it. They say it looks nothing like a shark."

"Boatmen like to boast," Shiptu said.

"You are right," Jubal said. They all stared into the flames for a moment. "But they boast about things that have truth to them. They might exaggerate, but they do not outright lie. Not all of them, anyway. I have heard the story from too many witnesses."

"What does it look like?" Milkah asked.

Shiptu laughed. "They all say something different."

"You laugh now," Jubal said, "but you were not laughing when that mangar bumped the boat earlier."

"I thought it was a bull shark. You know they have been seen as far upriver as Sippar."

Jubal chuckled and nudged Shiptu with his elbow. "You should have seen your face."

Shiptu rolled her eyes. "You should have seen yours."

"I was worried about my beautiful wife." He leaned over and kissed the top of Shiptu's head. She pushed him away playfully but couldn't hide her smile.

Milkah wrapped her arms more tightly around her legs. This was the time of night when her younger sisters would have settled around her, their soft warm skin touching hers as one sister nestled in her lap and another put a head on her shoulder. Milkah looked past Shiptu and Jubal to the smooth, calm river. The surface was as black as the sky. "Does Leviathan come this far inland?"

"Not that I have ever heard of," Jubal said. "But who can say what a beast might do?"

"It is too big for these waters," Shiptu said.

"Do you believe that, or just hope that?" Jubal asked.

Shiptu grunted. "It is common sense."

"What does common sense have to do with any of this? There is nothing common or sensible about a beast."

"We have never seen any sign of it. Not once in all the years we have traded along the river."

"That does not mean it is not there."

Shiptu gave a dismissive wave with her hand and the bangles on her wrist jangled. "It is only in the Great Water. And anyway, we made the sacrifices last time we were at the ziggurat. The gods will protect us."

"It is her God that sends it, not ours." Jubal pointed a finger at Milkah.

Milkah straightened up. "What?"

"It is His beast, they say."

"The One True God's?"

"That is what they say."

"I do not understand."

Shiptu released a sharp bark of a laugh. "Who could possibly understand your God? He does not come down to the ziggurat. He does not have a home. He does not inhabit the bodies of idols." She shook her head. "How could He send out the leviathan when He is not even here to do it?"

Milkah frowned. She didn't have an answer. A few days ago, she would have. But now, the words stuck on her tongue and her stomach churned with questions. "You have seen your gods? Really seen them?"

"Well, I have seen the idols, obviously. That is good enough. And I have seen the priests who speak to them. And the ziggurats where the gods live."

"But the idols do not do anything," Milkah said. "They cannot talk or move. What good is that?"

"Hush!" Shiptu made a sign against the evil eye again. "Do you want them to hear?"

"They cannot hear. They are made of wood or stone."

"They can hear. Do you not understand anything? You think like a child. You are not a child anymore, you know. You should be married by now. And yet you cannot see what is right before you. Everyone knows the essence of the gods inhabits their idols." Shiptu clucked her tongue. "And even if you refuse to worship the idols, you cannot deny that the gods themselves come down to the ziggurats."

"Stairways to heaven," Jubal murmured. "You have never seen anything like it. They stretch up into the sky."

"Anyone who can create a thing like that knows something about the gods," Shiptu said.

"That is true," Jubal said. "These are educated men, brilliant men. They understand mathematics, astronomy, medicine. You cannot know more than them."

Milkah's brow furrowed. "It is not that I know more—"

"Then you do agree with them?"

"No, I just—"

"If you had been to the cities, you would know better. You are a simple girl. Just wait. You will see, soon enough."

"Do they have an answer for Leviathan? Do they know what it is?"

"They do not need to," Shiptu said. "I already told you, he belongs to your God—the God who does not make sense."

Milkah didn't say anything else. After supper she lay awake for a long time, wondering what waited beyond the smallness of her village. And that night, she dreamed of a ziggurat that stretched into the sky and disappeared into the clouds.

She awoke with a start. The night sky still covered her. She propped up on one elbow to see Jubal standing beside the remains of the campfire. "What is it?" she whispered.

"Shh!" he hissed. His hand rose in a sharp motion for silence.

Shiptu was crouched on her sleeping mat, a knife clutched in her hand. Milkah could see the pale moonlight reflected off its blade. Shiptu pointed toward the east, beyond a copse of date palms. Then she tapped her ear, signaling for Milkah to listen.

A low roar erupted in the distance. Milkah stiffened. Lions. Her pulse ticked in her throat. Another roar. She glanced at Jubal. His body was tensed and ready. But they all knew there was nothing he could do against a lion. Nobles hunted lions for sport and paraded around with their skins draped over their shoulders. But to everyday folk, there was no glory in the hunt. There was only the need to survive.

Milkah strained to see into the darkness beyond their open camp. Shadows shifted in and out of the date palms, but they were vague and shapeless. Her inability to see the creatures made the fear brighter and sharper. That was why she had always been afraid of the river. When she was growing up, she used to hesitate when the other children leaped into the brown water. Her mind always wondered what was hovering beneath the surface, unseen.

The sound of a hoof stomping the earth brought Milkah's attention back to Jubal. He was harnessing Uruk. "Hurry," he whispered.

"They will hear us," Milkah said. "Should we not lie still?"

Shiptu shook her head. "They have already smelled us. Jubal is right. Better to be on the water."

Another throaty growl erupted from the darkness. A shiver ran down Milkah's spine. She shifted off her sleeping mat and began to roll it up. She tried to hurry, but her fingers fumbled as her attention jerked back to the noises. She could feel the goose bumps on her skin, the raised hairs, the thud of her heart in her ears. Her body was screaming at her to run.

Jubal tugged Uruk's lead and whispered to him in a low voice. "Come on, now. Let us keep you safe." The donkey shuddered and sidestepped, nostrils wide as it picked up the scent of lion. Jubal patted Uruk's neck. "Let us go. You are a good snack for them, so let us keep you safe, all right?"

A roar broke through the still air. Uruk startled and bolted toward the river. Jubal strained to keep his hands around the rope as he raced after the donkey, his feet flying and sliding over the mud.

"If the gods are with us, the lions have already caught an *onager* or a gazelle," Shiptu whispered as she hurried to pack up their belongings.

"And if they have not?"

"Then it is your fault for angering the gods. Last night you spoke against idols, and now look! If they come after us, we ought to leave you to them. Then maybe the gods will be satisfied and leave Jubal and me alone."

"This is not my fault."

"Just listen to yourself. It is so easy to do right, and yet you refuse." Shiptu slammed a bundle of dates into a basket then stood up. "Why can you not just do what is right, like the rest of us?"

"Maybe my God sent an onager for them to eat. Maybe He is keeping us safe, even now."

"Ha! After He failed to keep your family safe?" Shiptu whipped around and stormed toward the keleg, arms loaded with belongings.

"Wait!" Milkah clutched her sleeping mat to her chest as she raced after Shiptu. Milkah's bracelets clattered as she ran, and Shiptu spun around to glare at her. "Quiet!" she hissed. "Are you trying to bring them to us?"

Milkah pressed her arm against her chest to stop the bangles from jangling as she sprinted. She tripped over a clump of dirt, stumbled to regain her balance, and kept running. Jubal was already at the river's edge, securing Uruk to the rope that guided the keleg. He was still breathing hard from his race to the river. "What about you?" Milkah asked as he waved her onto the boat.

"I will be all right. Made it this long, have I not?"

The first rays of weak, gray light were appearing on the horizon, and Milkah could make out his face as he winked at her and grinned. Then he patted her shoulder and gently steered her toward the keleg. "Now, hurry. The lions are close."

CHAPTER THREE

Shiptu pushed into the keleg before Milkah, setting the little vessel spinning. Milkah glanced back at the date palms. The shadows were clearer now. She could make out sleek tan bodies, pacing along the trees. She stepped into the boat even though it was still rotating. Her body lurched sideways as soon as her feet hit, and she toppled onto a basket of barley.

Jubal didn't wait for her to regain her balance. "Walk on," he whispered to Uruk. The donkey sniffed the air. His eyes rolled with panic, showing the whites. He was as eager to run as the rest of them. The boat jerked as the donkey lunged forward. Jubal jogged beside him, breathing hard as he struggled to keep up. He turned back every few steps, without slowing his pace, eyes scanning the shadows that circled the date palms in the distance.

Milkah huddled in the keleg, closed her eyes, and pressed her hands against her ears. She wanted to be back in her safe, warm house, listening to her sisters argue over the last piece of flatbread. She wanted to be at her hand mill again, even though grinding grain was the job she disliked the most. She should have appreciated it more—all of it.

Now, dark water spread before her. Milkah shrank inward and kept her hands and feet as far from the river as she could. The moon had set and the sun had not yet risen, so there was no reflection on the surface—just deep, unending blackness. Milkah felt as if she could drop a stone into that blackness and it would just go on and on forever. It was not true, of course. The Euphrates was not a deep river. The boats that plied it had shallow drafts. But that did not stop her from imagining the bull sharks that crept into its waters. Or the leviathan, whatever that was. She imagined that it was slick and slimy, like the eels she used to catch for her mother to cook. And it must have teeth like a lion, sharp enough to pierce bone. Its eyes would be as soulless as those of the venomous snakes that lounged along the riverbank, baking in the sun.

Milkah's eyes stayed on the dark, smooth surface until the sun rose and fragile morning light transformed the black waters to a sparkling brown. Only then did she exhale and lean back against a basket of barley. But even then, she did not trail her hand in the water as Shiptu did. Perhaps she never would again.

"Did you mean it?" Milkah twisted around to see Shiptu's face. "When you said that it was my fault there were lions?"

Shiptu flicked her wrist in a dismissive gesture. "I did not say that it was your fault they were there. I said it would be your fault if they came after us."

"But they did not."

"No." Shiptu frowned and swatted at an insect. The sun was fully above the horizon now, and heat was beginning to radiate across the water. "But they could have."

The words grated on Milkah. She wanted to shout at Shiptu to see the truth, but that would never work. "Anything can happen at any time." She managed to keep her voice calm and steady.

"You know better than that," Shiptu snapped back. "The gods control the balance of the universe. They control the outcome of our lives." She raised an eyebrow. "You believe that about your God, do you not? Or have you finally turned from Him?"

Milkah's forehead creased. "Of course I believe that…." Her voice faded away. There was too much that she didn't understand, that she couldn't explain. Just a few months ago, the universe had been ordered and balanced. The One God had ruled over everything as He should. Now, that universe was spinning out of control.

Shiptu's face lit up with a look of triumph. "So you admit it, then?"

"What?"

"That God has punished you?"

"No."

"But you just agreed that He controls the outcome of your life."

"Yes, but…"

Shiptu chuckled. "See, it is not so hard to understand."

"Not when all is going well for you."

Shiptu paused as she gave Milkah a knowing look. "And there is a reason for that."

Milkah shifted her eyes to the distant village they were passing. She took a deep breath and let it out slowly.

"I have heard of a man like you."

"Who?" Milkah was barely listening now. She didn't want to hear anything else Shiptu had to say. She was too angry. And she knew what lurked behind that anger. Fear. Fear that Shiptu was right.

"I do not remember his name. He lives far away, west of here. We heard about him from a few different traders last time we made this trip." Shiptu turned toward Jubal. "What was the name of that man from the west? The one who God punished so severely?"

"The one who lost all his children and all his wealth in one day?"

"Yes! That is the one."

Jubal kept trudging along the riverbank as he thought. "I do not remember his name."

"Oh well, it does not matter."

"It does to him," Jubal said and chuckled.

"What happened?" Milkah asked.

Shiptu turned back to her and settled into a comfortable position, with her back wedged against a basket. "Kind of like what happened to you, actually. Let us see, I am trying to remember all the details." She let a hand slip lazily into the water as she considered. "He was at a feast. No, all his children were at a feast. That was it. And a storm came and knocked down the roof, killing them all. Not a single one survived. Then, just as the messenger arrived to tell him what had happened, another messenger arrived with more bad news. Thieves had attacked his flocks, killed his men, and stolen everything. There is more, I think, but I cannot remember." She glanced over at Jubal. "Did I get it right?"

"Something like that, more or less. Then the gods took away his health too, last I heard."

"Oh, yes." Shiptu nodded. "Covered the man in sores, head to toe. Like a beggar."

"He was wealthy as a king, before that."

Shiptu nodded again. "Lost everything. Everything."

The story made Milkah feel sick and small. She didn't like hearing about it. "Are you sure it is true?"

"Yes, of course. Everyone was talking about it the last time we were down this way." She shook her head. "Terrible thing." Her eyes cut to Milkah, and she studied her for a moment. "It does remind me of you."

"No, it is nothing like me." But even as she said the words, Milkah could feel the lie. Shiptu was right. The man's story was like hers.

"Except the sores, of course."

Jubal chuckled from the riverbank. "Our Milkah is still a pretty little thing."

"Thank the gods," Shiptu said. She and Jubal exchanged a quick glance, and they both smiled.

Milkah felt a little warmer inside, knowing that they cared about her, even after Shiptu's criticism. Shiptu was probably critical because she was worried. Milkah felt sure that the woman only wanted what was best for her.

"Jubal is right," Shiptu said. "You will make a lovely bride some-day. You have always been a pretty girl."

"No." Milkah looked down, into the water. "I do not want to marry anyone but Nahor."

"Nahor is gone, Milkah. But you are still here. Your life will go on, whether you want it to or not."

Milkah said nothing.

"Who knows? Maybe you will end up with a good man that you like better than Nahor. It could happen."

"I do not want to talk about it."

Shiptu sighed, leaned forward, and patted Milkah on the arm. "It will all work out. I promise."

"Did that man not—the one who lost everything—did he not see the leviathan?" Jubal shouted from shore.

"Oh!" Shiptu straightened up, and her eyes brightened. "There was something about that. No, wait." She shook her head. "He did not actually see the leviathan, did he?"

Jubal slapped his arm then wiped an insect away. "No, maybe not. But there was something about the leviathan in the story we heard, was there not?"

"Yes, I am sure of it."

They both sat in silence for a moment. "We will have to ask around," Shiptu said. "I wish I could remember."

"Gossip changes as it is told, so who knows? Better to get it straight from whoever it happened to. But from what I remember, God sent out the leviathan to punish the man." Jubal's forehead creased in concentration. "Or maybe he just let it loose, or... No, I am not sure." He looked at Milkah and grinned. "The best part of trading is hearing the latest news. We will find everything out, soon enough. And I am sure that a lot more has happened since then."

"So, you do believe in the One True God?"

"What?" Jubal looked surprised at the sudden change of subject.

"You said that Leviathan is the One God's creature and that He let it loose."

"Well, yes, your God controls it."

"So my God is real."

"All the gods are real," Shiptu said.

Jubal nodded. "Best not to forget any. I will sacrifice to your God as surely as I would any other. But I make sure to remember the others too. That is where you go wrong."

"This man, the one God punished, he worshiped the One God only?"

Jubal rubbed the back of his neck. "Yes, I believe he did."

"He did. That is a big part of the story." Shiptu pointed at Milkah. "See how this man is like you? He served your God and got punished for it, just like you. Or failed to serve Him well enough, I should say."

"No, that is not—"

"Job!" Jubal shouted. "That was his name!"

"Yes, that was it!" Shiptu smiled. "It feels so good to remember that. It was driving me crazy. Job of…" Shiptu wrinkled up her face. "Where was it?"

"The Land of Uz," Jubal said.

"Land of Uz," Shiptu repeated as she nodded. "Wealthiest man in Uz. Or used to be. Not anymore."

"No." Jubal shook his head as he trudged onward. "Not anymore."

The day passed slowly. Shiptu and Jubal switched places, and she led the donkey until the afternoon sun slid down its long arc toward the horizon. Structures appeared in the distance, and Milkah raised her hand to squint into the sun. As the boat coasted closer, the buildings rose higher, until she could make out the jumble of buildings more clearly. "Is it a city?" She sat up straighter.

Jubal laughed. "Just a village. Bigger than ours though. We will stop here, see if they have anything to trade."

"Then we will go all the way to the sea?"

Jubal looked away. Milkah didn't like the look on his face, but she didn't know why. "Sure. Shiptu and I always go to the sea. It is not that much farther from here. That is where we meet the boatmen who come up from the Great Water to bring all the things that we cannot get here. Gold, lapis lazuli, pearls, ivory—beautiful things."

"And the barley will pay for it?"

Jubal's mouth tightened. "Most of it, anyway. You ask too many questions." He leaned over and slapped the water. It splashed Milkah, and she shrieked then splashed him back.

Uruk brayed from the riverbank and twisted his head to tug at the harness.

"Calm down, now." Shiptu pulled the lead rope. The donkey arched his back and kicked his feet in a little dance of frustration.

Jubal chuckled. "He is ready to stop for the night."

Milkah watched as Shiptu struggled to force the animal forward. "You have been up to the city of Uruk, right?"

"Sure," Jubal said. "It is where we got the donkey. And his name, of course. More trouble than he is worth, really." But his affectionate smile gave away his feelings for the animal.

"What is it like?"

Jubal ran his fingers through his dark, curly beard. "Like any city, I suppose. It has its priests and temples, market stalls and craftsmen. And all the people living there, crammed into their stacks of mud-brick houses, like bees in a hive. And the palace, of course. Kings know how to live, that is for sure." Jubal chuckled. "I could get used to a life like that."

Milkah tried to imagine it all. She could only picture something that looked like her own village, but bigger.

"You will see soon enough. One city is not that much different than any other. Just wait until we get to Ur."

"I never thought I would see a city, especially not Ur. It has the highest ziggurat, does it not?"

"Oh, yes. It will change the way you think about things when you see it. No one could build something like that if the gods were not real—if they were not helping. They want to be seen and heard. They want a home to live in."

Milkah turned the idea over in her mind. Her neighbors had kept altars for their idols so that the gods could live inside their houses. It had never made sense to her. But she had never needed proof of God's presence before. Now, her fingers itched at the thought of holding something real and tangible—something made of stone and wood—that would make her feel safe and secure. She understood that craving for the first time, but she wouldn't give in. "My God does not need a home. He can live anywhere."

Jubal shrugged. "Maybe. Who knows what a god might do? Best not to take chances, though. We know the gods live in the ziggurats. How can you know where your God is, if He can be anywhere?"

Milkah didn't like the question. She pushed it aside and watched the structures on the river's edge grow larger as the boat slid closer. "Will we stop here for the night?"

"Yes."

"But I thought you said it is better not to stay near people when you are traveling—that they cannot be trusted."

"We know people here. It is all right."

"Oh. That sounds good, then."

Jubal winked at her. "But I will still sleep with one eye open. You cannot be too careful when you have a boatload of goods on you."

Milkah's brow furrowed and she looked away. She didn't like the idea of strangers, of people who couldn't be trusted. She had known the same people all her life. It had never occurred to her not to trust any of them. They had been as reliable as the landscape surrounding her, as sure and steady as the river and fields had been. They would always be there, sharing the same gossip, having the same quirks, sometimes saying the wrong thing to one another, or falling into some small dispute, but making peace in the end. They had all been in it together. They were all connected.

Now, she was approaching a village of people who had no connection to her.

"You will have a chance to ask about Job," Jubal said. "They might have heard something new."

Milkah felt a spark of optimism. Maybe meeting strangers wouldn't be so bad, after all. It could be exciting and interesting. She straightened her tunic and smoothed down the front of the coarse wool fabric. Her heart beat a little quicker at the thought of seeing people she had never seen before. She watched as they passed golden fields of *einkorn* and emmer wheat, the stalks of grain waving slowly in the warm breeze. A skinny boy with a staff waved and shouted from the riverbank. He was herding a flock of goats, and they bleated and butted one another then turned their attention to stare at Milkah as she sailed past. She waved back to the boy, and he smiled.

The sound of voices and the smell of cooking fires filled the air as they neared the tangle of mud-brick houses. Dogs barked and ducks waddled inside wooden pens. They quacked, ruffled their feathers, and stared at her with beady black eyes. Milkah realized that the village looked the same as her own, just with more houses and wider fields. The granary was bigger too. The nearest king would demand his share, of course, and the villages would make sure the harvest was safely stored for him and for themselves. Milkah wasn't sure if these villagers had to pay the same king that her village did. And in the end, it probably didn't matter. One king was the same as another, she supposed. They all demanded the same taxes, and they all fought one another. And whoever won would send his soldiers out to collect what the villagers owed him, same as the king he had fought before him.

Shiptu and Uruk stopped their long march, and she began to pull the boat toward the shore. Jubal leaped out when they reached the shallows and helped Milkah balance as she stepped out. The keleg rocked and Jubal steadied it, making sure that everything on board stayed dry. Children shouted and ran to the riverbank. They crowded around, talking fast and asking questions. The smaller ones jumped up and down and tried to peek into the keleg. "What have you brought?" they asked. Uruk brayed and sidestepped nervously as Jubal shooed the children away.

A middle-aged man with a thick midsection and heavy bangles on his arms strode toward them. The kohl around his eyes was freshly applied, and his thick black beard was neatly brushed. Milkah felt self-conscious as the sweet, rich scent of his perfume drifted toward her. She was not wearing any cosmetics, and she must look dirty and unkempt from the journey. She wished they had taken the time to stop and freshen up before meeting the villagers.

The man greeted Jubal and Shiptu warmly before turning to her. "And who is this? You have brought something extra this time?"

Jubal threw an arm casually around Milkah and let it rest across her shoulders. "She is a neighbor. Lost her whole family, so she is to come with us."

The man stared down at her thoughtfully for a moment, then looked at Jubal. Jubal nodded, and an understanding passed between them that made Milkah feel strange, but she couldn't quite put the feeling into words. The man's eyes flicked down to study her, then back up to her face. Milkah leaned closer to Jubal. She felt safe beside him, beneath his heavy arm. Whoever this man was, they knew him, so it must be all right, even though she didn't like the look in his eyes as he studied her.

"I am Urshanabi. My wife, Ninsun, has food for you. I am sure you are hungry."

Milkah nodded. "Thank you."

"Come on." Shiptu motioned for Milkah to follow. "Let us leave Jubal and Urshanabi to talk. I want to get something to eat."

Jubal lowered his arm and gave Milkah a gentle pat on the back. "Go on. I will be there soon. There will be stories that I do not want to miss." Milkah glanced back as she followed Shiptu, but Jubal didn't notice. He was too busy discussing something with Urshanabi. He shook his head as they spoke in low, quick voices. Then Jubal nodded, and they both smiled. Milkah turned back toward Shiptu and picked her way along the riverbank, up a winding path, and into the jumble of mud-brick homes.

"Shiptu!" A short, round woman appeared at the corner of a house. She carried a clay jar and wore a necklace of blue lapis lazuli and red carnelian beads. Her sandaled feet flapped on the sunbaked mud as she hurried toward them. "We did not expect you so soon."

Shiptu smiled. "We did not want to wait to bring you what we have." She turned to Milkah and motioned to the woman. "This is Ninsun." Shiptu's smile widened as she looked at Milkah, but it didn't reach her eyes. "Go on ahead and fetch the water. Let us catch up for a bit."

Ninsun handed Milkah the clay jar that she had been carrying. "Come back here with it." She nodded at the two-story home beside them. "This one is our house."

"All right." But Milkah hesitated. She didn't want to walk alone through the village full of strangers.

Shiptu waved her forward, the smile still on her face. "Go on."

Milkah tightened her grip on the jug and turned away. Ducks quacked from their pens as she passed, and a dog growled. A few children followed her, staring as she made her way down to the water's edge. "Who are you, and where do you come from?" one of the older children, a surefooted boy of ten or eleven, called out as he trotted after her.

"My name is Milkah. I come from a village like this, only smaller."

"Do you have any news?"

"About what?"

The boy shrugged. "I do not know. Anything." He kicked a stone and it skidded across the dirt, into the river. "Nothing ever changes around here."

"It is the same where I am from."

"But you came here, so something changed for you."

Milkah sighed. "That is true." She crouched down to fill the jug. The water felt warm and stagnant from the heat of the sun.

The boy stood beside her. He hopped from one foot to the other as he watched her. "I want to go downriver like you. I want to go all the way to the Great Water."

"Home is better," Milkah said. She stood up and wiped the lip of the jar to catch a drip of water.

"Easy for you to say. You have gotten to go places."

Milkah started walking back toward the rows of houses. "I would rather have stayed home. Be happy here while you can."

A look of frustration passed over the boy's face. "Do you not have any good stories to tell, at least?"

Milkah thought about the last month of her life. She shook her head. "No. I am sorry. I do not have anything good to tell."

The boy kicked another stone then wandered away.

"Wait!" Milkah called after him.

He spun back around. "What?"

"What news do you have? Have you heard about Job or Leviathan?"

"Yes. The grown-ups have been talking about a sea monster. That is why I want to go to the Great Water. That is where it lives."

Milkah stared at the boy. "Shouldn't that make you want to stay here, where it is safe?"

The boy paused and thought for a moment. "No. I would like to see what everyone is talking about. Wouldn't you?"

"No. I would rather go back home, to my own village." But even as she said the words, Milkah understood what the boy meant. There was something inside of her that stirred at the thought of seeing something secret and powerful, something that boatmen claimed was real but few had ever found.

The boy put his hands on his hips. "Lots of people talk about going places."

"Well, maybe you will get to, someday."

"My father says I will stay here for the rest of my life and nothing will ever change."

"I hope that he is right."

The boy looked surprised. "But—"

"You will understand if you ever do leave," Milkah said. Then she murmured, too quietly for him to hear, "After it is too late." A wave of homesickness gripped her so tightly that she had to clench her teeth to keep tears from forming in her eyes. "I have to go," she said and hurried toward the house where Ninsun and Shiptu were waiting for her.

CHAPTER FOUR

The ground blurred, and Milkah wiped her eyes in the crook of her elbow. Then she splashed a handful of water from the jar onto her face and forced a smile. She had to be strong. Shiptu and Jubal had done so much for her. She didn't want them to think that she was ungrateful.

Milkah took a deep breath and braced herself before she entered the courtyard. The voices of women and the smoke of a cooking fire met her as she rounded the corner. The smell of burning palm fronds and sunbaked mud felt familiar and safe as she stepped inside. The compound was much bigger than her family's had been. It had a spacious, roofed courtyard that shaded them from the sun and was bordered on all sides by two-story mud-brick structures.

"Milkah!" Shiptu stood up from where she had been crouched beside the fire. "There you are." Three girls sat on the ground near her, each one busy at work. The youngest, who looked around eight years old, ground grain with a hand mill, while another one plucked feathers from a duck, and the oldest, who seemed close to Milkah's age, ground spices with a mortar and pestle.

Ninsun sat between them on a low, backless stool. "These are my daughters." She waved Milkah over. "Come have a snack while you wait for dinner to be ready. You must be hungry."

"I am." Milkah smiled. "Thanks."

Ninsun picked up a clay bowl filled with dried fruit and nuts, grabbed a date for herself, then passed the bowl to Milkah. She plucked out a fig and leaned against the whitewashed wall as she ate. Afternoon heat hung in the air and pressed against her body as she listened to the women around her. Shiptu caught Ninsun up on the latest news from their village while her daughters finished preparing dinner. The scene felt so familiar and comforting that Milkah could almost pretend that she was back home, with her own sisters.

But she was not home, and the longing felt sharp and heavy within her as she studied the girls' faces and listened to their chatter. Everyone else's life was going on around Milkah, as if she had not lost everything. The realization felt bizarre, impossible. How could these sisters still have one another? How could they giggle and chat as if the world had not ended? She put down the bowl and pushed it aside. Her appetite was gone.

As the heat began to fade and long evening shadows crept into the courtyard, Jubal and Urshanabi strode inside. The women poured sesame seed oil into the clay lamps, lit the wicks, and arranged them around a large reed mat. Then they covered the mat with clay platters and baskets filled with unleavened bread, roasted duck, sheep's cheese, chickpeas seasoned with onions and garlic, apples, apricots, and pomegranates.

They all settled around the mat and reached for handfuls of food from the communal serving dishes. The tiny flames from the clay lamps flickered across the dim courtyard and cast shadows against their faces. Urshanabi smiled. The whites of his eyes gleamed in the lamplight. "It is good to have you here," he said to Milkah. She didn't like the way he looked at her, even though he was smiling. Guilt zipped through her as she sat at his table, eating the food he was generously providing. She told herself to stop judging him. Some men had a hardness behind their eyes, but it meant nothing. "Thank you," she managed to say.

"Have you been to the Great Water?" his oldest daughter asked. Milkah tried to remember her name. She thought it was Amarsin.

"Milkah has never been anywhere," Shiptu said. She and Urshanabi exchanged a glance and they both smiled.

"It is all new to me," Milkah said. She looked down and tore off a piece of bread.

"To be young again," Urshanabi mused. "When your whole life is before you, and so full of possibilities."

"Yes." Ninsun grinned. "What possibilities."

Shiptu giggled.

Jubal shot her a quick look, and she fell silent, but her eyes stayed eager. He turned to Urshanabi. "What is the latest about Job? Have you heard anything since we saw you last?"

Urshanabi chuckled. "That one has seen trouble after trouble. You would not think it is possible for it all to happen to just one man."

"I do not think it's funny," Amarsin said.

Urshanabi reached over and gave her an affectionate nudge. "Better to laugh than cry, right? Just be glad it is not happening to you."

"It will not happen to you," Ninsun said.

"You cannot know that," Amarsin said.

Ninsun frowned and dipped her bread in the chickpeas. "Of course I do. Did your father not go all the way to the ziggurat in Ur to offer sacrifices for you and your sisters? Do we not honor the gods and serve them?" She nodded toward an altar in the corner of the courtyard. "Look how we keep them fed." Bowls of fresh fruit lay at the feet of a metal figure.

"Your mother is right," Shiptu said. "We live in a world of law and judgment. Righteousness brings blessings, wrongdoing brings curses."

There were nods and grunts from everyone but Milkah.

"Job's friends tried to explain it to him," Ninsun said.

"That is right," Urshanabi said. "They all tried to get through to him. They sound like good men. They have more patience than I would have, that is for sure."

"So Job did not listen to them?" Jubal asked.

"No. Not last I heard," Urshanabi said.

"He just kept insisting that he had done nothing wrong," Ninsun said. She stuffed a date into her mouth, chewed for a moment, then added, "Such a shame."

Milkah's stomach felt tight and hollow. "But what if he had not done anything wrong?"

Laughter erupted around the mat.

"Really, Milkah." Shiptu rolled her eyes and reached for an apple slice.

"Even his wife had enough of it," Urshanabi said. "Told him to curse his God and die."

"I am not sure if she was trying to help or trying to be rid of him," Ninsun added.

Another round of laughter.

Milkah wanted to sneak out of the room and disappear. Nothing felt right. "But what happened to Job, in the end? What is he doing now?"

"Oh, I do not know." Urshanabi shrugged. "He was sitting around scraping his open sores with pottery shards, last I heard. Still is, I imagine."

"No." Ninsun lowered her hand from her mouth instead of taking a bite. "His God appeared to him, remember?"

Urshanabi shifted his leg and readjusted the fringed kilt he was wearing. "Ah, that is right. But I am not sure it makes a difference to the story."

Milkah leaned forward. "But what did the One God say?"

"Oh, something about being all powerful. Job should have kept that in mind."

"Well, maybe he did," Milkah said with more confidence than she felt. "Job did not curse God when his wife told him to, did he?"

"No," Urshanabi said. "Not that I heard, anyway."

"So he is still serving God," Milkah murmured to herself. The thought gave her a strange, unexpected hope.

There was a break in the conversation. The sound of chewing and the clatter of clay bowls filled the space. Jubal took a big swig from the clay jar, set it down, and wiped his mouth. "What was that part about the leviathan? We were trying to remember on the way here." He motioned toward Milkah. "She was curious about it."

"Who is not?" Ninsun said. "Seems like half the boys in the village are dreaming about becoming boatmen now."

"So, Leviathan is real?" Milkah edged forward.

"Sure," Ninsun said. "Plenty of boatmen say they have seen it."

"Shiptu says my God sends it out," Milkah said. "Is that true?"

Ninsun shook her head. "I have not heard that. Why would He?"

"To punish the unrighteous," Shiptu said. "Why would He not?"

"Hmm." Ninsun shoved a bite of roasted duck into her mouth and chewed. The grease glistened on her lips. "I guess that makes sense."

"But what did God say to Job about it?" Milkah asked.

"Oh, I have not heard about that," Ninsun said.

"You will get better news the farther you go downstream." Urshanabi glanced at Jubal. "Just be sure to bring it all back to us." He turned back to Milkah. "All I know is that the leviathan is huge, it lives in the depths of the Great Water, it has skin as thick as a soldier's leather shield, and it breathes fire."

Milkah leaned toward him, transfixed. If people could build towers into the sky, then why couldn't a beast roam the sea? She was learning that the impossible was possible.

Jubal laughed. "It does not breathe fire."

Milkah frowned as Urshanabi returned the laughter. "No of course not. But you should have seen Milkah's face. She believed it."

Milkah looked down.

"It is a child's tale, told to scare them into behaving," Ninsun said.

"Or a creation of the gods to scare *us* into behaving," Shiptu said with a sly smile.

Urshanabi chuckled. "Well, who knows? I have heard of stranger things. We know that the gods punish us with sickness, so why not a fire-breathing monster?"

Jubal shook his head. "A monster, maybe. But not fire breathing, surely."

"What about the blue fire in the sea?" Shiptu asked. "If that exists, then why not fire from a monster?"

"What is blue fire?" Ninsun's youngest daughter asked. No one answered her.

"Huh, well, when you put it that way…" Jubal scratched his chin as he thought about it.

"But what is blue fire?" Milkah asked.

"Sometimes the Great Water glows bright blue at night—bluer and brighter than anything you have ever seen," Jubal said.

"But how?"

Jubal shrugged. "It is a mystery. The priests say it is an omen, of course."

"The priests say everything is an omen," Ninsun said. Her tone held an edge of cynicism.

"They say everything is an omen because everything is an omen." Shiptu shot Ninsun a warning look. "And the gods are always listening." Everyone's attention slid over to the idol in the corner. The silent god stared back. There was an awkward silence. In the distance, the river slapped against the mud banks. A child shouted, and a dog barked.

"Will I get to see the sea turn blue?" Milkah asked after a moment.

Jubal reached for a serving of sheep's cheese. "It is up to the gods. It does not happen very often. Most people never see it."

"Best not to see it," Shiptu said. "Omens are almost always bad."

"Have you seen it?" Milkah asked.

"Once," Shiptu said.

"There is nothing else like it," Jubal said. "There is not a word for the color, really. Blue is not quite right. It was too bright for blue."

"And what bad thing happened after?" Ninsun raised an eyebrow.

"Well, the floods were especially bad that year," Shiptu shot back.

"The floods are bad most years," Ninsun said.

Shiptu narrowed her eyes. "And a fever took the neighbor's child."

"Children are always dying of fever." Ninsun popped a date into her mouth.

"What else have you seen?" Milkah asked.

"I have never seen it, but the boatmen who go down the Great Water say there is an animal as big as a house, with legs like tree trunks, and a nose longer than a man is tall," Shiptu said.

Ninsun laughed. "That cannot be."

"Boatmen love to tell tales," Jubal said. "They say the beast uses its nose like a hand, to pick things up." A round of laughter passed through the courtyard. "And its skin is wrinkled all over, like an old man's."

"And do not forget the front teeth," Shiptu said. "They are as long as spears and as thick as your arm." She giggled. "It is ridiculous. They have gone too far with that one."

"That is why no one believes boatmen," Jubal said.

"With good reason," Ninsun said.

"The trick is figuring out how much is real and how much is not," Urshanabi said. "A boatman's tale almost always has a kernel of truth to it."

Milkah spent the rest of the meal wondering what was real and what was not. She had never questioned anything before. But now she felt a terrible, insatiable need to know the true story behind everything. It was as if a door had opened and she couldn't force it shut again.

That night, as she lay on a sleeping mat beside Shiptu, Milkah wished to be home again, without any questions pricking her mind.

They nibbled at her like mice in a storehouse, slowly devouring the barley crop. Then, before anyone realized what was happening, the barley would be gone and the village would starve.

That's why the farmers prayed to Ninkilim, goddess of field mice, in hopes that she would keep her rodents from their granaries. Milkah had never thought that she needed to pray to anyone but the One God. And every year, He faithfully kept the storehouse safe. But now, in the dark room, enveloped in silence as the rest of the compound slept, Milkah wondered if the One God had ever had anything to do with it. Why would He bother to spare the barley but not her family? Maybe it was coincidence that the mice had not devoured the seeds for next year's crop. Or maybe it had been the intervention of some other god. Milkah rolled over and squeezed her eyes shut, but she could not squeeze out the doubt.

When she finally fell asleep, Milkah slept hard. When she woke up, she had no memory of dreams. She yawned and opened her eyes, expecting to see Shiptu on the mat beside her. But the mat was gone. There was no sign of the woman or her belongings. Milkah shot up onto one elbow. She had overslept. The thought made her want to cry. She had been determined to show how helpful she could be after all that Shiptu and Jubal had done for her.

Milkah stumbled to her feet, smoothed down the front of her tunic, and started for the door. Her hands flew to her hair, trying to tame the loose strands that had fallen from her braids. Then her hand moved to her throat as she realized that she wasn't wearing her jewelry. She doubled back, stooped down, collected the necklace, earrings, and bracelets she had inherited from her mother, then slid them into place as she strode away.

But when she went to push open the wooden door, it didn't budge. She frowned and pushed harder. Nothing happened. Her belly tightened, and a strange feeling swept over her. The door should open. She spun around and glanced across the cramped, bare room. She couldn't see out of the little square window. It was set too high, in order to keep out the heat. But she realized there was not enough light coming through. It must be earlier than she had first thought. Shiptu should still be here, sleeping.

Instead, Milkah was alone. And she was trapped.

CHAPTER FIVE

Milkah knocked on the door. She told herself that nothing was wrong. There had to be an explanation. She pushed it again, then knocked a few more times. "Someone will be here soon," she said out loud in order to make it feel true. She just needed to calm down and recognize that everything was all right. Milkah spun away from the door and paced the length of the room—only a few strides—then turned around and marched back to the door.

"It is nothing," she whispered to herself. But the sinking feeling inside her gut told her otherwise. An alarm was going off inside her head, even though she still couldn't quite understand what was happening. She knocked on the door again. When nothing happened, she pounded against the wood with the palm of her hand, then with her fist. She stopped for a moment, worried that there had been some kind of mistake and she would wake the entire compound for no reason. She tried a different, quieter approach, throwing her shoulder against the door in gentle thuds. Nothing happened. Instead, she bounced right off of the wood.

Something was wrong. This couldn't be a mistake or her imagination. Shiptu was gone. All of Shiptu's belongings were gone. And the door wouldn't open. Her heart pounded, and her palms began to sweat. "Hello?" she said in a loud voice. When no one answered, she hesitated, then shouted the word. "I am trapped in here!" she added. Then she slammed her fist into the door again.

"Someone shut her up before she wakes the entire village." The voice was muffled and distant, but she recognized that it belonged to Ninsun.

There were more low voices. Then the voices became raised, agitated. Milkah strained to make them out. "Someone help me!" she shouted.

Sandals slapped against the earthen floor of the courtyard. The sound drew closer. Milkah's heart beat harder with every step. There was a scraping sound, as if a heavy object were being pushed aside, and then the door flung open, just a crack.

Shiptu's eye peered in. "Quiet!" she hissed. "Do not ruin this for us."

"Ruin what? What are you talking about?" Milkah started to push the door open but Shiptu leaned against it. "What are you doing? Let me out."

"You are staying here, Milkah."

"What are you talking about?"

Shiptu frowned. "Just do what they tell you, and everything will be all right."

Milkah's brain moved slowly, as if it were wading through a marsh. She tried to make sense of what was happening. And then she noticed the necklace around Shiptu's neck. It was made of expensive lapis lazuli and red carnelian, shipped from far away. Not something found on the necks of simple village women. The last time Milkah had seen the necklace, it had been on Ninsun's neck.

The truth shot through Milkah like a clap of thunder. "You could not have done this."

Milkah couldn't believe it. She wouldn't believe it.

Shiptu's mouth tightened into a line. She said nothing. But her eyes grew hard and distant.

"How could you?"

Shiptu said nothing.

Disbelief shattered into desperation as Milkah realized that she had to convince Shiptu to let her go. Everything in her screamed to get out of the room. "I grew up beside your house. You were my mother's friend. Where is your compassion?"

"Should I have compassion on what the gods have cursed?" Shiptu shot back. "I trust their judgment."

"You were supposed to help me." The words came out in a strangled whisper. Milkah could not believe that her neighbor could betray her like this.

"I have to help my own family," Shiptu said. "And let the gods punish you as they will. Did I not give you a chance to turn back to them?"

Milkah shook her head and pushed against the door. Shiptu leveraged her weight against it, straining at the effort. "Jubal!" Milkah shouted past Shiptu. "Jubal!" He would make things right. He had always been nicer than Shiptu. He couldn't let this happen. He would never abandon her here.

Footsteps slammed against the dirt. There was a shuffling noise, and then Jubal's face replaced Shiptu's in the crack of the door. "Hey, now, no need for all this."

"She has sold me, Jubal!"

Jubal just looked at her.

"Jubal! Let me out."

He kept looking at her. Milkah felt a slow, sick horror crawl up her spine as she stared back. There was a strange detachment in his eyes. And somewhere, behind that, resignation. And perhaps even a tinge of sadness.

"Jubal, no."

He breathed in and let it out slowly. "I cannot let you out, Milkah."

"But you have to."

"No. I do not have to do anything you tell me to." He paused and stared into her eyes. "But you have to do what we say. See how that works now?"

Milkah's voice dropped to a pleading whisper. "You cannot be serious. You cannot sell me to them."

Jubal glanced behind him, then back to Milkah. "Well, I can, actually."

"Have you lost your mind?" she hissed.

"No." He shifted his weight against the door. He didn't have to strain like Shiptu did. He was big enough to keep the door shut with just one arm against it. "I am thinking clearly. This is a good thing for us." He gave a little smile, but it held no emotion. "You will be all right."

"No, I will not. You know I will not."

"The gods have already decided your fate. We are just going along with it."

"No. This is all you. You were supposed to help me."

Something flickered behind Jubal's eyes. Then he sighed. He looked tired. "Just do what Urshanabi says. He does not know you like we do, so he will not have as much sympathy. Do not get yourself hurt, all right?"

And then he pushed the door closed. Milkah stumbled back from the force of the movement. She stood frozen for an instant, then snapped back to life and launched herself at the door. "Jubal!" she shouted, louder than before. "Do not do this! You do not want to do this! I know you do not!"

Silence.

She kept pounding and shouting, and time seemed to stand still.

"Enough!" The words came out like a roar. Milkah flinched. This was a different voice. Urshanabi's. "Jubal is gone. You can shut up now."

"There has been a mistake." Milkah's heart pounded in her ears. "It is a mistake."

"No. There is no mistake here. You know that."

Milkah didn't know what to say or do. She hesitated. "Let me out."

Urshanabi laughed. "No, I do not think so."

Milkah swallowed the anger and let the fear show in her voice. "Please."

She heard movement, and then the door opened. He stood in the doorway, filling the space and towering over her. Her heart tapped against her teeth. He was going to let her out. Maybe he would let her go, maybe if she explained—

"You are going to be quiet now, do you understand?"

Milkah stared up at him blankly.

"What is done is done, and you cannot change it. So now you better make the best of it. You seem like a nice enough girl. I do not want to hurt you." He took a step closer. Milkah shrank back. "But I will." He stared down at her. His eyes were black and guarded, the eyes of the reptiles that sunned themselves on the banks of the river. He wasn't joking or laughing as he had been the night before. He was a different man today. So was Jubal, Milkah realized.

No, Jubal was the same—she just hadn't realized before who he really was. He and Shiptu had been planning this all along. Snippets of conversation came back to her like fragments of a bad dream. All the glances, the comments. They had known and they had tricked her. They had all laughed with her, joked with her, given her advice, and told her stories, and all the while, they knew what they were doing.

"No more shouting," Urshanabi said.

Milkah gazed up at him, frozen at the realization, unable to respond.

"Good. Just stay like that."

And then he slammed the door shut. Something scraped against the floor then settled against the door with a thud. Milkah knew there was no way out, but she tried the door anyway. It did not move. She could not believe it, so she kept trying to force the door open. But she did not shout anymore. Milkah knew that Urshanabi had meant what he said. So she pushed against the door quietly, until she couldn't stand up anymore. Then she slid down the wall and slumped onto the floor to stare into nothing, too numb with disbelief to cry.

Milkah didn't know how much time passed before she heard the door opening. She leaped to her feet and waited, her breath coming fast, her stomach burning. The door opened, and Ninsun's oldest daughter, Amarsin, slipped inside. She held a hand mill under one arm and a basket clutched in the other. Milkah looked over the girl's shoulder. She could make out the empty courtyard behind her.

"Do not think about it," the girl said. "I have seen what my father does to runaway slaves."

"I am not a slave."

"Say what you like, it does not matter."

"Of course it does. I am not supposed to be here—"

"They all say that."

"But—"

"It does not matter," Amarsin repeated as she set down the hand mill and the basket. "Do you not see that?"

"You are close to my age," Milkah said. Her voice had a desperate edge to it. "This could happen to you. You could be me. Help me, please."

Amarsin's eyes snapped to Milkah. "I could never be you."

"Of course you could."

Amarsin looked at Milkah like she was speaking to a child. "This does not happen to people like me."

"Of course it does! It just happened to me."

Amarsin looked irritated.

"Listen—"

"Stop. I already told you that nothing you say will make a difference."

"But if you will just listen to me. This was not supposed to happen. I am from a village just like yours. I grew up like you. Tell your mother."

"My mother will not help you." Amarsin stared at her. "Do you not understand? No one will listen to you now."

"But why not?"

"Because you are not a person anymore. Not really."

"But we all ate together last night! Was I not a person then?"

Amarsin shrugged. "Look, it is just the way it is. You are not like us anymore." She nodded toward the hand mill. "My mother says to make yourself useful while you are here."

"What do you mean, while I am here? Where else would I go?"

"How should I know? But you will not be staying here. No one like you does. There is no profit for them if you stay."

"But where—" The door shut before Milkah could finish the question.

A moment later the door reopened, and Amarsin set a jar of water on the dirt floor.

"Can you bring me something to eat?" Milkah asked as she bolted for the water. The heat was building in the small room, and her mouth felt dry and raw.

"They said to tell you to mill that basket of barley first. Do that and you will get something to eat."

The door closed again. This time Milkah heard the noise of the heavy object being pushed in place to block the door. She slumped onto the reed mat and took a long swig of water. It tasted old and warm. She made a face and set down the jug. Sunshine poured through the small, high window, painting a long yellow rectangle across the floor. Milkah watched the dust motes drift in the warm glow of the light. It must be afternoon now. She wondered how far away Jubal and Shiptu were by now. Had they disassembled the keleg to walk back upstream to their village, or were they still floating down with the current, toward the Great Water? She imagined Shiptu smiling as she ran her fingers across the necklace she wore. Milkah wondered if they would keep the jewelry or trade it as currency. The beads were worth a great deal, but she had no idea exactly how much.

As much as I'm worth, Milkah realized.

Outside, in the distance, she could hear children shouting and laughing. Their footsteps beat across the paths that wove through the houses. Then the voices and footsteps died away. A donkey brayed. Low voices of men, then a chuckle. Life was going on, outside the wall, as if nothing had changed.

"God, where are you?" Milkah spoke the words out loud. "God?"

Nothing happened. She felt only emptiness.

"Why have You taken everything from me? Have I not served You faithfully? The ones who worship the new gods say that they have to be placated because we offend them by accident. But You are not petty like the new gods. I know You are not." She felt the hot pinprick of tears behind her eyes. "The priests teach us that the gods only created us to serve their needs—to give them food and houses so that they can live in comfort. But I think that You created us for more than just that. I think You want something deeper from us. You do not just want sacrifices, do You? Shiptu told me that I should promise You my firstborn child to make up for my guilt. But if I do that, I am treating You like the new gods." Milkah slammed her fist against her palm. "I am innocent! You know that I am innocent! If I had done something wrong, I would admit my guilt. But I have not. You know I have not!" The tears spilled over to course down her face in a sticky stream. "You are not petty or childish like the new gods are. I know You are not." She wiped her eyes and nose with the back of her hand. "You do not punish us out of spite or because we broke some arbitrary, unknown rule. But I do not understand why this is happening. Look at what they have done to me. Why do You reward them for their evil and punish me for serving You? I am Yours, God. I have always been Yours!"

Milkah waited. This was when God should appear in a flash of light to rescue her. Or at least He should fill her with a strong, warm peace. But there was nothing. No voice shouted from the heavens. No small, still voice whispered from deep inside. Nothing.

When the door opened again, Milkah was still slumped on the floor, knees beneath her chin, arms wrapped around her legs. Ninsun appeared in the doorway, glanced at the basket of barley, and narrowed her eyes. "You have not milled anything yet."

"How could you do this to me?" Milkah hissed.

Ninsun didn't respond. Instead, she raised her eyebrows. "So, you do not want to eat? All right." The door closed, and Milkah was left alone.

Amarsin's words from earlier turned over in Milkah's mind. Milkah had never thought that this could happen to her, either. The universe had turned upside down and shaken her into places where she was not supposed to go. And now there was nothing that she could do but lie on the floor, curled up like a child, and wait for whatever would come next.

The sunlight faded from the room along with the sounds from outside. No one came back to feed her. Darkness crept into the space and covered her in a warm, humid blanket. She could smell the smoke of the evening cookfires and the damp breeze from the river as it whispered through the palm fronds beyond the window.

She began to hear the sounds of voices in the courtyard. The family was gathered around the mat, eating. Milkah wasn't hungry. She felt too sick and empty inside. The low murmurs continued until she fell asleep, her face stained with tears and her eyes swollen. Her last thought before drifting away was that she had been there, in the courtyard, eating with them just yesterday. When she had still been a person to them.

The next morning, Milkah woke up hungry. Her stomach ached and nagged to be fed. For an instant, she forgot where she was and what had happened. Then reality slammed into her, and she pushed herself up on one arm, heart pounding, eyes searching the room. Everything was the same as when she had fallen asleep. She stared into space for a few moments, then poured some water from the clay jug onto her hands and splashed her face. She drank a few sips then slumped back against the wall.

"What now, God?" she whispered.

The sun rose and the light slowly moved across the floor. Soon, Milkah's stomach was roaring at her. The door finally opened and Ninsun strode in. She glanced at the basket of unmilled barley and clucked her tongue. "So, you do not want water either? Is that it?" She scooped up the water jug in a quick motion, then spun around and strode out of the room.

"Wait!" Milkah called after her. "What is going to happen to me?"

"You are not going to eat or drink until you do what we say." Ninsun began to pull the door closed.

"No, I mean where are you going to send me? Amarsin said you are not going to keep me here."

"How should I know? We will sell you, and they will take you where they take you."

"Who? Who is going to take me away?"

Ninsun slammed the door shut.

Milkah decided that she wouldn't mill the barley. She would never do what they said. She would find a way to escape. But as she sat alone in silence, the heat built. The mud walls were seven feet thick to keep the interior cool, but the day was blazing. The walls could only do so much. Shadows slowly shifted across the floor, so she knew that time was passing. But it crept past slowly, like a hazy nightmare she once had, where her feet were caught in the river mud and, even though she tried to run, her body could not move. She had opened her mouth to scream, but no sound had come out. In the nightmare, she had been all alone, trapped in silence.

Soon, Milkah's throat burned and her mouth felt thick and dry. She swallowed and rolled over. Her body ached from exhaustion, hunger, thirst. The thought of just staying on the floor and never getting up again felt good. The temptation whispered to her like a lullaby. Maybe, if she just closed her eyes in this heat and didn't drink anything for another day or two....

But something stirred within her. Milkah remembered her mother's words about the One God. *"He has a plan for all of us,"* she used to say. *"Even when we cannot see it or understand it."* The belief tickled at her mind and pulled her back like a hand that reached into the water to draw out a drowning child.

The burning in her throat overwhelmed her. The need for water began to drive her mad. All she could think about was the feel of water inside her mouth, of cold crisp water pouring down her throat. The coolness, the relief. She had never experienced thirst like this before. The river had always been near her house, overflowing with water, ready for the taking. Now, she could hear that water lapping the banks, mocking her from the edge of the village.

Milkah pushed herself up and dragged herself to the hand mill. She began to cry, but there were no tears. And there was no sweat on her body. She was burning hot, but her skin was dry as dust in the sun. Milkah knew that in this heat no one could survive without water. She was already dehydrated. She wondered if Ninsun and Urshanabi would let her die of thirst. They wouldn't want to lose their investment, would they?

Milkah did not know. She had not thought that anyone would be capable of doing the things that Shiptu, Jubal, Ninsun, and Urshanabi had done over the last few days. She could not imagine what else they might do. Milkah knelt behind the mill's saucer-shaped stone then took a handful of barley from the basket and dropped it on top. She picked up the smaller stone and began to pound the barley husks. Her vision blurred and she saw stars as she brought down the stone again and again. She needed water. She leaned her weight forward to exert enough pressure to break open the husks. Then she had to grind them to meal. She leveraged her body and pushed down on the stone until her knees and fingers burned.

In the dim room, only the rectangle of light from the high window hinted at the day's passing. Milkah's knees had been rubbed red and raw from kneeling against the hard-packed dirt floor. Her hands ached from gripping the stone. They had left her with a large basket of barley, more than she had ever had to mill at one time before. And in the past she would have had her sisters to chat with as she worked. She had never felt so alone as she did now, locked in the room, sick with heat and thirst, her heart shrieking with grief and anger.

The door opened. Milkah lay on the floor beside the hand mill. Her vision pulsed in time with her heart, and she felt woozy if she tried to move. She did not shift her head to look up. "Good decision." It was Urshanabi's voice. She heard his footsteps move across the floor then stop beside her head. His fringed kilt rustled as he crouched down. "You made the right choice." His voice was louder now, closer to her ear. She still didn't turn to look at him. The dirt floor felt cool against her cheek. "How about some water?" She heard the jug thump on the ground beside her. Water sloshed. "Milkah, next time, do not make this so hard. I will not be as patient again."

She heard the thud of a solid object dropping onto the floor. "You have more work to do before you eat. I am not convinced that you have learned how this works yet."

Milkah waited until his footsteps crossed the room, the door slammed shut, and she was alone again. She rolled over to see a basket of barley beside her, as full as the one before. There was also a clay jar. She lunged for it and gulped down the good, cool water. Nothing had ever tasted so wonderful. Slowly she felt life returning to her body in a surge of energy. A wave of determination passed through her. She would survive. She would find her way home again. And somehow, she would find God along the way.

***

Milkah finished grinding the last of the barley as darkness seeped into the room and the sounds of the village fell silent. Her back ached and her knees were on fire. All she wanted to do was collapse onto the sleeping mat. But hunger drove her to the door. "I have finished," she said then knocked a few times. She leaned against the wall to wait, faint from lack of food. The room shifted in front of her, and she squeezed her eyes shut. Her stomach cramped and contracted, like clothes wrung out after a washing.

She could hear the family in the courtyard and smell the smoke of the cookfire, but they took their time coming. When the door finally opened, Milkah felt weak with relief. Ninsun held a loaf of unleavened barley bread and a bruised apple in her hands. Everything in Milkah howled for the food, but she stayed still and silent. Ninsun tossed the bread and apple onto the floor then brushed off her hands.

Milkah glanced down at the food. "Can I have more?"

"No. That is more than enough for a girl your size."

"But I have not eaten in two days."

"And whose fault is that?" Ninsun raised her eyebrows and stuck her hands on her hips.

Yours, Milkah wanted to shout. But she said nothing. She was too afraid that they would take away the little bit they were giving her.

Ninsun stared her down for a moment then ducked outside and came back with another basket full of barley. "Grind all of it by morning if you want breakfast."

Milkah stared at the basket. She would be up all night.

Ninsun didn't wait for a reply. She set the basket on the floor and strode back out the door. Milkah lunged for the barley bread, brushed off the dirt, and crammed it into her mouth. The flat, round loaf was gone in four big bites. And her stomach still howled for more. She picked up the apple, rubbed it against her tunic to clean it, and took a big bite. The flesh was bruised and mealy, but she was too hungry to care. She devoured it.

Outside the door, she could hear the familiar sound of the heavy object being pushed in place to lock her in. Muffled voices followed. "They should be here tomorrow," Urshanabi said.

"The same traders that came last time?" Ninsun asked. Her voice was more distant. They were walking away.

"I do not know," Urshanabi answered. "But it does not matter. We will get a good price, either way."

Milkah strained to hear the rest of the conversation, but she couldn't make out the words, only the murmur of their voices. And then there was silence.

Someone was coming for her. Milkah's eyes darted around the room, searching for a solution, an escape, a miracle. There was none. She was trapped. There was nothing she could do to save herself.

Tomorrow would come and they would take her away, forever.

CHAPTER SIX

Milkah was begging the One God to intervene when she heard the boatmen arrive. The shouts and unfamiliar accents floated up from the river, followed by the sound of a boat being dragged onto the shore. Her heart rocketed into her throat, and she pushed herself up from the sleeping mat. Her knees and back still ached from the hours spent at the grinding stone. The sunlight was weak and gray as it filtered into the small room, so she knew that it was early morning.

Milkah listened as the voices grew louder then filled the courtyard. They were there, just outside the door, ready to take her away. She stumbled to her feet, heart thumping inside her throat. She couldn't make out the words, but from the tone, it was clear they were haggling. There were sharp words, then cajoling ones, followed by a good-natured laugh. Then there was rustling and thudding alongside the low murmurs of quiet conversation. She could hear water pouring and dishes thumping on the reed mat. They were eating breakfast together.

Milkah paced the small room, waiting. Her stomach was tight and hollow. She was hungry, but even if they fed her she didn't think she could keep anything down.

And then, just as she was letting down her guard, she heard the familiar scrape and thud, and the door swung open. A tall, thin middle-aged woman with sharp cheekbones and a pointed chin stood in the entranceway. She was dressed in a colorful woven tunic that hung to her calves and left one shoulder bare. The metal on her headdress glistened, and the beads clattered as she turned her face to stare at Milkah through kohl-lined eyes. "Let us go." She made a quick, sharp motion with one hand.

Milkah didn't move.

"Peleg," the woman shouted.

There was a sigh, then a man strode into the room. He was big, with a belly that bulged beneath his tunic, a thick nose, and heavy brows. He shot the woman an irritated look but said nothing to Milkah. Instead, he crossed the room quickly and grabbed her arm. His wide, meaty fingers closed around her like a vice. He dragged her out of the room without bothering to speak to her.

Milkah's feet skidded across the dirt floor as she struggled to keep up. She glanced over to Ninsun and Urshanabi as she passed them in the courtyard. Eyes wide, she tried to pull away from the man and lunge toward them. "Do not do this!" The words came out in a gasp. Yesterday she had thought the worst thing was to have to stay with them. Now, she was desperate for the safety of the small room. There, she knew what to expect.

Something in Ninsun's eyes flickered. "Wait," she said.

The man sighed again, but he stopped. "What?"

Ninsun hurried to Milkah.

Milkah's heart thudded into her mouth. Ninsun would stop this. She would keep her here.

"You did not pay for the jewelry."

Milkah's stomach plummeted to the floor. Ninsun was not going to save her.

Peleg grunted. "Take it, then. I want to get downriver."

Ninsun reached out and grabbed Milkah's necklace.

"No, you cannot take that. It was my mother's."

"And now it is mine." Ninsun struggled with the clasp for a moment, then yanked it from Milkah's neck.

"And the bracelets, armbands, and earrings." Ninsun held out her hand.

Milkah froze.

"Give them to her," Peleg said. His fingers tightened on her arm. "Hurry."

Milkah slowly slid the jewelry from her ears and her wrists. She squeezed her hand around them, one last time, trying to remember her mother's face. And then Ninsun snatched them from her.

Peleg jerked Milkah's arm as he began to drag her out of the courtyard, and she struggled to catch her balance and keep up as he pulled her along. Two men were already walking toward the river ahead of them, hauling baskets filled with barley and jars of sesame seed oil. In the distance she could see a reed boat, bigger than any she had seen before. She realized that they must be closer to the Great Water than she had known, for this was a boat that could brave the sea.

The vessel was as long as ten men lying head to foot. The bundles of reeds that formed the walls were tied in thick rolls and all bound together in neat rows that curved upward at the stern and the bow. The entire surface was coated with sticky bitumen as extra waterproofing. There was a shelter on the open deck large enough to accommodate a handful of people if they crowded together. Two poles rose from the center of the deck, connected by slats of wood, like a ladder that narrowed to meet at the top. Ropes hung from the poles and stretched across the deck. This was nothing like the little keleg that had bobbed down the river to bring her here. This was a boat that could take her far away, to places she had never imagined.

Peleg tugged her arm, and Milkah realized that she had slowed her pace to stare. Everything in her screamed to turn and run, to not let them take her on the boat. She glanced back. The tall, thin woman was trudging after them, adjusting her headdress and swatting an insect. Behind her, Urshanabi watched from the doorway of his courtyard. There was nowhere for Milkah to go, nowhere to run or to hide. No one in this village would help her. She was just another captive to them. Her feet kept moving forward, even as her brain shouted at her to stop.

Another man stood at the boat, one who Milkah had not seen yet. He was loading the baskets that the two other boatmen brought him. They stopped and spoke for a moment, and then the man at the boat turned and looked at her. His face hardened, and she caught a flicker of anger. He dropped the basket that he was holding and marched toward her. He had pleasant, even features, and might have looked kind if his mouth had not been clamped into a tight line. He was of medium build and height and wore the simple wool kilt of a boatman.

"What is this?" he demanded as Peleg approached them. "We are only trading in grain and oil, remember?"

Peleg shrugged. "This one was a good deal. Why not add to the profit?"

The man's eyes flicked down to Milkah's and softened as they made contact. He swallowed, then looked back at Peleg. The anger returned to his face. "We are not taking her."

"Why not? What does it matter?" Peleg looked genuinely surprised.

"It matters to me. Leave her."

The woman caught up with them and looked at the man. She scratched an insect bite on her elbow and sighed. "What is wrong with you, Javen? Why should you care?"

"It is my boat," Peleg said. "And I am taking her."

"I did not agree to this," the man called Javen said.

"She is already paid for," Peleg said. "And I have a buyer in mind. He is looking for another woman, and she is just right." He looked down at Milkah, and his eyes swept down to her feet then back up again. He nodded. "He will pay in lapis lazuli. It is a good deal for us."

"You will get your share," the woman said. "No need to make a fuss." She held up a hand, studied her fingernails, then pushed back a cuticle.

"I told you, I do not want anything to do with this."

"Well, she is better off if we take her," Peleg said. "She will end up a lot worse off if we leave her here for the next trader to take." He scratched his beard. "If that is what is bothering you."

Javen stared at Peleg for a long, hard moment. Milkah could see the emotions boiling behind his features. His eyes flicked over to Urshanabi, who leaned against the threshold of his compound, arms crossed over his thick midsection, watching them. Javen's eyes moved back to Milkah, then to Peleg. "All right."

Peleg grinned. "I knew you would see common sense." He clapped Javen on the back. "What has gotten into you, anyway?" Peleg yanked Milkah forward and she stumbled.

"Let go of her arm," Javen said. "I'll take her to the boat."

"Do not let her escape, or you are paying for her." The woman's eyes narrowed. "And we both know you do not have the means."

"So, you will be taking her place, if she gets away," Peleg added. "You will pay the debt."

"Fine," Javen said in a quick, dismissive tone. "Just let go of her arm."

Peleg rolled his eyes and released Milkah. The woman laughed. "Always collecting your strays, Javen. Is this going to be like the time you tried to save that abandoned bird? The one with the broken wing. It died in the end, did it not?"

"No one touches her, all right?" Javen said, ignoring the woman's comment.

"Fine with me," Peleg said. "I already told you that I am selling her as a wife or a concubine, whichever he is looking for. It does not matter." He looked over at the two men loading the boat. "Leave this one alone, all right? There will be a bigger profit that way, and you will get your cut of it."

The men grunted in agreement and kept loading the baskets.

Javen leaned closer to Milkah. "Follow me," he said in a low, even voice. "It will be all right." She had heard those words before. Shiptu and Jubal had told her that, and then they had betrayed her. But Javen's tone was different, and there was no distance behind his eyes. Something deep inside whispered to trust him. She pushed that feeling away. No one would ever fool her again.

Peleg and the woman strode down the path to the boat, chatting in low voices as they went.

Javen's gaze traveled over Milkah's shoulder, to Urshanabi, who still leaned against the doorway, watching them. "Peleg was right when he said it is better for you not to stay here. We need to go." He didn't grab her arm or force her toward the boat. Instead, he just waited. Milkah's stomach churned. She couldn't stay here, but she couldn't leave. She just wanted to go home. But she had no home anymore.

Javen shifted his weight from one foot to the other. His eyes looked troubled. "I cannot stop Peleg and the others. They are going to get you on the boat." Milkah glanced back at Urshanabi then turned to Peleg. He caught her eye and stared her down. "Hurry up," he said then headed toward the boat.

Milkah took a step forward. Javen's expression was difficult to read, but it looked like resignation. Then they walked side by side to the water's edge. The hard-packed dirt on the path turned to mud as they neared the river. It squelched beneath Milkah's leather sandals and felt warm where it touched her bare toes. There was a ladder propped against the side of the vessel, and Javen held it steady as Milkah climbed it. He nodded to her when she reached the end and rounded the top of the reed wall. She dropped down onto the deck. The surface was covered with baskets of barley, jars of sesame seed oil, and bundles of woven cloth.

Javen disappeared back down the ladder. One of the other boatmen shouted from the shore, and she felt the boat rock then shift forward into the river. She stumbled and pressed a hand against the low wall for balance. Then Javen and the other man scrambled on board and pulled the ladder in, and the boat began to drift into the current.

Javen stopped beside Milkah, while the other men picked up long poles and pushed them into the water, guiding the vessel as it floated downstream. "We are almost to the Great Water, are we not?" Milkah asked.

"Yes."

"And then what?" Her eyes darted up to Javen's then back to the village on the shore. It was growing smaller. She could still see Urshanabi standing in front of his house, but his features were too distant to make out. He looked like a soft blur against the white-washed wall.

Javen's jaw flexed. "We will go down to Dilmun."

"Dilmun?" Milkah's breath caught in her throat. "But that is not possible."

"I have been there," he said in a calm voice. "It is possible. Where do you think the ivory, gold, and pearls that you have seen come from?"

"I am from a small village. I have barely seen anything at all."

"You will now." Javen smiled, but his eyes looked sad.

"Some people say Dilmun is not real—that it is where the gods live. They love beautiful things like gold and ivory."

"It is real enough. And there are no gods there."

"Who is there then?" Milkah hesitated, unsure if she should push him, or if she even wanted to know the answer. "Who are you taking me to?" The question came out quietly, almost a whisper.

Javen looked away. "There are plenty of rich traders there. They control all the trade that goes up and down the Great Water. I do not know which man Peleg has in mind, specifically." He breathed in and out. "I do not suppose it matters in the end."

The truth crept up Milkah's spine like the prickly legs of an insect. She shivered. "No, I suppose it does not."

"There are worse places that you could go." Javen's eyes flicked to hers then darted away again. "I have seen a lot worse happen to women like you."

"Yes. But this is bad enough."

"Yes," Javen agreed. "It is."

"I should be back in my village right now." Milkah hugged herself. The heat hung heavy in the air, but she felt cold inside. She wanted to ask Javen to help her, but she couldn't trust him. What if he told Peleg? Or what if he was only pretending to care, as Shiptu and Jubal had done to make it easier for them to sell her?

There was a long silence. Milkah could hear the soft rasp of Javen's breath and the slap of water against the boat. In the distance, a long-legged heron sprinted across the bank and lifted into the sky. "Have they fed you?" Javen asked.

Milkah shook her head. "Not much. Not for a while."

A muscle in Javen's cheek twitched. "I had to stay with the boat or I would have made sure—" He shook his head. "It does not matter now. I will get you something. You will not go hungry on this boat. I can promise you that, at least."

He walked away and ducked through the low doorway of the shelter, then returned a moment later with a dried fish and a flat loaf of unleavened barley bread. "Thank you," Milkah said as she took it from him. She tried to eat slowly, with dignity, but hunger drove her to devour it quickly. Javen watched with a frown on his face. Milkah wondered what that frown meant. She couldn't tell. She chewed a bite of barley bread and swallowed. "Why are you being so nice to me?" She tore off another bite and waited.

He didn't answer for a moment. Milkah regretted asking. Fear tickled her brain and made it hard to swallow her food. If she had pushed him too far, he might stop helping her.

Javen looked out over the flat water and the plains beyond. Invisible heat shimmered in the distance, forming mirages over the bare earth. "My God says to help the oppressed—the foreigners, the orphans, and widows. The ones who are powerless."

Milkah stopped eating. Surprise shot through her. "Which god?" she asked. "I only know one God who says those things."

"I serve the old God. The one who sent the flood. The One True God." His gaze turned to her. "You have heard of Him?"

"Yes. He is my God too."

He smiled. "I thought He might be. But I was not sure. Not many claim Him, these days."

"No, not many. They have forgotten the flood, even though it was not so long ago."

"Your God is not the one who sent the flood," one of the boatmen called out. He stood a few paces away, heavy wooden pole in hand. His bare legs were thin and sinewy, his cheeks hollow above a sparse black beard. "Enlil did. People were making too much noise, and he could not get any sleep. You never know what the gods might do, especially when they are irritated. But we were saved by a boat like this one, made of reeds." He shook his head and chuckled. "Every child knows that story. Do not listen to Javen. He is half crazy. And the gods will punish him for it, one of these days."

"The One God sent the flood to destroy the wicked," Javen said. "Because they were oppressing the powerless and shedding the blood of the innocent." His eyes shifted to Milkah. They locked on hers for a moment, and she felt something stir inside of her.

A laugh from the hollow-cheeked boatman shifted her attention back to him. "The gods do not care about that." He paused to wipe his brow with the crook of his elbow, his other hand still gripping the pole. "As long as we give them what they want, that is all that matters. Why should they care how we treat each other?"

"As long as we keep things running smoothly enough to maintain their temples," another voice called out from the other side of the boat. There was a splash as the boatman's pole hit the water. His stout, muscular arms moved in slow, careful movements, and he wore a thoughtful frown on his face. "They care because they do not want us to do anything that will destabilize society. Then the priests could not do their jobs, and people would stop leaving their offerings."

"God cares about people, not just stability," Javen said.

"The gods care about themselves, that is all," the somber-looking boatman responded. "And you would do well to recognize that, before it is too late. They want whatever benefits them."

Javen didn't answer. He just sighed and looked out over the water.

"What made you believe all that, anyway?" the hollow-cheeked boatman asked. "I have never heard any of it before I met you."

"I heard about the One God from a trader who had been east, to Uz," Javen said. "I liked what I heard."

"Uz?" Milkah's attention shot to Javen. "Have you heard of Job?"

"Yes. That is who the trader had been talking to. Job told him about the One God, and the trader told me."

"Do not listen to him," the somber-looking boatman called out from the other side of the boat. "Your God turned on Job. He has lost everything."

"And he still serves the One God," Javen said, too quietly for the man to hear.

"Is that true?" Milkah's eyes flicked to Javen. She hadn't realized how much she needed him to say yes. "That he has stayed faithful?"

"It is, last I heard."

"Then he is a bigger fool than you, Javen," the hollow-cheeked boatman said.

"I hear he still refuses to admit his guilt," the somber-looking boatman said. "Your God might restore him, if he admitted it."

"He might not have anything to admit," Milkah said. "He could be innocent."

The boatmen laughed. "Why do you not shut her up, Javen?" the somber-looking one asked.

"Because he is as crazy as she is," the other one responded.

"Everyone shut up." Peleg's voice boomed as he marched across the deck. The vessel rocked with his heavy footsteps. Milkah had not seen him since they boarded. He must have been inside the shelter, or behind it, blocked from view. "I will not have blasphemy on my boat. Do you want the gods to take away their protection?" He made the sign against the evil eye. "Have you not seen what can happen on the water?"

The men fell silent.

"And, Javen, stop talking to the girl." Peleg turned and glared down at her. "Go find Kalumtum." Milkah didn't like the coldness in his eyes. He looked as if he didn't care what she did or what happened to her, as long as she didn't cause him any trouble. She glanced at Javen, and he nodded to her. Milkah began to walk toward the bow, where the woman called Kalumtum must be, hidden behind the shelter. Even though the boat felt big to Milkah, it was actually small enough that she could see everyone and everything on board, except for what was inside or behind that cramped structure. Peleg's hand reached out and grabbed her arm. She froze. "Do not try to slip overboard. You will not get far. And I will make sure you regret it."

"She is not going to do that," Javen said. "Leave her alone."

Peleg's hand stayed on Milkah's arm for another moment. "No, I am sure she will not." His gaze turned back to Javen. "You both know the law and the penalties for breaking it. And do not forget that I know where your mother and sisters live, Javen. I will see to it that they pay the price for any wrong you do to me, if it comes to that."

"You act as if I have not been sailing with you for months. What do you think I am going to do?"

Milkah studied Javen's expression. She wanted to believe that he would try to help her, but she knew better than to think that. He wouldn't risk it. She shouldn't expect more from him than the food he had given her.

Peleg grunted. "I cannot mark her arm since I am selling her to someone else, so I have to be careful."

Milkah had only seen a few people with a brand or tattoo on their arm that marked them with their owner's name, but she had heard that the cities were full of them.

"I have always been able to depend on you, but..." Peleg scratched his jawline. "I do not like the way you talk to her."

"And how do I talk to her?" Javen kept his eyes on Peleg's with a strong, steady gaze.

"Like she is one of us." They stared at each other for a tense moment. Then Peleg released Milkah's arm without looking at her, turned, and walked away. She could feel Javen watching her as she rubbed her arm and made her way to the bow. The boat rocked beneath her feet and she felt queasy.

"There you are," a woman said as soon as Milkah rounded the corner of the shelter. She sat with her back against the shelter's reed wall, covered by its shade, with her legs stretched out in front of her.

"Are you Kalumtum?"

"Who else would I be? Do you see any other women on board?" She closed her eyes against the glare of the sun and popped a date into her mouth. "Take care of that."

Milkah saw the grinding stone at the woman's feet. Her body felt heavy as she stared down at it. She sensed the weight of the years ahead. This would be her life, day after day, until she died. Milkah looked over at the water. It stretched ahead, sleek and glistening, with the promise of freedom. She wondered what it would be like to jump into that water and swim away. She could already feel the cool waves lapping her skin, the softness of the mud beneath the soles of her feet.

"My husband expects bread when we stop for the night. What do you think will happen if you do not have the flour for it?" The woman sighed and popped another date into her mouth.

Milkah dropped to the floor of the boat and got to work.

Kalumtum did not speak to her, and the time crept by slowly. The sun passed overhead in its familiar arc as the sweat slid down her back. When she finally emptied the basket of barley, Milkah rocked back on her heels and wiped her forehead with the hem of her tunic. The cool of the evening had fallen, and the sky was bruised purple. The boatmen shouted to one another, their poles splashed, and the boat rocked from one side to the other. Milkah braced a hand against the floor to keep from toppling over. She watched as the boat shifted direction and eased onto the shore. The riverbank was quiet and empty. Marshlands spread out along the flat plane, dotted with palms and pockets of stagnant water. Tall marsh grasses bowed in the breeze.

Javen strode around the corner of the shelter. "Are you all right?" he asked in a low voice.

"Of course she is all right." Kalumtum waved him away. "What do you care, anyway? She has nothing to do with you."

His eyes moved from Milkah to Kalumtum then back to Milkah. "I am all right," Milkah said. He nodded. Kalumtum rolled her eyes, then stood up and brushed off the back of her tunic. Her beaded headdress jangled and her bracelets rattled as she moved. Javen slipped away, and Milkah heard him speaking to the boatmen, and then she watched as they scrambled down the side and secured the boat.

"Get the barley flour to shore," Kalumtum said. "And everything else you will need. It is all stored in the shelter."

Milkah rose to her feet, straightened her tunic, and ducked through the low door, into the small room. The tight space sweltered with hot air, trapped beneath the ceiling since midday. Milkah glanced around and saw a platter, an empty jar, a ceramic mixing bowl, and a stack of small leather pouches. She checked each pouch until she found the one filled with salt, and grabbed it along with the platter. The fresh evening air felt good as she ducked back outside.

Kalumtum was already climbing down the ladder. Before her face disappeared behind the side of the boat, she shouted to Milkah, "Do not drop anything." Then she was gone from sight. Milkah heard the woman's feet hit the mud then patter away. She doubled back to the hand mill and scooped the barley flour into a basket, then took it with her to the ladder. She tucked the clay platter beneath one arm and the jug beneath the other to free a hand for climbing. She hesitated, then set the basket and jug onto the floor of the boat. She would have to come back for them. She swung her leg over the side and tried to steady herself with her free hand. The ceramic platter slipped out from beneath her arm, and she jerked her knee up to catch it, then nearly toppled to the ground. Her stomach lurched into her throat and her toes tingled. It wasn't far to the ground, but a fall from that height would still hurt. And it would break the platter. She didn't want to think about what might happen then.

"Need a hand?"

Milkah's body relaxed at the sound of Javen's voice. She twisted her head to look down at him. He met her eyes and smiled.

She returned the smile. "Yes."

He reached up his hands. "Pass everything down to me."

An instant later everything was on the ground, and Javen was holding the ladder steady for her. She scampered down and began to pick up the cooking supplies. "Thank you," she said quietly, unsure how to feel. Jubal and Shiptu had been nice to her too. She remembered how Jubal had helped steady her as she stepped onto his keleg.

On the shore, Peleg had started a fire, and smoke curled into the air, rising in lazy tendrils to meet the purple sky. The boatmen stood knee deep in the river, casting circular nets into the water. For an instant, the scene felt peaceful, familiar. But she knew there was nothing peaceful here, not for her, not anymore.

"Hurry up!" Kalumtum shouted from beside the fire as she dropped a reed mat onto the ground and settled onto it.

Milkah hurried to her, set everything on the ground, and doubled back to the river with the empty jar. She looked for the cleanest stretch of water, away from the muddy eddies stirred up by the boatmen's feet. She filled the jar, then looked around for Javen as she walked back to the fire. He was wandering the marsh, collecting palm fronds.

When she reached the fire, Milkah set the clay platter beside the flames to heat. Then she dropped a handful of flour into the mixing bowl, poured in a splash of water, and sprinkled a pinch of salt. She watched the boatmen casting their nets as she stirred the dough with her hands. Their figures were black silhouettes against the orange glow of the setting sun. Beyond them, a flock of birds darted through the sky and a fish splashed in the dark water.

Milkah formed the wet dough into a flat disk and slapped it onto the clay platter. The heat of the fire warmed her face and pricked her fingers. She rocked back on her heels to wait. One of the boatmen whooped and trotted back to the fire with a wriggling net. "It is big enough for all of us," he said as he passed the mangar to Kalumtum. The fish was as long as his arm. Kalumtum shook her head and motioned toward Milkah. "I am not doing it as long as she is here to do it for me."

Javen reappeared from the marsh and added more fronds to the fire, then sat down beside Milkah as she cleaned and roasted the fish alongside the loaves of flatbread. She ate last, and in silence, as she listened to the conversation around her and the night sounds from the river. Insects trilled in the warm air, and a bird cried out in the distance.

After the last of the fish had been picked clean, Kalumtum brought out a honeycomb to share. She passed a portion to everyone but Milkah. She waited, but Kalumtum did not even look at her. It was as if she wasn't there at all.

A memory came back to Milkah of a time when she ate nuts and honey with her family. They had been lounging beside the riverbank in the cool of the evening, celebrating the birth of her youngest sister. The world had felt safe and bright then, with a lifetime of promises ahead.

The honey glistened in the firelight and made Milkah's mouth water. Everyone else was chatting and laughing as they licked their fingers and slurped the honey from the comb. Light and shadow danced across their faces and sparks crackled up from the flames. Milkah looked away and watched the gray moonlight shimmer across the river's surface.

Javen nudged her with his elbow. Milkah looked up as he slipped his piece of honeycomb into her hand. She wasn't sure how to react. "Thank you," she whispered. She took a small bite, and it was as sweet and good as she had remembered. It made her want to smile at Javen, but she held back. Shiptu and Jubal had given her small things too, breadcrumbs to gain her trust and lead her along the path they wanted.

"We will make it to Ur tomorrow," Javen said. He spoke low enough that the others didn't notice. They were too busy with their own conversations.

"What will happen then?"

"They will go to the ziggurat. Have you been to a city before?"

"No."

"I wonder what you will think of it."

"My imma was from—" Milkah had to stop herself. She knew that she needed to keep her distance, but it felt so good for someone to talk to her as if she mattered.

"She was from near here?" Javen asked.

"Near the coast. She told me about Ur." Milkah chuckled. "Warned me about it mostly."

Javen nodded slowly. "With good reason." He studied her expression for a moment, then asked gently, "Where is your mother now?"

Milkah didn't want to talk about her family. She hadn't meant to bring it up, but the memory was always there, like a shadow that dogged her footsteps. Sometimes it was all she could think about. Milkah wiped her mouth with the back of her hand. "Have you ever seen Leviathan?" she asked.

Javen didn't acknowledge that Milkah was changing the subject. Instead, he just gave a vague smile. "Not yet."

"Do you want to see him?"

"Maybe." He picked up a palm frond and fed the fire. Sparks exploded in the air and disappeared into the darkness. "Some say he is the One God's punisher. But others say…" He shrugged. "Well, I do not know. But I have heard that the One God created him to bring chaos to the world."

"That does not make sense. The One God is a God of order."

"I think that is the point."

"That it does not make sense?"

"Yes."

Milkah watched the flames dance and crackle in the darkness. "No one can know the answer to these mysteries, I suppose."

"No."

Her entire body ached with the need for God to explain Himself. But Milkah didn't want to admit that she might never have the answers that she needed. So she pushed the thought aside. "What have you seen besides Leviathan? You have been all the way to Dilmun. You must have seen lots of things that people claim are only myths."

Javen chuckled. "How about an animal with legs as tall as a man, and a neck as tall as one of its legs?"

Milkah laughed. "I do not believe you."

"And it is covered with big brown spots and has two little rounded horns."

"That cannot exist."

Javen smiled. "And yet, it does."

"Where did you see it?" Milkah leaned closer without realizing it. She laughed. "If you really saw it."

"South of Dilmun. Some men had captured it and brought it north, to the coast." His smile faded. "It did not live." He picked up a palm frond and picked at the edges. "Wild things should not be held in captivity." He frowned and peeled a long strip from the frond. "Nothing should."

The words hung in the air and made Milkah uncomfortable. If he felt that way, why was he here, working with Peleg? She could not believe that he meant what he had said.

"Do you think that we might see Leviathan on our way to Dilmun?" She was changing the subject again.

If Javen realized that, he did not acknowledge it. "Are you afraid that we will?" he asked.

"No, I…" Her brow crinkled. "I do not think so. I do not think there is anything left for me to fear." But even as she said the words, a cold wave of dread rose from deep within. If she closed her eyes, she could sense a black, endless pit yawning beneath her. There was no escape. There was no one to save her. She had learned that anything could happen.

And that it could be even worse than what had come before.

CHAPTER SEVEN

The scenery began to change as the boat drifted downriver. Throughout the morning, they passed marshland and long-legged water birds that waded in the shallows. Villages of barrel-roofed reed houses lay scattered across the banks. Men stood waist-deep in the water, casting nets. By midday, as they traveled farther, the shore grew more crowded. The villages grew larger. After a while, Milkah could smell and hear the villages before they came into sight. Goats and donkeys bleated and brayed, children shouted, and the stones of hand mills clicked and clacked. The scent of cookfires and animals filled the air.

Peleg and Kalumtum left Milkah alone as she sat in the stern of the boat studying the shoreline, but they kept an eye on her. She knew they were always watching. They would never let her slip away unnoticed. Milkah watched a child filling a jug of water at the river's edge and remembered all the times she had drawn water with her sisters. She could hear the tone of their voices, see the way they smiled, feel the warm mud beneath her bare feet. But that was all gone now.

Milkah heard a noise and turned from the water to see Javen walking toward her. His footsteps stayed steady as the boat rocked beneath his weight. "We will be there soon," he said. He lowered himself down to sit beside her and leaned his back against the side of the boat.

"I can tell. It is getting more crowded."

He chuckled. "Just wait."

"Will they let me see it?"

"They will have to." He frowned. "They will not let you out of their sight."

There was an awkward silence. Javen looked as if he wanted to say something. His eyes flicked over to Peleg, then back to Milkah. He stayed silent.

"What will they do there?"

"They will trade and leave an offering."

"Will you leave an offering too?"

Javen's brow furrowed. "Not at the ziggurat. I do not serve those gods." He looked confused.

"I know. You told me that. But some men like to hedge their bets. Especially before sea travel."

Javen's face turned serious. "You cannot hedge your bets against the One God. It is all or nothing with Him. Either you serve Him or you serve the others. You cannot have it both ways."

Milkah nodded. "That is what my parents taught me. But I just feel like…" She gave a little nervous laugh. "Never mind."

"What?" Javen looked at her with a kind but intense expression. "It is all right to tell me."

Milkah hesitated. "I, well…" By habit, her fingers went to her wrist to fiddle with her bracelet, but they found only bare skin. "It is hard to believe that God is still with me." Her gaze moved beyond Javen, to study the distant horizon. The flat line wavered in the heat haze. "He has taken everything from me." Her voice lowered to a whisper as she repeated the word, more to herself than to him. "Everything."

Javen waited for her to say more. The silence unnerved Milkah and pushed her to keep talking. "Or maybe He did not do it Himself. Maybe He just allowed it to happen. But does that detail matter in the end? Is it not the same thing, really? And, either way..." She could feel Javen's gaze on her, but she did not turn back to meet his eyes. She shook her head. "How can I ever trust Him again?"

Javen breathed in, then slowly exhaled. "I think it would be impossible not to have those doubts. But it does not mean that those doubts are true."

"The other gods—the false ones—are petty and unpredictable," Milkah said. "They do not actually care about us, as long as they get their way. That is why they are always having to be appeased. I believed that our God was different. That He was above that—that He loved justice. But now..." She frowned and studied a white bird as it waded in the shallows on long, thin legs. "He does not seem very different anymore."

"He has not abandoned you."

Milkah's head snapped around to face Javen. "Then what do you call this?" She heard the anger in her voice, but couldn't stop herself.

He flinched, then looked away. "I understand." His voice was soft and tinged with sadness.

Milkah clamped her mouth shut. She wished she could take back the words. Javen was the only person who might help her. If he turned against her, who would make sure that she got enough to eat?

He might even help her escape— No. She cut off the thought as soon as it popped into her head. Javen had been kind to her, but she couldn't trust him. And she could never expect him to do anything more than the occasional kindness. She would never expect more than that from anyone again.

"I cannot explain it to you, because I do not understand it myself," Javen said. "But our God is not the same, even though He still lets the righteous suffer. His love is there, despite it all. The other gods offer no love. It is all transactional with them. They do not care about us." He laughed and the corners of his eyes crinkled. "They are not real, of course. But even the people who believe in them do not think that they care."

Milkah stared at Javen. The words pushed up from her throat, even though she didn't want to say them. Her mouth opened as if someone else controlled it. "How can you call this love?"

The smile dropped from his face.

"Nothing He is doing to me is out of love. Show me that He cares, Javen. Show me." Milkah swallowed hard, her eyes locked on his, her skin hot and her heart pounding. "You cannot. Because here I am, betrayed, with no future. And do you know what happened before this? My entire family died. Every last one of them. You cannot know what that is like. So do not tell me that the One God is a God of love. And do not tell me that He is just."

Javen's gaze remained steady and even. "I knew something must have happened for you to end up here. I am so sorry, Milkah."

Milkah stood up. "Sorry cannot help me. Nothing can help me anymore." She stalked away and did not look back. Somewhere, deep inside, something stirred and whispered that there was help for her, even if it was not the help that she had imagined or hoped for. But the feeling was so soft and vague that she could not hold it. That peaceful whisper slipped away, lost behind the hurt and disbelief that had suddenly turned to rage.

Milkah sat alone as she watched for Ur to come into sight. First, they passed vast stretches of barley fields dotted with farmers, backs bent to their labor. Then the walls of the city appeared in the distance. At first, she could only make out a low white line. As the boat slid closer, the mud-brick walls grew taller and taller, rising like a fortress on the plain. She could see movement against the walls as a distant blur that slowly transformed into a swarm of people. Their clothing formed a vibrant moving rainbow, and their copper jewelry flashed in the sun. They milled around enormous city gates that stood, imposing and as cold as the scales of a fish shimmering in the sharp light.

The walls rose higher and higher, until they were so close that Milkah could see the soldiers standing with their spears, guarding the city. She watched in silence, overwhelmed by the height and length of the wall. She could only imagine what lay hidden on the other side. The boatmen shouted and the boat rocked as they dug their poles into the muddy river bottom. The vessel shifted direction and eased into an artificial canal that ran from the Euphrates around the side of the massive wall.

Milkah stared at the network of constructed waterways that led to the great city. She had helped dig and maintain the irrigation canals in her village, but they were nothing like this. These waterways carried big reed boats, like the one that she was on, and boatmen shouted all around her in different languages. Sunlight glinted off the water so that she had to squint to take everything in. Animals in wicker cages bleated and squealed from the decks, and boatmen splashed their poles in the water as they slid past one another.

Their boat wound through the noise and chaos to the end of the canal, where they dead-ended against the city wall. Unsmiling soldiers stood at the entranceway, pointing and shouting to the boatmen as they approached. Milkah watched as the boats clustered and formed a line. She stared at the men who towered above them from the gate's stone platform, waiting for the boats to file past. They wore shiny copper helmets that rose to a point above their heads. Their chests were bare above their calf-length kilts, but they wore leather capes across their backs with rows of metal disks sewn on as armor. Each one carried a dagger on his leather belt. They stared down with stony eyes, and Milkah looked away. She had never seen anything so intimidating as those armored men glaring down with spears in hand, demanding tribute.

The boatmen waited their turn, then poled the vessel into position alongside the soldiers. One of them thumped the butt of his spear against the stone platform and shouted down to Peleg to hand over the tax. He and Javen hurried to unload baskets of barley and stack them at the soldiers' feet. A scribe standing to the side made a notation on a clay tablet. He nodded to the soldiers and they waved them on.

As the boatmen eased the vessel through the gates, the canal opened into an artificial harbor where traders could dock their boats. Milkah estimated that there must be room for more than a hundred boats alongside the rows of wooden docks. A group of men with their backs and heads bare to the burning sun worked at one wall of the harbor, repairing a section that had crumbled. She figured they must be enslaved prisoners of war. How many of them had it taken to dig away the earth to create an entire harbor?

Milkah shifted her eyes from the men to scan the rest of the harbor. Sturdy walls blocked her view of the city and she wondered what lay hidden within. She smoothed the braids that twisted into a wide bun atop her head and wished for her jewelry. The people here would be sophisticated. They would be wearing the latest styles. She didn't want to look like a country bumpkin. Then she remembered who she was now. No one would even notice her. She did not matter to anyone anymore.

The boatmen steered the vessel alongside a dock and secured it with heavy rope.

"Let us go." Peleg motioned for Milkah without looking at her. Kalumtum followed behind him. She had put on crescent moon earrings that Milkah hadn't seen her wear yet. They were large enough to brush her shoulders and they swung and flashed in the sun as she climbed out of the boat.

Milkah scrambled up, eager to see beyond the harbor wall. Javen appeared at her shoulder. "Mind if I come with you?" His voice was soft and friendly. She felt a stab of guilt when she remembered their last interaction. She wondered if she had been wrong to take out her fear and frustration on him, or if she had been right to protect herself by pushing him away. "If you want to…" She tucked a strand of hair behind her ear that had fallen from her braids. "I thought maybe, after what I said…"

"It is all right. I understand." He reached out and helped her step from the boat onto the dock. It felt strange to be on solid ground, and she stumbled. Javen caught her and grinned. "Careful, now."

"Thanks." She managed a small smile. Kalumtum turned around and motioned for Milkah to hurry. Her crescent moon earrings slapped the side of her neck at the movement. Milkah picked up her pace as they strode across the wooden dock. "What about the boatmen?" she asked.

"They will stay on the boat with the trade goods until Peleg finishes bargaining," Javen said. "There are thieves everywhere, despite the penalty."

Mikah had not thought about that. Of course that would be the case here. It wasn't like her village, where everyone knew everyone. Although she would have thought that the harsh punishments would keep people from breaking the law.

They reached an open gate at the end of the dock with a soldier on either side, spear in hand. Each one watched closely as the small group filed past. Milkah hurried through with her head down. She didn't like the cold, impassive look in their eyes.

Milkah was immediately struck by the noise and the claustrophobic closeness of Ur. She had expected to see a vast space as they emerged into the city. Instead, she was surrounded by a tight maze of mud-brick houses. Her eyes darted back and forth, drinking in everything. The structures weren't very different from Urshanabi's compound. But there were far more than she had ever seen in one place before. And they were crammed together and stacked one atop another until she couldn't tell where one family's property ended and another's began.

Peleg and Kalumtum turned onto a narrow path that wound between houses. Then Peleg stopped and motioned her forward. "You stay with me. I am not taking any chances."

Milkah realized that if she found a way, she could slip away into the web of houses and disappear. But where would she go? And what would happen if they sent those soldiers after her?

Kalumtum fell into step behind Milkah, hemming her in. Even if she was brave enough to take the chance, they would never give her the opportunity. And if Kalumtum shouted out that Milkah had escaped, the law would be on Kalumtum's side. They would hunt her down. And they would not stop until they found her.

Milkah's head swiveled from side to side as they made their way down the narrow path. Walled courtyards and structures lined each side. She could hear the families who lived inside, just an arm's length from the busy street. A man with a donkey approached from the opposite direction. The donkey shied away and brayed, but the man tugged on the lead rope to force it forward. Milkah had to flatten herself against a wall to allow the animal to pass.

Smoke from cookfires drifted up from behind courtyard walls. The smell of lentil stew, roasted duck, baking bread, and broiled fish filled the air and mingled with the scent of animal dung and sewage. Shouts echoed through the narrow lane. Babies cried and children laughed. Women talked to one another as their grinding stones pounded a steady rhythm. The noise seemed to be coming from all directions—the alleyways running away from the street, the walled courtyards, the upstairs windows, and flat rooftops.

A woman yelled a warning, and dirty water splashed onto the street from above, barely missing them. Milkah sidestepped to avoid the puddle. People pushed their way past her, barely noticing she was there. They all just walked by one another, as if no one else mattered. Everyone was a stranger here.

Peleg turned into another side street. He led them past a house where an elderly woman swept the entranceway. The soft, lilting music of a lyre floated onto the street from behind the wall. Milkah wanted to stop and listen to the music, but Peleg was walking too quickly. She glanced back at Javen, who was following behind Kalumtum. They had to walk single file to allow room for the people filtering past in the opposite direction. He flashed her a grin then raised his eyebrows and motioned to the city around them. She nodded and returned the grin before turning back around.

The narrow street emptied into an open marketplace. Vendors sat on reed mats beside stacks of wares, shouting for buyers. Javen trotted forward, now that there was space to walk side by side. "So, what do you think?"

"You can buy anything here." Milkah stared at the endless displays of goods. There were spices, baskets of grain, stacks of lumber, semiprecious stones, jewelry, cooking oil, leather goods, gold, ivory, pearls, fruits and vegetables, freshly butchered meat, dried fish, colorful woven textiles, and pottery. It was too much to take in.

Peleg led them past a mat with ground spices piled onto clay platters. The rich scents of turmeric, saffron, and garlic hung in the air as they strode by. Then they passed a mat strewn with gold jewelry and shiny blue stones. A man was hawking jugs of barley beer from the next mat. Ducks quacked from a wicker basket, and a pig squealed from somewhere nearby. They were walking too fast, and everything felt like a blur of color and noise. Milkah realized that she couldn't recognize many of the words that she heard. Strange languages filled the marketplace along with strange clothing that she had never seen before.

They stopped when they reached an overweight bald man with heavily kohled eyes and gold earrings. He sat cross-legged on a mat, surrounded by baskets of goods. He smiled up at Peleg as they approached. "Headed south?" he asked.

"I am."

The man's smile widened to a grin. "Let us talk." He patted an empty space on the reed mat beside him. Peleg turned back to Milkah. "Do not leave my sight." Then he settled onto the mat while Kalumtum wandered away, her eyes fixed on a stack of dyed wool nearby.

"He will be a while," Javen said. "They will take their time haggling."

Milkah studied the bustling scene surrounding her. "There is so much to see." She turned to watch a woman on a litter carried by four men. She wore an elaborate headdress made of hammered sheet gold in the shape of leaves and stars. Her one-shouldered cape was dyed a rich red that matched the robe beneath it and the red beads of her necklace. Her gold earrings bounced with the movement of the litter.

"Are you going to look around?" Milkah asked Javen when she noticed Kalumtum winding through the stalls, leaning over to inspect the goods as she went.

"I would rather stay here with you."

Milkah felt a flicker of warmth. But she pushed the feeling away. He could be staying by her side in order to keep an eye on her for Peleg. They might have spoken about it without Milkah knowing. Or he might be planning to betray her in some way that she had not thought of yet. She had learned that kind words and smiles could hide the greatest of evils.

And yet, when Javen smiled, the enthusiasm reached his eyes and felt so genuine.

Milkah frowned and looked away. It was better not to think too much.

"Are you all right?"

"Yes. Of course." Milkah realized that her expression had given her away. She had to learn to be more careful, more guarded. She had never needed to hide her feelings before, and it went against her nature.

"Let us get you something to eat and drink," Javen said. His eyes were kind, but Milkah could sense them searching her. He knew that she was closing herself off from him. "Maybe then you will feel better."

"I am fine, really." She didn't want to owe him anything. Every kindness he did for her made her afraid that he would expect something in return. It seemed strange to think that way. In the past, it had never occurred to her that someone might have ulterior motives.

"Are you sure?" Javen looked at her with his warm brown eyes, and Milkah almost gave in. But she managed to shake her head and look away. "I am not hungry." She watched as a man with a basket full of fish strode past. Javen stood beside her in awkward silence for a moment. Milkah studied the milling crowd and wondered if she could disappear into it. But then where would she go? She glanced back at Peleg. His dark eyes flicked up to hers immediately. He was watching her while he haggled with the trader.

"There is no safe place for you here," Javen said in a low voice.

"What? Oh, no I was not..." But he knew exactly what she had been thinking.

Javen sighed. "You remember when we were talking about Job the day we met?"

"Yes."

"You said you lost everything. Job did too."

"Yes, I have been told that before." She remembered Shiptu's cold glare as she explained Milkah's guilt, comparing it to Job's. Her voice hardened. "And I have been told that he deserved it."

Javen looked surprised. "What?"

"They say he offended God in some way. Why else would he suffer?"

Javen's expression shifted into a frown. "No, that is not what happened at all. Job is the most righteous man in Uz. He might be the most righteous man anywhere, from what I have heard. Where did you hear otherwise?"

Milkah remembered the confident laughter at dinner the night before she was betrayed. "From everyone."

Javen shook his head. "People say all kinds of things to make themselves feel better."

"Yes, that is true." Milkah felt a spark of a connection when she heard his words, but she immediately tried to smother it.

"People like to rely on their own righteousness. They want to point fingers and go to bed feeling safe. Otherwise, how can they face the dark?"

"I do not think the people who told me about Job were righteous."

"No? Well, even so."

"I suppose they considered themselves righteous."

"Most people do."

Milkah nodded. She watched a woman haggling over a length of woven cloth at a nearby stall. "I had hoped that Job was righteous."

"Because that meant that you might be too?"

Milkah's attention jerked to Javen. "Yes."

"I understand."

"How? No one else has."

Javen took a deep breath and let it out slowly. "Evil struck my house too. Not as severely as it did yours, but I have known loss. The answers people had for me were not good enough. I used to leave offerings at the temples, and it did not do any good. I said the right prayers. I paid the diviners and healers to break curses and expel demons. None of it worked. So I finally decided that it wasn't as simple as everybody claimed. Then, when I heard about Job's God—the One God—it all made sense."

Milkah's mouth went dry. "How? What made sense?" She leaned closer, needing the answer.

Javen smiled, but it didn't reach his eyes this time. Instead, his gaze was far away. "It made sense that it cannot make sense to us. How can we ever understand the ways of God?"

"That is it? That is your answer?"

Javen shrugged. "Yes."

"It is not enough. I do not like it."

Javen's eyes stayed on something in the distance. "Neither do I. But that does not make it any less true."

Milkah could feel the tension in her shoulders, the tightness in her chest. She needed more than this. Javen's attention shifted back to her. He studied her expression for a moment. "What happened to your family?" he asked softly. "How did you lose them?"

Milkah looked down at her hands. There was a pale ring of untanned skin around her wrist where her bracelet used to be.

Javen exhaled. "I'm sorry. I should not have asked. You do not have to talk about it."

Milkah's eyes flicked up to his, and something broke within her. She couldn't resist the sincerity and gentleness in his voice. "It was not something that should have happened. I have heard of families all dying together from a plague or from war. So I know that entire families can be lost. But not like this…"

When she didn't say anything else, Javen waited but kept his eyes on her. The sounds and smells of the marketplace faded away as the past roared back. "Mad dogs attacked us in the fields. Some of us died right there. The madness took everyone else, except for my abba and youngest sister. Then, just when I dared to believe that we would be all right, they both drowned. It all happened so fast…" Milkah didn't know how to explain. "People said we were cursed. Then Shiptu—the woman who took me to Urshanabi—she told me about Job. And it made me feel…" Milkah shook her head. She had said too much. "Never mind."

"It is all right."

Milkah hesitated, but Javen's soft brown eyes convinced her to keep going. "When I heard about Job, I did not feel so alone anymore. I realized that I am not the only one to serve God and lose everything. And I know that I did not do anything to deserve it. But I cannot… I cannot feel Him anymore. There is no sign of Him anywhere. And, after what has happened since my family died…" She didn't finish the sentence.

"People who worship the new gods say that it is impossible to know if we have offended them."

Milkah nodded, and Javen continued.

"Eventually we will forget a ritual or we will say something we should not, or forget to say something that we should. Everyone is always looking over their shoulder, worried about what they might have done or failed to do. They are thinking, what if I opened a door to a demon? What if I accidentally exposed myself to something that could bring on a curse? What if my family has been cursed in a previous generation and I do not even know it? So they offer more sacrifices and work harder to appease the gods for all the sins that they do not even know they committed."

Javen shifted his weight and readjusted his kilt. "But I do not think our God is like that. I do not think that we are always at risk of offending Him when we do not mean it, or accidentally bringing a demon home, or opening a door to a curse. With Him, I do not think it is about what we do ritually, I think it is about what is in our hearts. How do we really feel about Him? How do we treat others? That is what matters to God, I think."

"But even if we do what you are saying—if we do right in our hearts—He might still allow our worst fears to befall us."

Javen sighed. He looked at Milkah as if considering what to say. "That is true. Job said that his worst fears had come to pass."

"Then what is the point of serving the One God?" Milkah spoke low enough that she wasn't sure Javen had heard. Even so, she felt a pulse of regret as soon as the words escaped her lips. Something deeper than fear pulled within her. But she didn't know what to do with that feeling, so she pushed it away. "Anyway, the priests would put a curse on you for saying those things."

"Of course they would. Or they would try, anyway. They would be out of a job if everyone believed like me."

"You are a radical." Milkah smiled as she said the words.

"I hope so. You have to be if you serve the One True God."

CHAPTER EIGHT

Milkah sat on the boat that night, feeling the gentle rocking motion as she watched the other vessels docked in the harbor. She studied the trail of moonlight skipping along the surface and the soft glow of oil lamps that pierced the darkness like little stars. Javen worked nearby, sorting baskets of grain.

Something caught Milkah's attention, and she squinted at the sleek black water. The shimmer of moonlight dipped and wavered along the surface. Milkah inhaled sharply. Something moved beneath them. She leaned forward. A current swirled. Then there was a splash. Milkah leaped to her feet. She squinted into the silent harbor but saw no more movement. The moonlight lay still on the water again.

"Something out there?" Javen asked. He glanced up briefly then looked back down at the basket in front of him.

"Yes." Milkah let out a nervous laugh. "For a moment I thought—" She shook her head. "Never mind."

"When you are thinking about sea monsters, you will find evidence for them everywhere."

Milkah felt her face flush. "I know it is silly. But you are right, it is on my mind."

"Why should it not be? Who would not have questions?" His eyes moved to hers, and she knew he was talking about more than monsters. She felt exposed after all that she had told him earlier that day.

"I have heard a new story about a sea monster." The voice came from the dock.

Milkah and Javen both turned to look. A tanned stranger wearing a worn woolen kilt and a copper armband stood alongside their boat. "I could not help overhearing you."

"Which sea monster?" Milkah asked.

"The leviathan."

Javen and Milkah exchanged a quick glance. "Come aboard," Javen said and waved the man toward them. "Sit and eat with us. We would like to hear."

The man nodded. "All right." He dropped onto the deck with the surefooted practice of a boatman. "Where do you come from?"

"Down the coast of the Great Water," Javen said. "Far from here."

The man nodded. "I have just gotten back from trading with an overland caravan upriver."

Milkah felt a stab of expectation. "They had not been to Uz, had they?" She felt embarrassed as soon as she asked. That would be too much of a coincidence.

The man's eyebrows rose. "As a matter of fact, that was exactly where they had come from."

Milkah's heart skipped a beat. "Tell us everything."

Javen ducked into the shelter, returned with a bowl of nuts and dates, and motioned for the man to sit. Milkah scooted over to make room. The small group formed dark silhouettes beneath the pale white moonlight as they huddled together. "Did you hear anything about a man called Job?" Milkah couldn't stop herself from asking right away.

The boatman chuckled. "Sure did. Everyone is talking about him."

"We have heard news, here and there, but not enough," Javen said. He reached for a handful of dates.

"What is the latest you have heard?" the boatman asked.

"That he was sitting outside in ashes, mourning the loss of all he had, and scraping his sores," Milkah said.

The man chuckled. "Oh, well, I have more for you."

Milkah grinned. She glanced over at Javen, and he returned her smile. His face was partially lost in shadow, but she could see his white teeth in the moonlight. She liked sharing a moment of excitement with him. It made her feel as if someone understood her. She couldn't remember the last time she had felt that way.

The boatman cleared his throat and cracked his knuckles. Milkah could tell that he was going to be a good storyteller. "You have heard that Job was struck down with disaster after disaster— all his livestock lost, all his children too. Then he took sick. Covered in open sores, as you know."

Milkah nodded.

"And all his friends warned him to repent. They gave long speeches, explaining to him that God punishes wrongdoers. Job insisted that he was innocent. So the friends explained that he just didn't realize that he was guilty. You know how easily that can happen."

Milkah's stomach sank. This was going to be the same story that Shiptu and Jubal had told. She didn't want to hear that version. She knew that news changed depending on who was telling it, but that there was only one real version. She believed it was Javen's. She needed it to be Javen's.

"Who knows if we have stepped on sacred ground belonging to one god or another? Or if we said the wrong thing? Or if we opened a door to a demon, hungry for human flesh?" The boatman paused for effect. "But Job did none of these things."

Milkah straightened up.

"Job was righteous."

"I knew it!" Milkah flinched when she realized that she had shouted the words. But the boatman just looked amused.

"Then you were right."

"How do you know?" Javen asked. "I heard he was righteous too, but I had no proof."

The boatman raised his hands, palms up. "God appeared to him in a whirlwind."

Milkah's eyes widened. "In a whirlwind?"

The boatman smiled. "That is right. A whirlwind. God swept in with a mighty rush of wind that hid Him from sight."

"Huh." Javen leaned back against the reed wall of the boat. His face looked pleased and thoughtful.

"What did God say?" Milkah dropped the fig she had been holding. There was no way she could eat now. "I have heard that He appeared to Job, but no one has been able to tell me the details."

"Well, first you have to understand what had been happening. See, Job knew that he was righteous. And after a while, that didn't sit too well with him. I do not blame him. And I do not think God blamed him for that either."

"Did he turn from God?"

The boatman shook his head. "No. But Job wrestled with Him. How could he not? He could not understand why God let him lose everything, when he had served Him so faithfully. And the more Job's friends blamed him, the more it tormented him."

"Yes," Milkah murmured. "I am sure it did."

Javen glanced at her but said nothing.

"So eventually, Job demanded answers from God. Who would not? Even the most righteous cannot bear to suffer that much. He could not stand it anymore."

"And did God blame him then?"

The boatman rubbed his chin with callused fingers. "No, I do not think He did. But, even so, no man has a right to accuse God."

Javen nodded. Milkah just stared, her pulse pounding in her ears as she waited to hear more.

"So, God came down in a whirlwind and told Job that he knows nothing."

"What exactly did He say?" Milkah leaned forward.

"Oh, well, there was a lot. He started by asking Job where he was when God laid the foundations of the earth."

Javen grunted. He looked amused.

The boatman glanced at him and smiled. "Pretty good question, right?"

"Yes."

"What else?" Milkah asked.

"He asked if Job was there when God put the stars in the sky. He asked if Job can make the sun rise, or if he can control the weather. God was there for all of it, of course, and He made sure that Job realized that. Then God pointed out the complexity of His creation, how every animal knows just what to do and how all of it works together somehow. So how can Job understand what is just or unjust? The universe is too vast, God is too great. Job sees from the tiny little perspective of his tiny little time and place. But God sees all."

Milkah frowned. "So, God is just. That is what you are saying— what God Himself said."

"Right. But how can Job see that? How can any of us?"

Milkah let out a long breath of air. The words felt right inside, but they didn't sit easy. She still wanted to understand.

"And that," the man said with a grin, "is where the leviathan comes in."

Milkah had almost forgotten their mention of the sea monster that had caught the boatman's attention in the first place. "Did God send it out to punish Job? I have heard that."

The boatman laughed. "Not at all. The leviathan is not evil. It is not sent to punish."

"But it does destroy," Javen cut in. "I am sure of that."

"Yes, it does."

Milkah's brow crinkled. "I do not understand."

The boatman laughed again. "I am not sure I do either. The leviathan is some sort of symbol of chaos within God's plan for creation."

"Just a symbol?" Javen's eyebrow shot up. He did not look convinced.

"A bringer of chaos, then. Who knows if it represents chaos or brings it? And I am not sure it matters."

"Of course it matters!" Milkah realized her tone too late. "I am sorry. I did not mean to snap at you. But none of this makes sense."

"How could a sea monster make sense? How could anything that God does make sense? That is the whole point. Life will never be predictable. It will never make sense, even if you serve God faithfully."

Javen nodded slowly. But Milkah shook her head. "That cannot be the end of it though. What happened next? God gave Job the answers? He explained why He allowed the righteous to suffer?"

"Nope."

Milkah flinched. "That is it? That is the end of the story?"

"That is it."

"It cannot be."

The boatman shrugged. "Well, God did confirm that Job is righteous—none of the suffering was his fault. And He made it clear that Job needs to trust in God's wisdom, not his own. So there is that."

"But…" Milkah looked from the boatman to Javen, then back to the boatman again. "That is it? Really?"

The boatman spread out his hands, palms up. "That is it."

"It is not enough."

"It has to be," Javen responded quietly.

"But it is not," Milkah repeated. There was nothing more that she could say. She had heard all that had happened to Job, and still nothing made sense.

And worse than that, she now knew that she was not safe. The reality settled deep within her, like a growing darkness. Who was to say that something worse wouldn't happen to her now? After all, God had allowed Job to suffer the unbearable—and then to suffer even more. And Job was righteous. He should have been safe.

Was there nothing standing between her and the abyss?

The next morning, Milkah fell out of a dream like barley seeds caught in the wind. "Get up. It is time to go worship."

Milkah opened her eyes and realized that Kalumtum was shaking her awake. "What?"

"I said to get up. We are leaving."

Milkah had just enough time to braid her hair and arrange it on top of her head before they filed off the boat.

"Carry this." Kalumtum shoved two baskets into Milkah's arms.

"Have we remembered to pack everything?" Kalumtum asked Peleg.

"Yes, of course." He sounded vaguely annoyed.

Kalumtum's face was tight. Milkah wondered why. She must be afraid that her god wouldn't accept the sacrifice.

Milkah was trying to get a grip on both baskets when Javen appeared at her side. "I will take this," he said as he scooped one of the reed baskets from her hands. Milkah nodded. "Thank you." The morning was already sweltering hot, and sweat dripped down her forehead. She wiped her face with her bare arm and watched the boats entering the harbor as the small group strode down the dock. The sun's rays poured over the water and set it ablaze in shades of pink and gold.

Milkah turned to Javen and whispered, "I did not think you would come to the ziggurat. You can see it there in the distance."

Milkah raised her eyes in the direction he pointed and saw the tallest structure she had ever seen. It seemed to reach the sky.

"I would rather not," he said. "But I do not want you to have to go alone. And they are not going to let you out of their sight, so…" He shrugged.

Milkah stared at him for a moment. "Why do you not want me to have to go alone?"

Javen rubbed the back of his neck. "Oh, I do not know. It is not a place... Well, I do not like it there. I do not think you will either." He looked sheepish. "I thought it might help to have a friend."

He was coming along just to make her feel better, even though he didn't want to go. The realization warmed her inside. She tried to push the warmth away but couldn't. She smiled at him instead, even as she berated herself for doing so. He returned the smile.

"Move on," a soldier's deep voice bellowed beside them. Milkah startled, then hurried ahead. She had not been paying attention to where they were going. They passed through the gates, then wound through the maze of houses again but soon veered off in a different direction. For a while, everything looked the same as the day before. Houses stood side by side, sharing walls with their neighbors, and the sounds of families cooking breakfast drifted from inner courtyards. Donkeys blocked the narrow street and brayed when their owners tried to force them to move. A stray dog dashed out of an alleyway to disappear down another lane. The ditch running through the street reeked of sewage, and puddles of stagnant water littered the thoroughfare. Milkah tried to avoid them. Her sandals left most of her skin exposed, and she didn't want the dirty water to splash her bare toes.

She was too busy avoiding puddles to notice the wall looming ahead of them. When she finally looked up, Milkah stopped short. The bricks towered like a fortress, warning her away. The sound of chanting rose from behind the wall to mingle with the scent of incense and the bleating of animals. A cold chill shivered through her.

They entered through a decorative gate that opened into a spacious outer courtyard. Milkah skidded to a halt and stared. People filled the open space, holding baskets of grain, fish, fruit, and spices. Others clutched bolts of brightly dyed cloth or jars of barley beer. Milkah was caught in the swirl of colors and noise. The bustling space was a city within a city, overwhelming her with the buzz of activity.

Behind the crowd lay a row of whitewashed structures. Milkah watched the people going in and out. Many of them were temple slaves, barefoot and wearing simple, undyed kilts, hurrying to wherever they were needed. She recognized the priests by their shaved heads and knew that the women she saw with them must be priestesses. The priests and priestesses were all fine-looking people, with strong bodies, who must have been chosen from the most elite families. Milkah stared at them, wondering what it would be like to ascend the ziggurat's stairway to heaven and converse with your god.

"No," she whispered to herself. She had to hold strong to the truth that their gods were not reachable. They did not exist. But the priests and priestesses looked so confident in their finely woven wool skirts and glittering jewelry, chins raised with the haughty assurance of someone with access to power and answers.

Milkah wanted that access too. She wanted answers.

Milkah could see into the courtyard of one of the buildings as they walked past. Women sat at low tables as they pressed reed styluses into tablets of wet clay. She had heard that priestesses were educated just like men, although she had never seen evidence of it before. But of course, she had never known anyone who could read or write. It wasn't possible in her village, even for the boys.

Sick and injured people waited in line outside of the next walled courtyard. Some stood, shuffling and muttering, while others lay silent on stretchers, carried by family members with tight, desperate expressions. Beyond the open doorway she could hear the low incantations of the priests chanting their healing magic. A shout rose from beyond the door, then a high-pitched scream that sent a shudder down her spine. There was another shout, followed by a strange howling. The chanting sharpened in intensity until the howls turned into the shrieks of a trapped animal. Milkah turned away. The sounds from that courtyard made her feel wrong inside, though she could not explain exactly why.

Peleg made the sign against the evil eye as they strode past. Kalumtum refused to look. She kept her gaze straight ahead, her lips a firm line.

"What is going on in there?" Milkah whispered to Javen.

"They are exorcising demons to heal the sick."

Milkah nodded. It was common knowledge that demon possession caused many sicknesses. The vague, sick feeling that something was wrong continued to creep through her body, even as she moved past the building. She realized that the entire complex felt as strange and disturbing as the exorcism she had heard. "I think the demons are everywhere here," she murmured, half to herself.

Javen's eyes cut to her. "You are right about that."

Milkah swallowed. "I can feel it." She looked over to meet Javen's gaze. "That is why you did not want me to have to come here alone, is it not?"

"Yes." He scanned the crowd. "They do not seem to feel it. But I always did, even before I gave myself to the One God. Something always felt dark and wrong about this place. And now, well…" He shook his head. "I can barely stand to set foot within the walls."

"But you did."

His attention turned back to her. He nodded, his eyes steady. "I did."

Milkah knew what he meant, though he did not say it. He had come to this terrible place for her sake. She wanted to reach out and take his hand. It was a silly impulse, and she stamped it down. But her heart beat a little faster at the thought.

A priest cloaked in the skin of a giant mangar strolled past, the silvery-yellow fish scales sparkling in the sun as he moved. He ducked into a structure filled with priests with shaved heads wearing heavy gold jewelry. They crouched over low tables, pressing their reed styluses into clay tablets and conversing with one another.

Milkah could see that some of the men weren't priests. They had unshaven heads, and their sleek black hair was neatly styled in waves, like their beards. Their finely woven kilts and gold earrings, necklaces, armbands, and heavy makeup marked them as wealthy men. "What are they doing in there?" Milkah asked Javen.

"They are handling business. Real estate transactions and trade deals, mostly. A lot of the property in the city belongs to the temple. The priests manage it all in the name of their god, but"—he grinned and shrugged—"in the end, it is just business. They make a great deal of money and have a great deal of power." They kept walking, and Milkah craned her neck to watch the men inside the complex as they passed. "That is why they all have to be educated as scribes," Javen added. "They have to keep records of all their business transactions, their holdings, their profits, all of it. They see it as acting as caretakers for their god, of course."

"And what do you see it as?" Milkah asked.

"A way to get what they want."

They passed a pen filled with goats and sheep. The smell of animal dung mingled with the scents of sunbaked mud and sweat. A priestess was examining the animals, tapping a finger against her chin as she considered. Then she pointed toward a ram. A slave rushed forward to pull it from the pen. "She is a diviner, is she not?" Milkah asked.

"Yes." Javen frowned. "They will slaughter the ram, and she will prophesy based on the signs she reads in the organs."

"I have seen enough," Milkah said.

"You have not yet seen what we came for." Javen nodded ahead of them. "Surely you can see how close we are." He glanced over to her. "Be prepared. The ziggurat will dazzle you, even though you will try to resist."

"I have heard that it puts the fear of the gods into everyone who sees it."

"It seems to. People say no one could build such a wonder without divine help."

"What do you say?"

Javen considered for a moment. "That people do a great many things they should not do, with or without anyone's help."

Milkah laughed. "You say the strangest things sometimes."

Javen flashed a smile. "It does not mean I am wrong."

"No. It does not." Milkah returned his smile, and it stayed on her face longer than she meant it to.

The wall to the inner courtyard drew nearer, and Milkah felt her belly tighten. She didn't want to feel excited, but the energy of the crowd was contagious. Like them, she wanted to see something great and wonderful, here on earth. She tried to fight the anticipation that zipped through her veins, but she could not push it down.

And then they were passing through the ornately carved gates, to the grand courtyard, the home of the greatest monument to the gods ever built. To the false gods, she reminded herself as she stepped inside the walls. The reminder fled from her as soon as her eyes beheld the wonder that towered all the way to the sky.

CHAPTER NINE

Milkah sucked in her breath and stared, unable to move. The great step pyramid loomed over her, rising higher and higher, until it seemed to touch the very heavens. She craned her head back and squinted against the sun to take in the full height of it. She could not understand how anything made with human hands could be that high. How had they done it? Even with thousands of slaves to dig the earth and bake the bricks and haul them one after another... No. It still seemed impossible.

The massive structure rose in three levels, with a triple staircase across the front so that the priests and priestesses could ascend toward heaven to worship Nanna, the god of the moon. In the middle of the pyramid rose a grand staircase, while the two smaller staircases angled upward from opposite corners of the base level.

The effect was that of an angular, artificial mountain, a place where the gods were known to live. There were no mountains on the plain, so the people had created their own mountain to bring the gods to them. Except this mountain gleamed and glistened in the sun as the rays caught its shimmering painted bricks. The outer edges of the first story were a deep, foreboding black. The second and third stories were painted a bold, bright red that reminded Milkah of a fiery sunset—or the blood of slaughtered animals.

A shrine stood atop the highest level, its enameled brick walls glazed a deep blue as rich and pure as water.

Milkah felt dizzy beneath the heat of the sun, staring upward, her head thrown back to take it all in. A hand touched her arm. "Are you all right?"

She heard Javen's voice but could not look away from the ziggurat. "Yes…I am fine."

"Remember, it is just a building. No different from any house, only bigger." She could hear the tension in his voice.

"Yes. Just a house…" But it didn't feel like it was just any house. It was grand and glorious, unlike anything she had seen or imagined. It made her feel weak and small inside, but strangely important too. People like her had built this. Was there nothing that people could not do?

She frowned and pulled her eyes away. Her mother had warned her about the ziggurats. She said that there had been one not too long ago, taller than anything ever built. But the One God had come down and scattered the people who built it, because they had thought the same thing Milkah had just been thinking—that they could do anything if they could create such a marvel. When she had heard the story, Milkah had believed that she was above all that, that she would never think such things. But she had never looked upon a ziggurat before. She had been arrogant to believe that she would be immune.

This is why they build them, she realized. It created a fever in the soul, to see such wonders.

"Come on." Peleg glared at her. "You are holding everyone up."

Milkah glanced behind her to see people stopping short, then sidestepping around her. Javen dropped his hand from her arm, and she hurried ahead. The skin felt bare where his fingers had been, and she wished that he would touch her again. It had made her feel safer to have a friend in this strange, unearthly place.

Milkah kept her eyes on the ziggurat as they neared its base. Stacks of offerings covered the bottom steps of the grand staircase. A small child rushed forward to set a bolt of colorful cloth onto a step, then looked over at his mother. The mother smiled, and the child skipped back to her. She kissed the top of his head and took his hand.

Milkah crept closer, her gaze fixed on the gleaming building towering above her.

"I can help you."

Milkah's attention jerked to a woman standing beside her. "What?"

The woman stared at her through dark eyes lined with kohl. Her eyebrows were painted with kohl as well, and drawn together to form a single line above her eyes. Her eyelids were painted a beautiful shade of blue, and her lips were stained red. She wore an elaborate headband made of bronze and blue beads and gold hoop earrings that hung to her shoulders. "I can help you," she repeated.

Milkah glanced around. Somehow, she had lost Javen in the crowd.

The woman eased closer. "I see something in you." Her unblinking eyes pierced Milkah. She felt as if the woman could peer down into her soul. The feeling made her shiver.

"You are a priestess?"

"Yes."

"I do not... I do not need your help." But even as she said the words, Milkah could feel the desire within. The woman's words tugged on her with the force of water flowing downriver. She could feel herself being swept away.

The woman slowly cocked her head and studied her. "But you do need help."

Milkah's jaw flexed. She glanced away again, looking for Javen, but only saw strangers. She turned back to the woman. A quiet warning whispered inside of her, but something else pulled at her too. Something that made her feel powerful and in control. "How can you help?"

The woman smiled. Her eyes pierced a little deeper into Milkah. "You have been deeply troubled, yes?"

Milkah frowned then nodded.

"Your life has taken a strange and terrible path."

"Yes." Milkah's heart contracted. How could this woman know?

"I will break the curse. And then I will divine your future. I know that you want to know."

Milkah knew that she should say no. She had felt the wrongness in this place. And she knew that her God did not allow diviners or fortunetellers. But something in the woman's eyes had caught hold of her. The priestess could help her. She had answers. She had a hidden power, access to knowledge, to secrets. Milkah's mouth felt dry, and her pulse pounded in her ears. What would happen if she said yes? Could this woman break a curse from her? Would her life fall back into place? Could a priestess really tell her what her future held?

Everything within her yearned for answers. Why had her family died? Why had she been betrayed? What would happen to her when they reached Dilmun? Was there a way for her to be free again? The One God had not answered her. And He had not saved her from destruction.

"Let me help you," the priestess said. Her voice was smooth and promising, like the warm waters of the Euphrates. Milkah could sink into them and drift away. It could be so easy to have answers, to have hope again. Everyone else here was doing this—and they must be getting something good from it. Why else would they all come here?

The priestess watched her as the seconds ticked by, each one echoed by the pounding of Milkah's heart. Sweat beaded above her lip, and she wiped it away. Maybe the One God wouldn't mind. What could it hurt? Wouldn't He want her to have answers? To be at peace? Her belly surged at the hope of it.

But something deeper whispered within her. Milkah squeezed her eyes shut. She could feel the quiet warning. It filled her core with a silent knowing. And as she listened to it, a prickly sickness began to creep across her. She opened her eyes again and stared at the woman. The feeling of wrongness grew within her. She couldn't explain it or understand it, but she knew it was there.

"No." Milkah shook her head, then said the words quickly, before she could change her mind. "I cannot."

The woman's brow crinkled. "But why not, dear girl?"

"I just cannot. My God does not allow it."

The woman looked sad. "I wanted to help you. I would have helped you." And then she stepped away and faded into the crowd. Milkah felt a stab of remorse as she watched the woman go. She shook the feeling away, and a heavy wave of relief rushed through her, even though her heart still burned for answers.

"Hey!" Peleg's voice roared through the air. "Where have you been?"

Milkah flinched. "I just looked up and you were gone. I am sorry. There are so many people."

He grabbed her arm, and his fingers closed with the force of metal. "Do not. Leave. My. Sight."

"I will not. I promise." Milkah caught a glimpse of the priestess in the crowd. Their eyes met, and the woman stared at her with those sad, knowing eyes before she turned away and disappeared behind a group of priests.

"There you are." Javen jogged over. His eyes moved to her arm. "I will watch her."

"No you will not. You already lost her."

"So did you."

Peleg grunted, but he released Milkah's arm. "We need to leave the offering."

"I was worried about you," Javen whispered as they hurried toward the base of the ziggurat.

"I was all right."

Javen glanced over to Peleg, then back to Milkah. He lowered his voice. "Do not try to run."

"I did not."

Javen nodded, but his expression was still troubled. "If Peleg thought you had…" Javen shook his head. "Never mind. Just do not try. You will not get away with it here."

"He knows that I just got separated in the crowd," Milkah shot back in a whisper. "It was only for an instant." But her belly prickled with worry. She needed to be more careful.

"Here." Kalumtum waved them over to where she stood at the base of the grand staircase. Milkah went to her, even though she wanted to run in the opposite direction. Javen followed. "I am giving this to you to offer," Kalumtum said as she flashed Milkah a proud smile. "You see, I am not who you think I am. I take care of what belongs to me." She held up a jug of barley beer. "Take it and give it to Nanna." Her smile widened. "You are welcome."

Milkah didn't move. She felt Javen tense beside her. A few beats passed. Her heart thudded inside her ears. Kalumtum stared at her. Milkah could sense the warning in the woman's eyes. She swallowed hard. It would be so easy to give in and lay the jug on the step. It would only be a little thing to do, and it would stop Kalumtum's anger. The temptation roiled within her, telling her to stop making this harder than it had to be.

"Go on." Kalumtum shooed her toward the steps. "I am giving it to you so you can pray for our safe travel on the Great Water."

Milkah didn't move. Her face burned with shame, even though she knew that she was doing nothing wrong by resisting.

Kalumtum's smile faded. "You are not taking it? What is wrong with you?"

Milkah didn't answer. She wanted to sink into the ground. It felt like everyone was staring at her. The pressure bore down on her with the weight of a stone. She knew she would pay for this. Kalumtum would not accept any offense against her or her god.

Peleg stormed over to them. "What is this? The girl will not take it?" His gaze cut to Milkah, and he glared down at her as if she were one of the specks of dirt beneath their sandals. "Are you that ungrateful?"

"It is not that. I just cannot—"

"Who does not leave an offering to Nanna? What is wrong with you?"

"My God does not allow it."

Kalumtum snorted. "The God who has let you end up where you are? Ninsun told me your story."

Peleg burst into laughter. "She has a personal god? Not much good, is he?"

Kalumtum laughed too. "As if your God could compare to Nanna."

Peleg motioned for Milkah to take the jug of barley beer. "Enough. Get it done and let us go."

Javen stepped between them. "Leave her alone and let her serve her God. What does it matter to you?"

Peleg gave a dismissive wave. "You serve a strange God too. Of course you would stand up for this."

"It is not right," Kalumtum said. "She belongs to us. She does not get to keep her own gods. She has to serve ours now."

"She will serve the God she wants to serve," Javen said. "Same as me." His eyes sharpened and his face hardened with resolve. "If you try to force her to serve your gods, then I will not sail with you to Dilmun."

Peleg crossed his arms. "I will get another boatman."

"One you can trust? And one who has the experience to go that far south?" Javen gave Peleg a steady look. "You sure about that?"

Peleg stared back at Javen for a few beats. His jaw clenched and unclenched. "Fine. But I do not want to hear anything about your God." He turned to glower at Milkah. "And do not dare utter a word against our gods while we are at sea. If you do, I will throw you overboard myself. I will not have you risk all our lives."

Milkah stared back, her heart beating too fast to answer. She nodded her head, eyes wide. Then Peleg spun around and marched to the grand staircase. Kalumtum flounced after him. Milkah exhaled. "Thank you."

Javen shook his head. His eyes still glittered with anger. "You do not have to thank me. It was the right thing to do. I would never let them—" He cut himself off. "I will do what I can for you." His gaze met hers, and she felt the determination behind his dark brown eyes. They stayed on her, steady and strong. "I hope you realize that."

Milkah's skin felt hot. She didn't know how to answer, so she just stared back at him. But for the first time, she dared to believe that he was telling the truth. She held the gaze for a long moment before dropping her eyes.

At the base of the ziggurat, Peleg and Kalumtum laid baskets of barley and fruit, the jug of barley beer, and a length of cloth.

"What will happen to all of it?" Milkah asked. The steps were piled with food and drink.

"The priests will take it to feed Nanna."

"And then what?"

"They must eat it themselves." He chuckled. "Because their god sure does not. I do not know exactly how it works, but I do know that these offerings help keep the temple complex running. It takes a lot to feed and clothe all those priests, priestesses, and slaves."

The sound of voices filled the air above them, and Milkah turned her face upward. She shielded her eyes with the blade of her hand and squinted into the sun. Priests and priestesses moved along the outer edges of the shrine on top of the ziggurat. The inner chambers of the shrine were hidden from view, to keep the mysteries of the gods. Milkah couldn't make out the details because of the distance, but she could see the blurs of color as the people circled the structure.

A lone voice began to sing, and the unearthly tune drifted down the ziggurat to fill the courtyard. The worshipers fell silent, and all eyes turned heavenward. A chorus of voices from above joined in the song. The low beat of drums erupted. The deep rhythm pulsed through the air and inside Milkah's chest. Far above, the priests and priestesses wound past one another in a strange, slow dance, arms outstretched toward their god.

Suddenly, in the midst of the beautiful music and hushed crowd, Milkah was overcome with joy that she had not given into the ziggurat's temptation. This was not her God, and these were not her priests. Her God had no priest or house. He lived wherever He wanted. Her mother had said that maybe, one day, God would ask His people to build Him a house, and He would fill it with His own priests. But not yet. The world was still young, and He filled all of it with His glory. He could not be contained. He could not dwell in a single structure, no matter how tall or magnificent it was.

For the first time in a long time, Milkah felt right inside. And she felt proud of her God—the One True God.

They set sail the next morning. The two boatmen who had guided them to Ur stayed behind, unwilling to go so far south. They made their living poling boats up and down the Euphrates and would not risk the unknown dangers of the Great Water. As the boat slid away from the dock, Milkah watched as the two men strode away, their belongings slung over their shoulders in woolen bags.

One of them whistled and the other hummed along. Milkah wondered where they would go next.

She found a place to sit beside Javen as he maneuvered the boat through the harbor. Peleg stood at the opposite end of the boat with a pole in his hands. Sweat beaded across his forehead, and his face was red from the heat and effort.

"Can we manage without the boatmen?" Milkah asked.

Javen nodded and used his elbow to wipe the sweat from his brow without taking a hand from the pole. "Sure. We will put up the sails as soon as we can. Those men do not know how to sail. Peleg hires them when we are on the river, but once we go into the Great Water, we are always on our own."

They slowly wound their way through the congested harbor, to the city gates. They paid their taxes again, and Milkah looked away from the soldiers' hardened eyes as Peleg and Javen unloaded the baskets of barley and jugs of barley beer. As soon as they were out of the soldiers' earshot Peleg muttered, "They get you coming in and going out. Who do they think they are?"

Kalumtum laughed. "The ones with the weapons."

Milkah watched the soldiers grow smaller and smaller as the boat drifted down the canal. Beyond the city, on the other side of the waterway, she noticed a gleaming whitewashed wall, guarded by more soldiers. "What is in there?" she asked Javen, careful to keep her voice low enough that Peleg and Kalumtum couldn't hear.

"The burial ground. The kings and queens are laid to rest there. And a lot of others too, who will not be remembered. They buried twenty-eight women there alongside the last king to die. All of them killed so they can follow him into the afterlife to serve him there."

"Do you think they had a choice?"

"Oh, I doubt it. They would have been enslaved women, I am sure. Although they may have believed what they were told. It would have been easier that way."

They both stared at the walls.

"They sent them to the afterlife with silver ribbons in their hair," Javen said after a moment. "Not that it matters."

"You do not think it does?"

"No. There will not be any division when we reach the other side. The enslaved will be free, the rich and the poor with be on equal terms. Beggars will dine with kings."

"It is a nice thought, but it sounds like a child's fantasy. What makes you believe it?"

"I heard that Job believes it. If God declared him righteous, it must be true. Besides, it just feels right, does it not? Why should the powerful keep their power? How many powerful men are truly righteous? And, anyway, what would their power mean to God? They will be nothing before Him. We are all equal when it comes to that."

"Hmm." Milkah liked the thought. Being free and equal had not mattered so much, back in her village, when all the women she knew were equal to one another, more or less. She had not thought to consider it. But now it was all she could think about.

Milkah stared at the burial ground until rows of date palms and mud-brick buildings blocked her view. She slouched back against the wall of the boat, tired of straining her eyes to see.

"You said that the boatmen cannot sail. But you can?" Milkah gave a nervous laugh. "I mean, you know what you are doing out there in the Great Water?"

"Yes. I can sail. So can Peleg and Kalumtum. They spend most of their lives on this boat, going back and forth, back and forth."

She turned her head to look up at Javen. "What about you? Is that how you spend your life, going back and forth?"

He shrugged and kept his eyes on the waterway. "I guess it has been." He smiled, and his expression looked as if he were thinking of something far away. "Hopefully it will not be forever."

"What do you want to do instead?" Milkah squinted against the sun so that she could see his face better.

He breathed in and out, then shrugged again. "I guess I would like to see my family."

"And stay there, with them?"

"Yes."

Milkah waited for him to say more. When he did not, she took a chance and pressed him. "Why are you not with them now?"

"My father died. He taught me how to sail, and after we lost him, I had to take his place on the water. My mother and sisters depend on me now. It is not a bad life, but it keeps me too far from them."

"How did he die?" Milkah shook her head. "I should not have asked."

Javen hesitated. "At sea."

"I am sorry."

Javen nodded. There was an awkward silence. The water splashed as he moved the pole in and out. A child's shouts drifted from the shore.

"Are you afraid to make the journey?" Javen asked after a moment. "I did not want to tell you what happened to my father, but you are no fool. You already knew the risks of sea travel."

"I suppose it is worth the risk for you, if you make it to Dilmun and back."

Javen's face hardened. "Yes. If we make it."

Milkah looked over the water as Javen and Peleg steered the boat onto the Euphrates. The sound of the boat traffic on the canal faded as they caught the current and began to drift downstream. "The answer is yes, I am afraid of the storms," Milkah said.

Javen nodded. "So am I."

Milkah's attention jerked to him. "You are? But I thought…"

"That a boatman would not be afraid of what the Great Water brings?" He chuckled. "We are afraid because we know what to expect. And losing my father to the sea did not help."

There was an awkward silence. "I am sorry," Milkah said after a moment, even though she had already told him that.

"We knew the risk. My mother always warned us that he might not come back one day." Javen sighed. "But you always think it will not happen to your family. Other men go out and do not come back, but your father, he will always come back because he has to, right?"

"Yes." Milkah remembered how safe she had felt growing up, when she still believed that evil could not touch her house. "I understand what you mean."

Javen's eyes moved to hers. She felt a connection so strong that it made her mouth go dry. "When the people you love die, you realize that anything can happen."

Milkah's body tensed. "That is exactly how…"

Javen nodded slowly, eyes still on hers. "I know. I have felt that too—that sense of safety that shatters when your worst fear comes upon you."

Milkah stared into his eyes for a moment. Then she swallowed and looked down. "It is why I doubt the One God now. I almost gave in at the temple. I wanted answers so badly."

"But you did not give in. And that is what matters." Javen shifted his gaze to the current that ran alongside the boat. He stood in silence for a moment. "You know, it is why I turned to the One God."

"Because your father died?"

"Yes. And we lost our boat with him, so we had no way to live after that. I was desperate to feel…" He frowned. "I do not know. I needed to know that someone cared what happened to us."

"And you believe that the One God cares?"

"Yes. I am sure of it."

Milkah gave a humorless laugh. "So I have come close to losing my faith while you have gained yours."

"I do not think you are losing your faith. I think you are finding a deeper one."

Milkah shook her head. "I always had faith. Before, I mean."

"I know. I am sorry—I did not mean that you were lacking faith before or that God wanted you to go through this to strengthen it. I do not believe God works that way. I just meant that you will come through this closer to God, somehow."

"I know I should not say this, but…it does not feel worth it."

Javen shrugged. "You cannot help how you feel. And there is no right or wrong way to feel. It is actions that matter. And you resisted at the temple. You are stronger than you realize."

Milkah did not respond.

"It is not good what has happened to you," Javen added. "But God can bring good out of it, even though that seems impossible."

"It does seem impossible."

"Job must have felt the same way."

Milkah grunted. "God came down and spoke to him. At least Job knows he matters. He was worth God's time."

Javen did not respond right away. The pole slid through the river, and water splashed the side of the boat. The noise and smells of the city felt distant now. Milkah turned to look behind them. The massive walls of the city looked small and insignificant, as if Ur were nothing but a child's toy.

"He might appear to you in other ways."

Milkah turned back to Javen. "How?"

"I do not know. But He has His ways. He reached me, did He not? He used a trader to do it." Javen looked down at the water. "He used Job. I never would have heard about the One God otherwise."

"Do you think that makes it worth it to Job? To have lost everything?"

"I do not know. Probably not. But it is something good that came from it. And I am sure more good will come out of it too. We will just never know it."

Milkah watched the eddies of water swirl around the boat as it disturbed the surface of the river. "I just wish that God would appear to me like He did to Job. I need to know that He is there. I need a sign."

"I do not think all of us get that."

"But that does not mean I will not."

Javen smiled. "You are right. It does not." But his eyes did not look convinced. "What sign would you like?"

Milkah furrowed her brow. "Oh, I do not know."

"You sure there is nothing you are hoping for?"

Milkah thought about how tales of Leviathan had followed her down the river. She had not been able to shake those images. "All right. I guess there is something." She hesitated.

"Go on. I will not laugh, I promise."

Milkah shifted her weight. "You know how God used Leviathan to show Job that the world is beyond our understanding and control?"

Javen nodded.

"And that we cannot come close to being as powerful as God, since He created a creature that is so much more powerful than we are?"

"Uh-huh."

"Well, I need to find Leviathan. If I do, then I will have my proof that it is all true and that the One God is in control."

Javen said nothing. He just stood in the bow of the boat, looking at her. After a moment he nodded. "I understand what you are saying. But few boatmen have ever seen the leviathan. And if they do—that is if they are actually telling the truth—they wish that they never had."

"I need to see him."

Javen sighed and nodded again. "All right. I will help you."

"You will?" She sat up straighter. "How?"

"I will pray that God sends you the sign you need. And I will keep watch with you."

Their eyes met, and Milkah felt the promise in his gaze. "Thank you."

Javen's expression faltered. "You might not thank me if we find him."

CHAPTER TEN

Milkah could smell salt in the air, and she sensed a subtle shift in the landscape. A cry caught her attention, and she looked up to see a gray-and-white bird with black-tipped wings soaring above the boat. She had never seen one of its kind before.

"It is a seagull," Javen said. "We are almost to the Great Water."

"It just floats up there, as if invisible fingers were holding it by a string." She cupped a hand over her eyes to shield them from the glare of the sun. "What a funny little thing."

"You will be seeing a lot more of them."

Javen was right. Soon the sky was dotted with seagulls. They surveyed the boat with beady black eyes before one dived from the sky to grab a loaf of flatbread. The others followed to fight over the crumbs, screaming and flapping as they attacked. Milkah leaped up, startled.

Javen laughed and Milkah relaxed. She saw the amusement in his eyes and joined in the laughter. "I did not expect them to come so close."

"They take their chances for bread."

Milkah watched the flock of seagulls as they rose from the boat and fled back to the sky, squawking as they went. When Milkah looked back at Javen, she discovered that he was already watching her. His amused expression had softened to something else. The look in his eyes made Milkah feel warm inside, as if he saw into her heart and mind and appreciated what was there.

He dropped his gaze as soon as she caught him staring. His face reddened, and he cleared his throat. "Look." He pointed across the bow of the boat.

They had reached the Great Water. Its surface spread out in front of them as far as Milkah could see. She squinted and tried to make out the end. There wasn't one. "But how can it just go on and on like that?" The sparkling blue sheet ran all the way to the horizon, where it blended into the sky in a gray haze.

Javen smiled. "I do not know. And it goes a lot farther than you can see from here."

"It does?"

"Yes. And they say that beyond the Great Water there is an even greater water." He shrugged. "But who knows? Maybe it is just a story people tell." He pulled the pole into the boat and set it aside, then stepped to the center of the vessel, careful not to rock it. Milkah watched as he hoisted a large sail, slightly wider at the top than the bottom. The cloth snapped as it caught the wind and the boat took off, into the endlessness. Milkah gasped then laughed. She liked the feeling of soaring across the water. It was the closest she would ever get to flying.

Milkah gripped the side of the boat and watched as the banks of the Euphrates slid away, until the boat was completely surrounded by water. Air whipped past her ears and blew strands of hair from her braids. Sunlight glinted across the surface of the water and winked at her. She twisted around slowly, taking it all in. Above her lay the empty sky, around her the empty sea. She had never felt so small before. Nothing had ever felt so vast or powerful as that great expanse of water. It was bigger and greater than the ziggurat had been. Something about that made her feel afraid but also in awe of what God could create. No human being could do this. That tower of bricks back in Ur seemed laughable in comparison.

Javen stayed at the sail, eyes set with concentration. He adjusted the ropes, and the boat eased back toward the shore, until they were running parallel to the beach. "We will stay on this course," he said with a quick glance at Milkah. "It is not safe to go out farther than this. Boatmen never let the shore leave their sight." He frowned. "Or that is the idea, anyway."

Milkah didn't voice what she suspected he was thinking too. His father had not been able to keep close to shore, where it was safer. A storm could come up suddenly and blow them into the deep, where they would never find land again, either. "Protect us, God," Milkah whispered before she realized what she was doing. It occurred to her that she had not prayed since the day that Urshanabi and Ninsun locked her away and she had begged God to set her free. Now, the wind took her whispered prayer and swept the words into the sky. Milkah looked up, and for the first time since that terrible day, she felt a shimmer of hope that God might be there, listening to her.

Maybe it was just the fear of the unknown that made her turn toward Him, but she felt the desire nonetheless. "Thank you," she added, and a tiny glow of warmth filled her belly. Milkah let the warmth sit there, as familiar as her mother's cooking fire had once been, and closed her eyes. She knew that the feeling wouldn't stay, but she would try to hold it as long as she could.

"Look," Javen shouted.

Milkah's eyes flew open. She saw a fish as big as a man leap from the water then dive gracefully beneath the waves. Another soared from the water, then another and another. She watched, transfixed. "They are following the boat!" She leaned over the side to see them better. Their skin was as smooth and slick as wet leather, and their mouths curved into playful smiles.

"They do that sometimes," Javen said. He was smiling as he watched them.

"They will not attack us?"

"No. They have actually been known to help people sometimes. They are good to have around. They keep the sharks away."

The sleek bodies slid in and out of the water, one after another, like children playing a game. As they drew nearer, Milkah heard a whistle and a click. And then, as quickly as they had appeared, the fish all dived beneath the water and disappeared. She stared into the sea, hoping to see them again, but they were gone.

"I have never seen a fish do anything like that before," Milkah said. She shook her head and grinned. "I have never seen a fish look like that before either."

"There are strange fish in the Great Water. In fact, I am not sure that those are actually fish. They do not act like fish. They act more like dogs, following the boats and playing in the waves, as strange as that sounds."

Milkah kept staring at the water, but the surface remained smooth and empty.

"And they breathe air like you and me," Javen added.

"But how can they live in the water, if they breathe air?"

Javen shrugged. "They come up to the surface to breathe through the top of their head."

"Stop it. That cannot be true."

"But it is. You watch them long enough, you will believe it."

Milkah's grin faded as she thought about it. "If creatures like that can live in the Great Sea, then why not Leviathan?"

"Why not?" Javen agreed.

Milkah didn't take her eyes from the water for a long time after that.

Kalumtum made sure that Milkah ground barley as they sailed. She crouched in the stern of the boat, near Javen, pounding the millstones over and over again. As she worked, they passed small fishing villages that dotted the shoreline. The houses looked small and squat in the distance, and the noise of the people and animals was lost in the crash of the sea. Sometimes they passed fishing boats bobbing on the water and could hear the voices of the fishermen drift across the surface. The men cast nets into the sea and hauled them in again as the sun beat down on their bare shoulders.

Whenever one of the fishing boats appeared in the distance, Javen's expression would turn serious and his eyes would stay on the vessel until they drew close enough to make out the men on board. As soon as he saw the nets, the tension released from his body and he would nod to Peleg. Peleg would nod in return and their boat would sail on, skimming across the sparkling, rolling water.

"What are you looking for?" Milkah asked Javen when he took a break to eat an apple and sip water from a clay jug. She straightened her back and set down the grinding stone.

He wiped his mouth. "What do you mean?"

"Every time we see a boat you stare at it. I can tell you are worried."

Javen took a bite of the apple and chewed. Milkah sensed that he was searching for the right answer. He swallowed and shrugged. "Not worried so much as aware."

"Aware of what?"

Javen sighed and turned the apple in his hand. "Sea monsters and storms are not the only things to worry about at sea."

"Pirates?"

Javen nodded. "We will all end up enslaved in a foreign port if they catch us. If we survive, that is."

Milkah instinctively looked out over the water. She saw nothing but a flat, empty plane stretching all the way to the horizon. On the other side of the boat, she could make out a brown strip of shoreline in the distance. She wondered if she would end up better or worse off if pirates captured them. Worse off, she decided. As bad as things had turned out for her, she knew that they could be even worse. That was one thing she had learned from losing everything. There were things to fear that she had never known to fear before. She had come to sense a threat behind every corner. "Why be a trader then? It does not seem worth the risk."

Javen threw the apple core into the sea and took a swig of water from the jug. "This is what I know. And the risk pays off. It is more than enough to support my family." He stood up and stretched. "And I am not sure that it really matters. Disaster seems to strike when you least expect it, wherever you are."

"It struck me in my own fields, in my own village."

Javen nodded.

"But I think you may be rationalizing the risk. You cannot pretend that there is not a greater chance of death on the sea than on land."

Javen chuckled. "We all tell ourselves what we need to hear in order to do what we have to do."

Milkah straightened her legs and leaned back onto her hands as she considered that. "You know, maybe you are right. I do not think it really matters."

"No?"

"Not if God is sovereign."

"You sound like you are finding your faith again."

"I said if." But Milkah had meant what she said. Something was shifting within her, even though the change was so small that she almost couldn't feel it. The vastness of the Great Water gave her the sense that there had to be something greater than her. "I will know for sure if I see Leviathan."

Javen rubbed the back of his neck. "You cannot always choose the sign you want. Do not set yourself up for disappointment."

Milkah looked away. "I need this. God knows that."

"God knows what we need better than we do."

Milkah didn't have an answer for that.

"What is this about the leviathan?" Peleg shouted from the bow of the boat. His footsteps followed his voice and the boat rocked from side to side under his weight.

Milkah looked up at him but didn't respond.

"She is curious, that is all," Javen answered for her.

"I hear a boat was lost to the leviathan between here and Dilmun not too long ago." He locked eyes with Milkah. "That monster will take a boat down like *this*." He snapped his fingers and grinned, but his eyes were not smiling. He leaned closer to Milkah until she could see the pores on his nose and the small, pitted scars on his cheeks. "So do not think about trying to swim for shore. You have no idea what monsters lurk just beneath the water, waiting for you. I have seen a man go overboard and never come up again. He did not drown. Something got him." Peleg stared at her for a moment before he turned around and strolled back to his post, whistling as he went.

Milkah glanced up at Javen. He looked irritated. "Do not listen to him," Javen said, low enough that Peleg couldn't hear. "He is trying to scare you because he is worried that you will try to escape before we get to Dilmun. He knows that anyone who grew up on the river can swim." Javen's eyes flicked to Peleg then back to Milkah. "He will not tie you up because Kalumtum does not want to grind the barley herself." He shifted his weight from one foot to the other. "And anyway, I would not let him." Javen's face flushed red. She could sense that he was telling her more than he wanted to admit. "I told you that I will do what I can for you." His eyes moved back to hers. "I meant it. Do not give up hope. Wait for…" He frowned and turned his attention to where Peleg stood beside the sail. "I cannot say anything more. I have already said more than I should."

"Wait for what? What do you mean?"

Javen shook his head. "I have said too much. And I do not want to make promises I cannot keep. But do not lose hope, Milkah." His jaw flexed. "There might be a way out of this for you."

"How?"

But Javen didn't stay to answer. He hurried back to his post, leaving Milkah to wonder if she should dare to hope.

They camped on the beach that night, and Milkah baked them bread with the barley she had ground, just as she had done on the banks of the Euphrates. The evening felt the same as that one, except now the air smelled of salt instead of mud, and waves lapped the shore. The days took on a predictable rhythm after that, sailing beneath the sun, then camping after it set as darkness spread across the sea. Milkah loved the sunsets best of all, when the fire died down and the world became as still as the purple sky, and the water reflected the color like a copper mirror.

During the long days at sea, Kalumtum kept Milkah busy at the hand mill. But Milkah always managed to keep her eyes on the water, searching and waiting. One afternoon, when the sunlight glinted across the surface and forced her eyes downward, Milkah thought she caught a glimpse of movement far away. She dropped the grinding stone and cupped her hands over her eyes to block the light.

There was nothing there. Milkah waited. She was sure she had seen something. The seconds ticked by as her pulse tapped inside her temple. Then, in the distance, a huge, dark form slid across the surface of the water. Milkah leaped to her feet. "Javen!"

He was at her side in an instant. She could feel his arm against hers, barely touching, but warm and familiar. Milkah knew that he would have an explanation for what she had seen. "Could it be…?"

Javen squinted into the sun. They waited. "What did you see, exactly?" he asked after a moment.

"I do not know. Something big and dark. It just surfaced for an instant, and it was too far away to see what it was."

Javen's eyes roved back and forth, and then he put a hand on Milkah's arm. "Look," he whispered. He pointed to the water right in front of them. Milkah stared down, unsure of what to look for. Then she slowly realized that the water was the wrong color. It was too dark. At first she thought it was a shadow. But then she realized that it was moving. Milkah gasped and took a quick, jerky step backward. Whatever was in the water was hovering directly beneath them. Suddenly the boat was too small. She was too small. The entire world was too small to hold such an enormous creature.

"It is all right." Javen's voice was low and even. Milkah wondered if he was telling the truth or just trying to keep her calm. She stumbled to the side of the boat and saw the same darkness filling the water. The massive body slowly rose, until it no longer looked like a shadow. Milkah could make out the rough, gray skin, covered in bumps and scars. She rushed to the far side of the vessel and the beast was there too. "It cannot be!" Milkah shrunk back, to the center of the boat, and pressed her back against the mast. "Nothing can be that big." Whatever lurked beneath the boat was as big as an entire row of houses. Bigger, maybe.

Kalumtum crouched in the bow and made the sign against the evil eye. Peleg was as still as a statue, watching with tight lips. No one spoke. No one moved. They all watched as the creature slid through the water, close enough to touch, right beneath them. The only sound was the hammering of Milkah's heart in her ears.

Long, hard moments passed before the dark body narrowed into a tail as the creature slid past them. They watched as it slowly eased through the water, traveling on. A deep, ragged breath escaped

Milkah's lips, and she realized that she had been holding it in. Peleg let out a nervous laugh.

A blast of mist shot up from the sea, and a sliver of wet, gray skin appeared. Milkah stared and realized that it was the top of the animal's head. The sharp rasp of breathing filled the silence. As it hissed in and out, Milkah remembered what Javen had told her about the smiling fish they had seen earlier. This beast was breathing air, just like those fish did, just like she did. She felt a strange connection at the realization. Right beneath the surface, under the wavering water, she could make out a huge eye. It stared at her, unblinking. Milkah stared back, transfixed.

Then the creature sank downward and disappeared. Milkah's attention darted back and forth, searching. She ran to the other side of the boat. But the water was empty.

"It is gone," Kalumtum said and made the sign against the evil eye again.

Milkah realized how weak her knees were, and she slid down the side of the boat and sat down hard. "You all right?" Javen stooped down beside her.

"That was not…" Milkah shook her head. "No, it could not have been."

"No, it was not the leviathan. You see these huge fish sometimes. They do not seem to attack ships, but they do overturn them sometimes. Maybe by accident." Javen shrugged. "Who knows?"

"It came so close to the boat." Milkah's heart still pounded in her ears. She couldn't quite believe what she'd seen.

"It was a close call. If it had surfaced a moment sooner…" Javen lifted his hands in a gesture of helplessness.

"Everything feels so random, so chaotic." Milkah shook her head as the realization came to her. "We could just as easily be drowning right now as sitting here, talking."

Javen sighed. "It feels that way."

"It just feels that way, or it is that way?"

"I do not know."

"Do you really believe that God intervenes when it comes to something like that?"

"I do. He created the world and everything in it, did He not? He made Leviathan and has power over it, so of course He can control what happens to us."

"Then why save us from that giant fish but not from the storm that took your father or the mad dogs that took my family?"

Javen didn't say anything for a moment. He studied the palm of his hand. "I cannot answer that. But I know God can. And that has to be enough."

CHAPTER ELEVEN

The days ran together beneath the blazing sun and salt-scented wind. Milkah's lips became dry and cracked, and her skin blistered. She learned to walk the length of the boat without stumbling and how to identify the fish that swarmed the surface whenever she tossed an apple core overboard.

"I could almost like it here," she said to Javen as they sat in the stern of the boat eating their noonday meal. The words felt wrong as soon as she said them, and she frowned. She was adjusting to a life that she wanted to fight. Still, a strange feeling surged through her as she realized that when the journey was over, she would miss this time at sea with Javen. After this, there would be no more moments that felt like freedom. She would never fly across the water again, wind whipping through her hair and salt water stinging her eyes while Javen laughed beside her. She would never see Javen again.

Milkah looked away. She didn't want to care. She had tried to resist his kindness. And even now, she wasn't sure that she could trust him. Except that he had proven himself in small ways, over and over. Milkah picked at the fig in her hand but did not eat it. Javen could still turn on her, as the others had. But why would he?

But then again, why had the others?

"I have always loved the Great Water," Javen said. He leaned back against the side of the boat and sighed. "Despite everything." He glanced at her and hesitated. "I have liked this journey more than any other."

"Why?" She was afraid to hear the answer.

He looked down at the barley bread in his hands. "Because you are here this time."

His voice and his expression seemed so sincere. Milkah thought about their quiet conversations beneath the blue sky or the night stars, when it felt like they were the only two people in the world, even though Kalumtum and Peleg were always hovering nearby. When the two of them talked, she felt as if Javen understood her. She felt like she wasn't alone anymore.

But she could not be sure that he was truly on her side. And even if he was, their conversations would end soon. He would let them sell her to a stranger in Dilmun and abandon her to a life of servitude. She hardened herself and pushed the need away. "I did not ask to be here." Her voice came out flat and distant.

Javen's expression shifted and his eyes looked tired. "No, you did not." He stood up and brushed off his fringed kilt. "I am sorry. I should not have said what I did." He stood there for a moment, his figure blocking the sun. She could sense his uncertainty. Then he turned and walked away. Milkah wanted to shout for him to come back and finish the meal with her. She had been enjoying their conversation. But she said nothing. It was better this way. She needed to keep her distance, no matter how charming and kind he seemed.

Milkah ate alone in silence after that. She kept her eyes on the water as she nibbled her loaf of barley bread, straining to see any sign of the leviathan. Occasionally she glanced over at Javen, across the boat. He never looked back at her.

A few small fish leaped from the water, silver bellies flashing in the sun, before they splashed beneath the surface again. Milkah wondered why they jumped like that, but she didn't want to ask Javen. So, instead, she just wondered. The fish did not reappear, and there was nothing to watch but the still, flat water that stretched without end before them. The sun sparkled across the surface like the jewels that the wealthy men and women in Ur had worn.

They passed a small fishing village, and Milkah squinted into the distance until she could make out the shapes of people in the shallows, throwing their nets into the sea. The voice of a woman carried on the breeze, then drifted away, into silence. She looked back toward the horizon and noticed something different. Milkah shifted her weight as she studied the distant, white blur. Maybe it was just a trick of her eyes. Or a low cloud, hovering just above the waterline. She dropped her gaze, rubbed her eyes, and took a bite of her barley bread.

When Milkah looked back again, the blur was closer and more defined. She stiffened. Her eyes narrowed as she strained to make out any details. Whatever it was, it was coming closer. The blurred edges had sharpened into corners. A sail. It must be a sail. But she could not be sure.

Milkah glanced over at Javen. He was busy adjusting their own sail. She moved her attention to Peleg. He was arguing with Kalumtum. Their voices were low but heated, and her gestures were sharp and frustrated. No one but Milkah was watching the water. She didn't want to approach Javen after pushing him away, but that was better than trying to talk to Peleg or Kalumtum. She glanced back at the white shape on the water, then pulled herself up and walked over to the center of the boat, where Javen was adjusting the ropes.

"Javen?"

He looked surprised to see her, and then his face fell into a frown. "What is wrong?"

"I do not want to make a big deal out of nothing. But I think there is a boat out there. And it is coming closer."

Javen's attention jerked to the horizon. His jaw tightened. "Hey, Peleg! Are you not watching the water?"

"Yeah, yeah, I am watching." But even as he spoke, his eyes were on Kalumtum, not the sea.

Javen's gaze cut to Peleg, and his jaw clenched tighter. "There is a sail out there. You are not watching."

Peleg's head spun around to see what was out there. "Look what you have done now!" he shouted at Kalumtum then stormed to the side of the boat. She glared at him and stalked into the shelter. The cloth flap that covered the doorway dropped behind her. Peleg lifted his hand to his brow and squinted toward the sail. "It is moving fast."

"I do not like it," Javen said quietly.

Peleg's face hardened. "I do not either."

"We just passed a fishing village," Milkah whispered to Javen. "It is probably a fishing boat, right?"

Javen didn't answer. His eyes were on the distant sail. The vein in his throat pulsed.

Milkah could hear the rasp of her breath and the quiet slap of water against the hull of the boat.

"I want you to go into the shelter with Kalumtum." Javen's voice was even and calm. Too calm. Something about his tone made her stomach feel hollow.

"What is wrong, Javen?"

"It is not a fishing boat. Please get in the shelter. And if they come closer, find a place to hide. Get beneath the bolts of cloth, or behind the baskets." He rubbed the back of his neck, his eyes still on the boat, his jaw tight. "Do what you can."

Then, as if everyone had suddenly come awake, the deck flashed with movement. Milkah dashed into the shelter while Peleg rushed for the sail along with Javen. As she ducked through the cloth door, she could hear the whir of the ropes in their hands. Their voices were low and sharp, the words lost in the wind. The boat tacked then picked up speed. She lost her balance and stumbled as she hurried toward the stack of baskets against the back wall of the shelter.

"Hurry!" Kalumtum commanded. "Hide me." She pushed a basket aside and stepped over a jug of fresh water. Then she pushed another basket aside, crouched down, and wedged herself against the wall. "Push them back in place."

Outside, the sail snapped in the wind. Ropes whirred as the men adjusted them. Peleg shouted something that Milkah couldn't make out. "Milkah!" Kalumtum motioned for her to hurry. Milkah reached for the baskets and shoved them in front of Kalumtum. She left a sliver of space, just large enough to slip into. Javen shouted something from outside, but the wind whipped the words away before she could make them out. Her belly churned as she darted behind the baskets to wedge herself beside Kalumtum.

"What are you doing?" Kalumtum looked at Milkah as if she had lost her mind.

Milkah gave her a similar look. "Hiding with you, of course."

"Oh no you will not." Kalumtum kicked the basket in front of Milkah and it toppled over. "Get out."

Milkah froze.

"Get out!" Kalumtum's voice rose to a shriek.

"But I have to hide." Milkah couldn't understand Kalumtum's reaction. "Javen said I should. It is all right."

"Who cares what Javen says? He did not pay anything for you. He has no say in what happens to you. Now, get out." Kalumtum shoved her away.

"But why? Why will you not let me hide too?"

"Because if they see you, they might not bother to look for anyone else. Let them take you, what does it matter?"

Milkah's brain moved slowly. She couldn't quite comprehend that someone would do this to her. But of course they would. She was no longer a person to Kalumtum.

"Put the baskets back and hide me," Kalumtum ordered.

Milkah moved stiffly, without thinking. She stacked the baskets in place and backed away slowly. The boat rocked beneath her feet. They were still flying across the water. She knew that Peleg and Javen were working the sails as best they could. But what if it wasn't enough? Her stomach twisted, and her heart thudded in her throat. After all that she'd been through, how could this be happening? Suddenly, all she wanted was the safety and security of the past few days. At least she knew what awaited her at the end of the journey. If the pirates overtook the boat, she would be hurtled back into the unknown. And what would happen to Javen? Would they take him too? Or just cut him down, right in front of her?

Milkah eased toward the cloth covering the doorway. Behind her, she could hear Kalumtum's ragged breath from behind the baskets. She could sense the fear and desperation in the small, sweltering space. The waiting was unbearable. Whatever happened, she needed it to happen soon. Milkah reached out and shifted the blanket a tiny bit, just enough to peek through a sliver of an opening. Her sweaty palms felt sticky against the rough wool.

Outside, Javen stood at the sail, his mouth set in a firm line, the wind whipping through his hair and flicking his kilt. He turned his head from the ropes to the sea behind him, then back to the ropes. Milkah couldn't see the boat following them, but she knew it was there. Their boat tacked to the side and her shoulder slammed against the door jam. Peleg passed into view. He was gripping a rope and his red face was slick and shiny with sweat. Then he stepped out of sight again.

"What is happening?" Kalumtum hissed from across the small room. Her voice sounded muffled behind the baskets of barley.

"I do not know. I cannot see. They are still working the sail."

"If the pirates make it aboard, you go up to them. Lead them away from here."

Milkah ignored Kalumtum. She kept her eyes on Javen as he struggled to push the boat harder. He kept checking behind him every few seconds, his expression hard and determined. "Now is the time for Leviathan to come, God," Milkah whispered. "Bring him here. Please." She imagined the monster's great, snakelike body twisting and coiling from the sea to block the pirates' boat from theirs.

But for what seemed like a very long time, nothing happened. Milkah was sure she could see the movement of the sun across the sky, so much time had passed as they waited and watched. Milkah crouched at the doorway, still keeping watch as the sun slid downward. She watched the fear on Javen's face fade into exhaustion, but the dread stayed in his eyes. As long as that look was on his face, she knew that they were not safe. She imagined the pirates' boat slicing through the water like the sharks that followed the fishing boats, sleek, silent, and full of violence.

As long as the wind held, they could keep tacking and fleeing across the water. But as soon as the wind died, they would be overcome. There would be more men in the pirate ship, each with an oar, and they would row until they caught Peleg's boat. And that would be the end for all of them aboard, one way or another.

The sun continued to slide downward. Milkah realized that she was hungry, but her stomach felt too queasy to eat. Slowly, the sky faded into a dark purple, then blackened. Stars flickered awake and spilled across the blackness, illuminating the sky with tiny, white pinpricks. "Thank You, God, that there is no moon tonight," Milkah whispered. Clouds crept quietly across the sky, blotting out the stars one by one. She watched until the deck filled with darkness as thick as the water beneath them. For the first time since the pirates appeared behind them, Milkah felt a surge of hope. "Thank You for the darkness, God. Hide us within it."

Milkah crept to the back of the shelter and collected jugs of fresh water and a couple of loaves of stale barley bread. Then she stole outside, eyes darting toward the open sea. She saw nothing but darkness. "Javen," she whispered as she moved toward the white sail, the brightest thing in the landscape of black.

"Milkah. Are you all right?"

"Yes, of course. But are you all right? I have brought food and water."

"Thank you." Javen didn't take his attention from the ropes in his hands or the sea in front of them. "I am starving. But I am glad you waited until it was dark. They were close enough to see us clearly by the time the sun set. Better if they do not know that you are aboard."

"Where is Kalumtum?" Peleg asked.

"Still hiding."

Peleg grunted and took a loaf of barley bread from her hand. He shoved a big bite into his mouth, chewed, and swallowed, then grabbed one of the water jugs from her. He drank it down in fast, hard gulps, then wiped his mouth with his forearm. "We have a chance if this darkness holds."

"It is in God's hands now," Javen said. He adjusted a rope, and the boat's path shifted slightly. Then he reached a hand toward Milkah without taking his eyes from the water. She put the barley loaf in it, and his warm, callused fingers closed around hers. She wanted his hand to stay there on hers, making her feel safe, but he pulled it away to bring the bread to his mouth. He tore off a bite with his teeth without ever taking his other hand from the ropes.

"You should have left a sacrifice at the ziggurat," Peleg said between swigs of water. Milkah could feel his cold, hard stare on her. "If they catch us, it is on you. I never should have taken you. You have been a curse on us from the beginning."

"She has done nothing wrong, Peleg."

"Ha! Defying Nanna like that? And what other gods has she offended?" Peleg took another sip of water and swallowed. "We ought to throw her in, see if that pacifies the gods."

"She has done nothing wrong," Javen repeated, his voice harder this time.

"Refusing to honor the gods is not nothing," Peleg muttered.

"You will have to throw me in first," Javen said. Milkah could not make out his expression in the darkness, but she could hear the determination in his voice.

Peleg didn't respond.

"And who will get you out of this then?" Javen asked. "We both know that you cannot sail as well as I can. They would have caught us by now if I were not here."

"They might catch us anyway." Peleg sounded irritated, like a child realizing that he would not get his way.

"And they might not."

There was a long, tense silence. Only the whir of rope and the splash of water echoed across the quiet. "You forget that my God does not live in the ziggurat. He is here with us now, and He hears our prayers without a bribe. When we sacrifice to Him, it is out of love, not fear. And it is not to convince Him to give us our way."

"Well, Nanna is up there, right above us." Peleg pointed upward, toward the invisible moon. "And maybe he is hiding tonight because Kalumtum and I did what was right and left him a sacrifice."

"The moon is not out because it is the time of the new moon. It has nothing to do with Nanna."

Peleg snorted. "And why do you think they are chasing us down during a new moon? See? It still goes back to Nanna. Think about the timing of it."

"Nanna cannot control when a pirate goes after us."

"Stop blaspheming on my boat. I will not have it. You will get us all killed."

Javen did not respond. He was focused on something else. Milkah could hear him murmuring softly. She wondered if he was praying.

"And what good is your God anyway?" Peleg asked. "What good has He done for Milkah? What good did He do for that man everyone is talking about? What is his name?" Peleg stopped for a second to think. "Job!" he shouted after a moment. "What good has He done for Job?"

"Quiet," Javen said in a detached tone. "The pirates might be close enough to hear. Water carries sounds. You know that."

"Answer my question," Peleg said, this time in a harsh whisper.

"He showed Job that the universe does not operate on cause and effect. God's ways do not always add up, from what we can see."

Peleg laughed. "What kind of god does not respond to our sacrifices or our obedience? You do right, and the gods do right by you." He nodded toward Milkah. "That is why people like her get what they deserve. You cannot feel sorry for someone like that. They have done it to themselves. Can you not see?"

"We have a boat of men pursuing us who will enslave you, same as her, if they do not kill you first." Javen's words were soft but edged with emotion. "If they catch us, does that mean you are getting what you deserve?"

Peleg made a strangled sound of frustration in the back of his throat. "Shut up, Javen, and just get us out of this."

"I am," Javen said. "No," he added quietly. "The One True God is."

Milkah realized the boat was tacking hard to the right and had been for some time. She had been too distracted by the argument. Peleg must have realized it at the same time. "Where are we going?"

"To the shore."

"You know the shoreline here?"

"I cannot see any better than you."

"Then what are you doing?"

"I do not know. But it just feels right." Javen pulled a rope and knotted off another one. "We will find out when we get there."

"You are taking a risk, Javen. You might go straight into one of their villages. They have to live somewhere near here. This is a dangerous stretch of coast."

"I know." Javen's hand stayed steady on the rope. "But I would be taking a risk to stay on the water too. As soon as the clouds clear, they will be able to make out the white sail. And if the clouds do not clear, the sun will rise eventually, and they will be sure to see us then. You know that they will not stop until they have caught us. They know we are traders."

The boat cut through the darkness. Everyone stopped talking and strained to see past the black wall ahead of them. But there was nothing to see but more blackness. Time crept by before a quiet rustling arose in the distance. "Palm fronds," Milkah whispered. They were almost to the beach. And then the bottom of the boat scraped sand, and the vessel shuddered. Milkah jerked forward and grabbed the mast to catch herself.

Javen brought down the sail quickly, then shoved the rope into Peleg's hand. Peleg tied it off as Javen climbed over the side of the boat. There was a splash, and then the boat rocked to the side. Peleg sighed and followed Javen into the water. Milkah felt the boat sway and rock, then slowly inch forward. Peleg groaned as he strained to push the vessel.

"There is an inlet," Javen said. Peleg responded, but Milkah couldn't make out the words. The boat lurched forward, then lifted as the bottom cleared the sand. The two men scrambled back onto the boat. Peleg's heavy body hit the deck with a thud as he toppled onto his side. Javen managed to land on his feet then leaped back up fast, like a cat. He offered Peleg a hand, but Peleg waved it away and pushed himself up with a grunt.

Peleg and Javen hurried to grab a pair of wooden oars, dipped them into the water, and eased the boat forward. Water splashed as the oars swept through the water. A bird cried out from the shore, unseen in the darkness. They could not make out where they were going and Milkah's body tensed as she waited for the boat to strike something. But the vessel kept sliding through the water, slowly but surely.

"What is happening?" Kalumtum whispered from behind Milkah. She heard the cloth flap rustle in the darkness. Footsteps followed. "Are they gone? Where are we?"

"I think we lost them. We have found an inlet."

"How?" Kalumtum asked. "You cannot see anything out here."

"My God told me," Javen answered. His oar slid through the water, then rose, and then splashed into the water again.

Kalumtum hesitated. "Your God speaks to you now?" She sidled closer to him. "How?"

Milkah heard Javen's hand thump his chest. "In here."

Peleg snorted. "This stretch of coast is littered with inlets. You just got lucky, that is all. Your God had nothing to do with it."

"Listen to you. You of all people know that nothing happens by chance. Did you not just say that when disaster strikes, it is because the gods allow it to punish us?"

Peleg snorted again. "We are not safe yet."

But Milkah knew that they were. She could sense it. God had spoken to Javen's heart. She knew He had. This was not a coincidence. The tension seeped from her body as the boat slid slowly forward, through the unknown. Wind whispered through the palm fronds, and an unseen animal splashed into the water. The oars kept rowing.

They were safe, but where were they? No one could know until the sun rose.

CHAPTER TWELVE

The sun rose bright and brilliant the next morning. Milkah woke from where she lay huddled in the stern of the boat. She pushed herself up on an elbow to peer outside. They had beached the boat on the shore after traveling as far up the inlet as they could. Now, the morning light illuminated the land that had been shrouded in darkness the night before.

Peleg and Kalumtum lay on the other side of the boat, still sleeping, but there was no sign of Javen. Milkah stood up, stretched, and scanned her surroundings. The narrow inlet was bordered by dry, sandy coastline dotted with rocks and grass. There was no sign of people or animals. There was no smoke from cookfires in the air, no bleating of goats or shouting of children. A splash caught her attention and her eyes darted to the shoreline. Something had just slid into the water and disappeared.

Milkah heard rustling behind her and padded to the other side of the boat, careful not to wake Peleg or Kalumtum. She saw Javen striding through the grass. He waved and smiled when he noticed her. Milkah smiled back then worked her way down the ladder propped against the side of the boat and hopped onto the sandy shore.

"Good morning," Javen said as he approached.

"Are we all right here?" Milkah peered over his shoulder, into the vast, empty expanse. A dry breeze rolled across the land and carried wisps of sand with it. She wiped the grit from her eyes and turned back to Javen.

He nodded. "There does not seem to be anyone around. It is a good hiding spot."

"You have been exploring?"

"Yes. I took a look around as soon as it was light enough. I did not want to take any chances." He looked toward the boat.

"They are still asleep."

"I am not surprised," Javen said. "It was a late night."

"For all they know, the pirates are camped right beside us."

Javen chuckled. "They take too many risks, even though they do not realize it. They do not think anything can ever go wrong for them."

"They are self-righteous, you mean."

Javen shrugged, but his eyes glinted with amusement. "Most people are, I suppose."

Wind whipped through the seagrass and rippled the stalks. Milkah took a deep breath and let it out slowly. "I think I like it here."

"It is peaceful," Javen said.

"Yes."

Javen looked at her for a moment and hesitated. Then he grinned. "Take a walk with me?"

Milkah almost refused, but her heart won over her head. She wanted to wander this strange, lonely beach with him. She even wanted him to slip his hand in hers as they strolled, side by side. The thought made her feel embarrassed and foolish, so she tried to put it aside.

"All right," she said and fell into step beside him. The sand was warm and soft beneath her bare feet. "You saved us last night," she said after a moment. As soon as the words left her mouth she wondered if she had said too much. But it was true. Without Javen she was sure they would have been overtaken.

He shook his head. "No, it was the One God. I felt led to turn toward land when I did. I had been praying, asking Him to show me a way. And then…" He kicked a stone on the beach. "I do not know, I just felt it, deep down, in here." He patted his belly.

Milkah nodded.

They walked a few paces in silence.

Javen scratched his head. His hair was uncombed, the dark curls loose and out of place. "It makes me wonder, though."

Milkah glanced up at him and saw that his expression was troubled.

"There have been so many times that I have prayed and have gotten no answer. Why this time?" A bird swooped down, splashed into the water, and darted back into the air with a fish clutched in its beak. Javen looked over to Milkah. "You have been wondering the same thing, have you not? You must have."

"Yes. Of course. It makes no sense to me."

Javen bent down and picked up a stick of driftwood. "We always prayed before going out to sea." Javen turned the stick in his hands. "Nothing felt any different the day my father was lost. There was no warning in my belly, no feeling from the One God. Nothing." Javen threw the stick into the inlet. It hurtled end over end, then landed with a little splash. "Why not then? Why this time?"

"I do not know." Milkah watched the stick catch in the under-tow and slide back toward the shore. "I have asked myself the same thing over and over again."

Javen gave a solemn nod. "I know you have."

"It is one of the mysteries of God. I know He protects us, but…" Milkah threw up her hands. "Sometimes He does not. Sometimes the worst still happens."

"It seems that way." Javen looked at her and grinned. "But not always. Not today. Today our God kept the danger away. He spoke to me. I want that to be enough. I just want to be thankful for that."

"Me too."

They walked on in silence, the sand crunching beneath their feet.

"Look at this." Javen crouched down and picked up a shell. He stood back up, brushed it off, and studied it. "Here," he said. Milkah held out her hand, and he dropped it in her palm. The curved white shell felt cool and slick against her skin. "It is beautiful." She tried to hand it back to him, but he shook his head. "It is yours."

"Thank you." She ran her finger across the shell as they walked. The thoughtfulness of the small gift made her feel like someone cared. She glanced behind them. The boat was far away, just a small dot on the shoreline. "Javen, do you think…" She tried to figure out how to say the words. "There is no one around."

Javen's face clouded. He looked away. "I tried, Milkah. That is the reason I went out alone this morning. It was not just to look out for the pirates. I thought there might be a chance for you."

"You mean…?"

He looked back at her. "Yes. I wanted to find a way for you to escape." He shook his head and turned away in frustration. "But there is no fresh water anywhere. It is just empty desert. We would not last." He ran his fingers through his hair. "And let us say we tried. We could walk for days and not find anything. Or we could run into one of the villages where the pirates live. They are all over this stretch of coast." He shook his head. "The only way we are getting out of here is by boat."

"That is why Peleg slept on board last night?"

"Probably. Although I would not abandon him to die here. But I might have tried to get you out, then sent help to come back here...." He shook his head again. "It's a child's dream, thinking that way, though. You know the law. And the threat to my family. If we are caught..." He did not have to finish the sentence. "But I just keep thinking that there has to be a way."

"I cannot believe this." Milkah squeezed her hands into fists. "Here we are, with no one to stop us, and we still cannot leave."

"That is all I have been thinking since I woke up this morning."

"There has to be a way."

"There will be, if God provides it." Javen looked around at the emptiness surrounding them. "But it is not here."

"Do really you think that He will? He has not stopped all of the bad things that have happened to me so far."

"He stopped the pirates from finding us, did He not?"

"Yes, but—"

"Then we know He is still watching over us. We know that He still stops bad things from happening—at least some of them." Javen frowned. "At least one of them."

Milkah thought for a moment. "Who knows what else He might have stopped? How many disasters might have happened that we will never know about?"

Javen smiled, although his eyes were still sad. "Yes. That is right. I had never quite thought of it like that before."

"It is a good way to think, if it is true."

"It has to be true."

"Yes."

Javen's hand brushed hers as they walked. Milkah didn't pull hers away. Instead, she looked up at him. His eyes warmed and he let his fingers stay against hers as they strode forward. Milkah's heart flip-flopped in her chest. The touch of his skin made her feel safe and free, even though she was trapped on the beach. She hesitated, then closed her hand around his. His eyes shot to hers in surprise. Then he tightened his fingers around her hand and his eyes looked happy for the first time in days. They walked in contented silence for a moment before Javen sighed and looked down. "I am sorry I have failed you, Milkah."

She leaned closer to him until her arm was against his. "You have not failed me, Javen." And she knew that she meant it.

They spent the rest of the day hidden in the inlet in case the pirates were still looking for them. A boat full of trade goods was a prize that they would not easily give up.

"We will have to eat from our food stores," Javen said. "We cannot risk smoke from a fire."

Peleg frowned but did not argue. They spent the day on the beach eating dried fish and stale bread. Javen took the time to check over the boat and make a few minor repairs. Kalumtum lay on the beach beneath the sun and ordered Milkah to fetch her fresh water and dates. Milkah stayed by Javen's side as much as she could, and they chatted about everything, from their favorite foods to their childhood fears, to their fondest memories. Milkah felt herself drawing closer to him, like a boat drawn down a swift current.

But then, just as she began to let go, reality stabbed through her, reminding her that this would not last. Dilmun awaited, and only the One God could save her from it. "Please, God," she whispered as she watched Javen, the sunlight highlighting his tousled black hair as he grinned down at her. "Save me from what is coming. Let me stay here with Javen, somehow."

They lingered another day, just to be safe. "Come out into the water with me," Javen said after they had eaten breakfast. He raised one eyebrow and grinned at her. The morning was already stifling, and the sun beat across her bare shoulder like a hammer. So she waded into the warm, salty inlet after him. The sand squished between her toes, and she reached for his arm to steady her. He smiled and took her hand. All around them, the water glistened gold beneath the sun, and the sky was so blue it hurt her eyes. "I do not want this to end," she whispered, loudly enough for only the One God to hear. Her heart ached in the midst of that happiness, because she knew that it was only for a moment, and then it would be gone forever.

They set sail the next morning. Their fresh water stores were running low, and they couldn't risk another day. No one could be sure how long they would have to travel before they reached an oasis. "I thought you knew these shores," Kalumtum said to Javen as the wind filled the sail and they drifted out of the inlet, into the Great Water.

"I do," Javen said. His mouth was set in a grim line, and Milkah wondered if he ached as much as she did at the thought of leaving their desert hideaway. "But we came ashore in the dark, without any sight of landmarks. And before that, we were traveling for hours in the dark, with no way to keep track of where we went."

Kalumtum sighed. "This has been a harder trip than usual. It cannot be over soon enough." She made a sign against the evil eye and settled into the shade beside the shelter.

"Harder than usual when I am doing all your work for you?" Milkah muttered, too softly for anyone to hear.

Kalumtum closed her eyes and sighed. "Wake me up when you figure it out, Javen. And Milkah, get back to grinding. And salt those fish that Peleg caught this morning. Actually, do that first, before they rot in this heat. Put them out to dry after you salt them. Then get back to grinding."

Milkah looked back at the inlet as it disappeared behind them. Then she turned to the pile of slimy fish waiting to be cleaned, salted, and dried. As she worked through the pile, her attention stayed on the water, as usual. God had answered their prayers to escape the pirates. Maybe He would answer her prayers to see the leviathan. Then she would know for sure that He was still there and that He was in control.

The day passed slowly. After a while, she forgot to be afraid that the pirate sail would reappear on the horizon. Sweat trickled down the back of her neck as she knelt over the grinding stone, scraping and pounding. Her knees burned and her throat felt raw. She licked her lips and leaned back on her heels. The time spent in the inlet felt as far away as the moon. "Do you know where we are yet?" she asked Javen when he passed by her.

Javen frowned, and his face looked troubled. She didn't like the expression. "No."

"Are we lost?"

"No. Not exactly. It is easy to get confused along this stretch. Everything looks the same. I will see something familiar soon. I am sure of it." But his expression did not look sure.

"So, do you have some idea of where we are?"

He nodded and scanned the shoreline. "Sure. There is a desert for a long way in both directions from here. I just do not know exactly where we are on it."

"So, it is all right?"

"It is all right." He flashed a crooked grin. "The One God is in control, remember?"

Milkah paused. "I still have not seen Leviathan. When I see Leviathan, then I will know."

Javen's smile faded. "God led me to the inlet. Try to hold on to that."

"There are inlets all along this stretch of desert." Peleg's voice. His heavy footsteps rocked the boat and he appeared around the corner of the shelter. "I already told you that we were just as likely to turn into an inlet as not."

Javen didn't answer.

"Well, what do you have to say to that?" Peleg asked.

"My God does not need defending. I know what He did. And so does He."

Peleg laughed. "Come on." He threw an arm around Javen's shoulder. "Take a look at this." He nodded toward the strip of land running alongside them. "I think it looks familiar." They walked to the other side of the boat, leaving Milkah alone to get back to her grinding.

Time slid by, until every muscle in her body ached and she had to stand up and stretch. The boat tacked suddenly, and she took a step back, trying to regain her balance. Her foot got tangled in a coil of rope, and suddenly the sky was wheeling above her and she was hurtling backward. She kept falling. Panic ripped through her. Where was the deck? It had all happened so fast, so unexpectedly.

And then the cold, hard sea slapped her body. Her brain registered what was happening as she plunged beneath the surface. She was being dragged by her foot, still entangled in the rope attached to the boat. Her sinuses burned with inhaled water. She clawed at the rope and managed to loosen her foot, then hung on for dear life to the knot at the end of it, gasping for breath as her head shot out of the water. She sputtered and spit and gasped again.

As soon as she caught her breath, Milkah screamed. "Javen!" she shouted. "Javen! Help!" A sudden, sick panic overtook her. If she lost her hold, the current would sweep her out to sea, and there would be no way for her to get back to the boat. She would drift away, farther and farther from shore, forever. "Javen!"

She heard shouting, and then Javen's body appeared above her on the boat, silhouetted by the sharp light of the sun.

"I cannot get back to the boat!"

Peleg and Kalumtum appeared beside him. "Get her!" Kalumtum shouted at Peleg. "She is getting away!"

Milkah tried to call for Javen again, but water filled her mouth. She coughed and went under. When she resurfaced, still coughing, eyes burning, Javen was gone.

"Peleg!" Kalumtum screamed. "Do something!"

"Well, what do you want me to do?" he yelled back at her. He gestured toward Milkah in a sharp, agitated motion. "She is gone."

"But you have to do something! I paid a lot for her. I gave up my favorite necklace!"

"What do you want me to do? Risk my life? Will that bring your necklace back?"

Milkah felt she was caught in a strange dream, drifting farther and farther away. Their voices carried over the sea, as sound often does across the water. None of it felt real anymore.

Then Javen reappeared. He launched himself over the side of the boat and dived into the water in a graceful arc. A rope whirred behind him, following him into the sea. Milkah realized that it was tied around his waist. "I am coming," he shouted as soon as he resurfaced. "Hold on. Keep fighting."

"Javen!" Kalumtum shouted. "What are you doing?"

"You will get yourself killed!" Peleg shouted. "And then what will happen to us? You are a fool."

Javen ignored them. Instead, he cut through the water, eyes locked on Milkah. "Milkah. I am almost there. Stay strong. Keep fighting. Do not let go of the rope."

Milkah held on as hard as she could. Her arms and her lungs burned.

"I am almost there."

"Bring her back, Javen!" Peleg shouted. "I will give you a cut if you do."

Milkah struggled to keep her head above the surface as Javen sliced through the water toward her. His eyes were hard and determined. Her heart pounded in her ears, dreading the moment when the rope came up short and jerked him back. That would be the end. No one would be able to save her then.

But Javen kept easing closer, until Milkah could hear the heavy hiss of his breath and see the saltwater beaded across his face and hair. She gasped and lunged toward him with the last of her strength. "Javen!" And then she was in his arms. His skin felt wet and cold, but his arms were as strong as ever as they locked around her.

Milkah felt her body collapse. She had given all she had. Her face began to slip beneath the waves. Javen kicked harder and managed to pull her above the surface. "I have you," he murmured. "Stay above water. We are going to be all right. I promise."

Milkah's legs had turned to stone. She had never been so exhausted. The world moved in slow motion around her, as if her body couldn't keep up with her brain. "I cannot keep going."

"You do not have to. I have you now." Javen glanced over his shoulder. "Pull us back!" he shouted. "Now!" Peleg and Kalumtum grabbed the rope and tugged. Kalumtum slipped and skidded across the bottom of the boat. "Brace your feet," Peleg shouted right before he stumbled. "Brace yours," Kalumtum shouted back to him. Milkah felt a yank on the rope. Slowly, she and Javen began easing through the water, back toward the boat. He kept his arms tight around her, kicking hard to keep them afloat. "We are almost there," he whispered. "Hold on a little longer."

She could hear grunts coming from the deck, following by muttering. "She will pay for this," Kalumtum said loudly enough for her to hear clearly.

"Do not listen to that," Javen whispered. "Just keep your head above water."

They kept sliding through the waves, until Milkah's back bumped against something solid and she realized they had made it. Peleg's thick, hairy hands reached down and clasped her beneath each arm. Then she was in the air, moving backward, the reed wall scraping her skin. She rounded the top and plummeted with a hard thud onto the deck of the boat. Her hip and shoulder exploded in pain where they hit. She lay in a puddle of water, sputtering and coughing as Peleg hauled Javen up into the boat. She heard him breathing hard as he collapsed beside her.

"Are you all right?" Javen asked from the floor beside her. His breath was still coming hard, and his chest was moving up and down too fast.

"Yes."

"Thank You, God," he murmured, then closed his eyes and let his head drop onto the floor.

She was saved. They both were.

But for what purpose, she did not know.

CHAPTER THIRTEEN

Peleg accused Milkah of trying to escape, but Javen cut between them. "Where do you think she was trying to go?" Javen demanded, his voice raised, his fists clenched at his sides. "The open sea?"

Peleg grunted.

Javen's jaw tightened as they stared at one another.

"I fell overboard," Milkah said, huddled against the side of the boat, still trying to catch her breath. "It was an accident."

"You know it's true because she called out for help," Javen said. "If she had gone over on purpose, she would have just slipped away and let herself drown quietly."

Peleg turned to glare at Milkah for a long, tense moment, then grunted again and stalked away.

Javen sank down beside Milkah and shook his head. "He should have realized that."

"He does now, thankfully." Milkah shivered, even though the blistering sun had already begun to dry her wool tunic. She did not want to think about what might have happened if Peleg had not seen reason.

"You are sure you are all right?" Javen asked.

"Yes. But are you?" Guilt and fear twisted through her mind as she watched Javen slowly recover his breath. He had given all he had to save her.

"I am good."

But she could hear the fatigue in his voice. He was slumped against the side of the boat, half sitting, half lying. "Are you sure?"

"Yep." He managed a weak smile.

Milkah felt so much emotion that she didn't know how to put it into words. Javen could have stood by, as Peleg and Kalumtum had. He didn't have to risk his life. But her life meant something to him. She had been so full of doubt for so long, but now she knew.

He cared about her.

She was not just a commodity to him. He was not trying to gain her trust in order to use and betray her. "Thank you, Javen," she managed to say. "You did not have to do that." She felt her face heat up at the words, knowing there was more behind them that she could not express.

Javen lifted his head and opened his eyes to look directly into hers. "Of course I did."

"No, you could have let me drown."

"I could never let that happen. Never."

Milkah hesitated. "Why not?"

Javen frowned and looked away. Saltwater slapped against the boat. Seconds ticked past. "Because you matter to me." His face was tense and serious. Milkah could sense how much it cost him to say the words.

"You matter to me too," she whispered before she could stop herself.

"But it is not enough." Javen's expression hardened even more.

"It is. I am here. I am safe."

Javen breathed in slowly, then closed his eyes and exhaled. "Not for long. I saved you just so that you can be thrown to the wolves in a few days from now. I am sorry, Milkah. I am so sorry."

"Do not be sorry. You risked your life for me. It is in God's hands now."

"Do you believe that? Really and truly?"

"I…" Milkah looked out over the sea, automatically studying the whitecapped waves for signs of the leviathan. Her search had become second nature. "I think so. I am trying to, anyway."

Javen nodded, eyes still closed. "You are not the only one I could not save." Milkah could hear the ache behind the words.

She waited a moment. "Do you want to talk about it?"

"I was with my father when we lost him. A rogue wave hit. Have you heard of those?"

"No."

"Sometimes a huge wave just comes up out of nowhere. No one knows why. They say it must be sent by the gods. Of course, those gods are not real." He shrugged his shoulders. "I do not know if the wave that hit our boat was sent by the One God or not. I do not believe it was. But it is hard to understand why He allowed it." Javen sat with his head against the wall, eyes still closed. "The wave over-turned our boat and swept us both away. The current took him in one direction and me in another. I washed up on shore and he never did. And that was that. I never saw him or the boat again."

"Javen, I am so sorry." Milkah wished there was more that she could say. She longed to reach out and touch him, but she did not move.

"I have never gotten over my being saved while he was not. He was a good man."

"So are you," Milkah said quietly.

Javen didn't respond.

"There is nothing you could have done."

"I have told myself that a thousand times. But I still do not believe it. Not deep down, in here." He tapped his chest.

"Now I understand why you want to help me. Why you risked your life to save me today."

Javen's eyes flew open and his gaze pierced into her. "You deserve to be saved."

"I did not mean that you do not care..." Milkah tried to find the words. "But you are not just trying to save me."

Javen's attention shifted to the horizon beyond them. He swallowed hard as he stared into the distance. "You are right. Something inside me believes that if I can save you, it would somehow make up for failing my father."

"You do not have to make up for something that was not your fault. But regardless, you have done it. You saved me today. You can let go of that burden now."

Javen thought for a moment, then shook his head. "No. Not yet." His gaze swung back to hers. "You are not saved yet. Not fully."

"You cannot control what happens to me. You have to put it in God's hands." Milkah gave a small, ironic smile when she realized what she had just said. "Now look who is the one arguing for God. It seems we have switched places."

Javen sighed. "Faith is not static. It waxes and wanes like the moon, depending on our season of life, do you not think? When it is at its thinnest, all we can do is trust God to catch us if we slip."

"Maybe that is when He reaches out to us the most," Milkah said.

"I like that idea."

"I do too."

They sat in silence for a moment. Javen's breath rasped in and out as he stared out to sea.

He shook his head. "But how can we bear it if He does not answer our prayers to save you?"

"I do not know. But we will, because we have to. Suffering will always come eventually. That is why we need Him. Because He sees us through it."

Javen's jaw clenched and unclenched. "He could prevent that suffering in the first place."

Milkah sighed. "I suppose He could. But can we understand how those things work? Is that not why God made Leviathan? To demonstrate that?"

Javen's expression softened. "Still on about your leviathan." He gave her a faint smile that crinkled the corners of his eyes.

"Yes, I am." Milkah raised her chin and flashed her own proud smile. "And I am going to see him. Then I will know I am right."

Javen moved his hand to hers and gently held it. His skin was warm and reassuring. She wanted to sit there in the sun, holding his hand forever, feeling safe and loved.

"Let us make the most of every moment that we have together, while we can," he whispered.

Milkah squeezed his hand in response because she did not trust herself to answer. Her heart was too full and too panicked, all at the same time.

Evening fell as Javen and Peleg steered the boat to shore. They all climbed down the side as the first stars winked awake. Darkness spread across the shore like a blanket. Milkah wanted to wrap up inside it, close to Javen's side, safe and content. Instead, she gathered palm fronds for the fire and made the barley bread, then roasted a fish that Javen caught. She and Javen sat close beside each other as they ate, their shoulders touching just enough for Milkah to know that he was there, steady and dependable. They didn't speak throughout the meal. Peleg and Kalumtum did all the talking, mostly about the profits they would make in Dilmun and what they would do with their windfall.

Every now and then, Javen would catch Milkah's eye and smile at her. Then she would feel the warmth catch inside and spread through her like a gentle wave. She wanted to lean her head on his shoulder, but she didn't dare. Not with Peleg and Kalumtum watching. Milkah was already worried that Peleg was suspicious of Javen. She had seen Peleg watching him and recognized the resentment in his eyes. Peleg was afraid that Javen would figure out a way to steal his property, as if she were a bag of barley or a copper armband that he might spirit away.

While Milkah cleaned up from the meal, a strange light caught her attention. She stood up, brushed off her tunic, and crept toward the shore. "Javen," she whispered. "Look."

The sea glowed a bright, unnatural blue. The color stretched out in long, undulating fingers that flowed within the waves. Whenever a wave crested, the blue shone brighter and lighter, then shifted back to a darker, glowing blue. Beyond the garish blue lay a deep, black sea, quiet with secrets.

"I have heard of this," Milkah said when Javen reached her side. "But I never thought I would see it."

They stood silently for a moment, utterly transfixed. The waves crested and fell as the blue shimmered and shone from within. "It is not possible," Milkah added, the awe forcing her voice into a whisper.

"I have only seen this twice before in my life," Javen said. "It is very rare. I never thought I would get to share it with you." His hand reached for hers in the darkness. The heat of his callused fingers felt right as they wrapped around hers. "Come on. Let us go in."

Milkah's attention jerked to him. "Can we?"

"Yes. It is not dangerous."

Milkah grinned. "All right. I would love nothing more than to be inside that beauty. It is like another world."

"Then let us disappear in it, even if just for tonight."

"We are almost to Dilmun, are we not?" Milkah wished she hadn't said the words as soon as they left her mouth. They almost broke the enchantment.

Javen swallowed. "Yes. This is our last night together."

"Then let us make it one to remember." Milkah took a step forward. Warm, blue water washed over her bare toes. She gasped as the glowing light swept across her skin.

Javen lifted her hand to his mouth and kissed it, then stepped forward with her. They exchanged a quick glance, then sprinted into the swirling, shining light together. Water splashed as they ran, splattering their clothes and dampening their faces. Milkah could not stop smiling. She squealed when the water reached her waist and the light surrounded them. The wild, living mystery wrapped around them, as if they had passed into a hidden land of dreams.

"You should not touch that!" Peleg shouted from the beach.

"It cannot hurt you," Javen shouted back.

"It is a bad omen," Peleg said.

"Maybe," Javen said. "Maybe not. Who can know?"

Milkah wondered how anything so beautiful could be dangerous.

"The gods are speaking," Kalumtum shouted. "We ought to listen."

"Then what are they saying?" Javen asked.

"I do not know," Kalumtum said.

"Then how can you obey?"

Kalumtum grunted. "You are a fool, Javen."

"Because I do not believe in gods who cannot be understood?"

"No one can understand your God either."

"That is true. But my God has a steady character. I do not understand what He does, but I understand who He is. Your gods act on whims. They have no character, no faithfulness. My God does."

Kalumtum spit and made the sign against the evil eye. "What does it matter, if you cannot predict what your God will do any more than we can predict what ours will do?"

"It matters." Javen smiled in the pale glow of the cerulean waves. "It just does."

Kalumtum shook her head from the shore, then muttered something to Peleg that Milkah couldn't make out.

Javen squeezed Milkah's hand as they stood waist-deep in the water, watching the blue swirling around their bodies. Milkah traced her finger through the water. Everywhere she touched turned a lighter, whiter blue, before fading back to the darker glow. The world had transformed into a fantasy land and anything was possible. "Maybe it is a sign from our God." She turned to look up at Javen. His face was lost in shadow, save for the faint blue glow reflected across it. "Maybe He is telling us that He is here, in all His glory, ready to save us."

Javen smiled, pulled her close to him, and kissed the top of her head. The brilliant blue billowed around them and lapped against their skin. "Maybe," he whispered. Milkah could feel the need and hope in his words. It echoed her own and made her entire body ache as they lost themselves in the beauty and wonder, despite the fact that her world was about to end.

Peleg and Kalumtum slept on the boat that night. Milkah knew that it was to keep her and Javen from sailing away in the night to leave them stranded on the beach. Kalumtum lay beside Milkah in the shelter, pressed against her side, so close that any movement would have alerted her. When Javen stirred in the night across the deck, Peleg shot up to watch him. There was no opportunity to sneak away under cover of darkness. And even if there had been, the landscape was empty and hostile, with no sign of fresh water anywhere. They would not last long if they tried to traverse that barren countryside. Peleg and Kalumtum need not have done anything to trap them. Their surroundings created the prison.

The next morning dawned clear, a good sign that felt particularly significant after the appearance of the mysterious blue lights the night before. "The sky looks like God is announcing that He will bring good to us," Milkah said to Javen as they set sail. Memories of the night before still warmed her inside. She would never forget that once-in-a-lifetime moment surrounded by a glowing sea. And she would never forget that Javen held her hand and shared the beauty with her. "I think it is going to be all right, somehow."

Javen shifted his gaze from the ropes in his hands to her face. "You have found your faith again."

"It is hard not to believe that God is with us after last night. Only God could create such a wonder."

Javen nodded then turned his attention back to the sail.

Milkah did not want to leave his side. Even though new hope rose within her, her belly still quivered with dread. If God did not intervene, they would reach Dilmun by nightfall. She could not hold all the emotions at once and found herself staring out to sea, falling into a strange numbness.

"Still looking for the leviathan?" Javen asked.

"Yes. I am still hoping…"

Javen glanced up, toward the sun. He said nothing, but the hard lines on his face showed that he knew they were drawing closer to their destination.

"Tell me about Dilmun," Milkah said. She drew her knees beneath her chin and hugged her legs. "But only the good things."

Javen nodded. He understood what she was asking. "It is in the desert, surrounded by a vast wasteland. But underground springs flow into it, creating a lush oasis in the middle of nothing. There is green everywhere."

"I like the color green."

Javen nodded. He didn't say what they both knew. There was nothing good waiting for Milkah amid that green.

They talked all morning, until the noon sun beat down from directly above them with the force of a hammer. Milkah kept watching the sea the entire time. She was so busy looking for a sign of the leviathan that she didn't notice that Javen was watching something else. When she finally tore her eyes from the sea, stood up, and stretched, Milkah saw the crease in Javen's brow. His attention was not on the water. It was on the sky. She followed his eyes to see a gray haze on the horizon that stretched upward in a billowing cloud.

"Is everything all right?" she asked.

"Sure." But his voice did not sound as confident as Milkah would have liked. And his eyes kept flicking back to the cloud. She switched her attention back and forth from the sea to the sky after that. After a while, the sky that had been blue just a few hours earlier became dappled with gray, then completely covered. The sun was blotted out, its heat weakened through the heavy cloud cover. Milkah stopped watching the water. The darkening sky had taken hold of her. "It is closing in fast," she said.

Javen's jaw clenched, then unclenched. "It is."

"Should I be worried?"

Javen smiled, but it didn't reach his eyes. "What difference would worrying make?"

Milkah looked toward the land. She could barely make out a thin hint of brown. "We are far from the beach."

"The weather has been trying to push us out to sea all day. I keep having to fight to keep us close to land." He glanced over at the shore. "Hey, Peleg!" he shouted. There was a shuffling sound inside the shelter, and then Peleg appeared a moment later.

"Yeah?"

"We have got to head to land." Javen nodded toward the sky. "I do not like the look of that."

"I do not like it either," Peleg said.

The ropes slid through Javen's hands as he adjusted the sail. Wind billowed and snapped against the cloth. The boat shifted suddenly. A fat raindrop hit Milkah's face. She wiped it away and frowned. Another raindrop hit, then another. And then the sky opened up and a deluge of water struck them. Javen's expression changed, and Milkah knew they were in trouble. His knuckles turned white as he struggled to keep hold of the ropes. Wind whipped across the water and slammed into the vessel. It rocked and rolled as a wave rose with the power of an invisible hand to slap the side of the boat. Milkah tumbled to the floor and crashed against a basket. Everything had happened so fast. One moment they were all right. The next moment the sea had come alive, clawing at them with angry fingers.

"Javen!" Milkah shouted, but the wind swept her words away.

Lightning flashed and thunder boomed so loudly that she could feel it in her bones. Milkah braced herself as another wave crashed over the side of the boat, drenching her and knocking the vessel sideways. She rolled and skidded until she thumped into the reed wall, which had suddenly become the floor. Then with a mighty heave, the boat slammed back down and the floor was the floor again.

Panic surged through Milkah as she turned toward Javen. Rain fell in sheets, nearly blocking her view. He and Peleg were both fumbling with the sail, their faces hard, eyes set and determined. They were shouting to one another, but the wind tore the words away before Milkah could make them out.

She caught movement in the corner of her eye and saw Kalumtum scrambling across the deck. Another wave swelled beneath them, raising the boat higher and higher while she fought to hold on. Then the wave collapsed and the boat fell in a sickening drop that left Milkah's belly in her mouth. She caught a glimpse of Kalumtum sliding across the boat before the bottom slammed back against the sea and rattled her teeth.

Everything in Milkah screamed to run, to hide, but there was nowhere to go. There was no place safe. The sea was a swirling, living beast all around them, ready to devour. "God!" she shouted into the howling wind and salt spray that stung her face. "How can You abandon me now? After all that has happened? Where are You?" She felt a vague desire to believe, but it was sucked away by the wind. She had survived tragedy after tragedy, only to be destroyed now. The bitterness caught in her throat and took her breath.

A jagged streak of lightning exploded from the sky and speared the water. Thunder erupted in a noise louder than she had ever heard before. The air shook from the impact, and her ears rang.

And then there was a firm hand gripping her arm. "There is nothing we can do," Javen shouted loudly enough for her to hear. Rainwater streamed down his face. "Stay with me." He pulled her to him. His skin was slippery with water, but she felt the strength of his arms around her. "Stay with me."

"We are not going to make it through this," Milkah murmured. She did not know if he heard her. Thunder tore through the sky again, and another wave lurched beneath them. The boat rose in what seemed like slow motion. Milkah felt as if everything was happening in a faraway fog. It could not be real. She watched the bow tip higher and higher, until the water disappeared and there was only sky in front of her. And then the boat rose higher still. She heard a scream in the distance and vaguely realized that it was Peleg. The sky grew bigger and bigger in front of the boat, until her feet lost their grip on the floor.

"Do not let go of me," Javen shouted into her ear as they tumbled backward, down the length of the boat. The sky wheeled overhead, and Milkah was overcome with confusion as the sky and boat switched places and the rain roared over her. And then she plunged into the water. Her mind moved slowly, but her feet knew to kick. She surfaced, gasping for breath, and flailed in the water as she looked around her. "Javen!" Her heart thudded in her ears. "Javen, where are you?" The sea surged beneath her, and she felt herself rising on a wave, until she saw the boat below her. Then she plummeted down, and water rose like walls on either side of her.

She was alone.

The water was closing in. This was the end. The sea would cover her and she would be pushed under, deeper and deeper, never to see the sky again. "I worshiped You!" she shouted with her last breath, before the walls of water collapsed onto her. "I trusted You! Where are You now?" Never had she felt so alone or abandoned. Not even when she buried her family beneath the floor of their home, one by one. Not even when she learned that she had been tricked and betrayed. There was a unique terror of being trapped in endless, roaring water with no escape.

The water crashed over her head. Everything in her erupted in panic as her instincts fought to breathe. The force of the waves propelled her downward. She kicked and struggled, but she couldn't reach the surface. Her eyes flew open. Saltwater burned them as she searched for air. What was up and what was down? Her lungs were screaming now. All she wanted was to breathe. She had to breathe. She had to find the surface.

Everywhere was water. Up, down, all around was water. There was no way out. She wanted to use her last breath to shout at God and demand to know how He could let it end this way, when she finally had hope. She and Javen might have found a way, somehow, to escape and be together. He loved her. She was no longer alone.

And then God allowed a storm. How many storms would a righteous God allow one woman to bear?

Milkah's body shuddered. She had to breathe. Her lungs would force her mouth open soon and she would suck in water. The edges of her eyes sparkled with black. She had to find the surface.

Need and anger struggled within her while the water fought against her. As darkness covered Milkah's vision, she felt a knowing inside, a whisper that spoke in silence but was louder than the thunder. The silent voice did not condemn her for her anger and fear. The Speaker understood her bitterness and loss. Warm acceptance flooded her body. Live or die, she realized what mattered was bigger than her, bigger than she could ever imagine. Everything that she had ever known or experienced was smaller than a single drop in the vast sea that drowned her now. And the One God was vaster than the vastest sea.

She understood, now. Not completely—not even close to completely—but enough.

Suddenly the words tumbled through her mind before she knew what she was saying. They came from that place of truth deeper than herself. *God, please deliver me. But even if You do not, I am still Yours. I do not know why this is happening, but I know You do.*

A final surge of energy rocketed through her. Milkah kicked as the need for oxygen crushed her chest. Everything burned. She kicked again. And then, suddenly, her head popped out of the water and air rushed into her lungs. She gasped again and again, each breath coming in fast, desperate wheezes. Then another wave closed over her head, and she held her breath as it pushed her under. But this time, she surfaced again.

"Here!"

Milkah's head jerked around at the familiar voice.

"I am here!" Javen was in the water behind her. He struggled against the roaring current, eyes focused on hers. She kicked toward him, and his hand shot out to grab hers just as a wave washed over them. His hand stayed locked around hers. They came up sputtering and flailing, but they were not alone anymore.

"He heard me," Milkah shouted.

Javen's grip tightened around her.

"I do not know what will happen now, but it does not matter anymore." Another wave poured over them. The current tried to tear Milkah from Javen's grip, but his hand stayed around hers. They surfaced together, spitting and gasping for breath. "I am His, whatever happens."

"As am I," Javen said.

"I am not afraid anymore," Milkah said.

"Neither am I."

CHAPTER FOURTEEN

Milkah and Javen clung to one another, helpless leaves on a river, as the waves tossed them. Never before had Milkah understood the full power of God. But now she realized that a God powerful enough to create a storm like this had to be more powerful than the storm itself. That made His power beyond comprehension.

Milkah's strength was fading and so was Javen's. Each time a wave crested over them, he was slower to resurface. Her fingers were numb from clutching Javen's hand, and her legs could not keep kicking. The water had turned to quicksand. She could feel herself slipping away.

They did not have much longer.

A flicker of color caught Milkah's eye. Something beige was moving in the water. For a strange instant, she thought that it was the leviathan, cutting toward them, bearing the storm in its wake. But as she wiped the saltwater from her eyes, she saw that the beige object was bobbing up and down in the waves. "Javen!" She tugged on his hand. He was slow and sluggish to respond. "Look, there is a basket." It was as large as Milkah and buoyant enough to float on the water.

A look of fierce determination flashed through Javen's eyes, and he pushed them both forward. Milkah sensed that it was his last surge of strength. "Help us, God," she whispered before saltwater filled her mouth. She spit and coughed. Javen's hand kept pulling hers. They worked together, swimming side by side to slowly make their way toward the basket.

But every time a wave came, they would lose sight of the basket as the sea tossed it in a new direction. With each kick, it floated farther away, as if the water were playing a cruel game with them. Milkah felt her hope draining as her chest burned and her vision blurred. "Take me as Yours, God," she murmured. She would die belonging to Him, no matter what He did or allowed the sea to do.

A wave rose in front of them and the basket crested atop it, spinning and bobbing. Then the wave sucked it down, directly at them, and it crashed across their shoulders. Javen lunged and grabbed the basket then treaded water as he struggled to push Milkah onto it. His head sank beneath the water, but he kept pushing her upward until her fingers locked onto safety. The basket lay sideways, and she managed to shimmy higher onto it until she was out of the water from the chest up. The current tugged at her, but the basket kept her afloat. Hope surged through her.

Javen's grip loosened, now that Milkah was safe. But her grip did not. She tightened her hold on him and pulled as hard as she could while clinging to the basket with her other hand. Javen emerged from the water coughing and spitting. His free hand flailed upward and caught the edge of the basket. Milkah struggled to pull him up beside her. He was too heavy. "Javen!" she shouted. She was losing her grip on him. Then the sea surged beneath them and swept his body onto the basket, alongside hers. He sputtered and gasped, then looked over to her, eyes wide with surprise. "We made it?" he said, then more forcefully, "We made it!"

Another wave swept over them. But this time they bobbed along the surface and spun in a circle before dipping down into the trough, then back up again. "God is here, in the storm," Milkah shouted. And she knew it with all her heart.

They rode out wave after wave, clinging to the basket. Time moved with agonizing slowness, until the squall blew itself out as abruptly as it had erupted. The darkness eased back into light as the clouds dissipated. Sunlight broke free and its rays shone across the water in a golden path. Soon, the sky was a bright blue dome again, the sea calm and flat.

Milkah and Javen looked around, dazed and exhausted. Nothing quite felt real.

"I think we are going to live," Javen said.

Milkah heard herself laugh out loud. It was a strange reaction, but it felt good. "Yes, we are."

A thought struck her. "Where are Peleg and Kalumtum?" She turned her head from side to side, searching the vast expanse of water. "And where is the boat?"

"Gone," Javen said.

"Drowned?"

"Who can know for sure? It is in God's hands now. We will never find them again. They have been blown miles away from us by now, if they managed to survive." His face made it clear that he didn't think they were alive. He swallowed and closed his eyes for a moment. His expression shifted, and Milkah could see the struggle within him. His eyes opened. "You know what this means?"

The truth dawned on Milkah.

"You are free," Javen said.

"God saved me with the storm."

Javen just looked at her. There was nothing else to say. The reality of what God had done, or allowed to be done, was too overwhelming.

"I did not see it while it was happening. I was too afraid."

"I do not think anyone sees what God is doing while He is doing it."

Reality washed over Milkah in waves. Not only was God at work in the most terrifying and mysterious of ways, but she was free to live again. After being condemned to a life in captivity, she had been given a new chance. Nothing would ever bring her family back, but somehow, miraculously, she had been given her life back again.

And she would live it to the fullest. She would serve God, and she would cherish every single day.

Milkah's eyes swept the sea around her. She didn't care that water surrounded her and that she felt as small and powerless as a speck of dirt. She didn't care that there was nowhere to go, no sign of land and safety. Her faith had roared back like a lion.

"We have to make it to land now," Javen said. His face was serious. She could see the concern in his eyes. "We cannot survive for long out here like this."

Milkah didn't hesitate. "We will make it," she said. And she knew it was true.

The sun moved slowly across the sky as they drifted in the deep, endless blue. They didn't know how far they had been swept out to sea. And there was no way to fight against the current anyway, so they let it take them. "It is in Your hands, God," Milkah said as she stared at the horizon line, where blue met blue and blurred together. Water and sky stretched as far as she could see.

"He may not take us back to land," Javen said. His gaze was firm and steady, and not afraid. Milkah knew he could sense the peace too.

"No, He might not. But we will still make it, in a way."

Javen gave a little half smile. "I think I understand what you mean. Live or die, God is in control."

"There is a comfort in that, whether or not we like the outcome."

"I would rather die here with you than live without you," Javen said. "That is what would have happened if the storm had not come."

Milkah's heart felt so full that she could not respond. Instead, she leaned her head against his shoulder as the water lapped the sides of the basket and the sun dried their hair. As the day plodded by, her skin felt hot and tight and her lips cracked. Javen warned Milkah not to drink the saltwater, no matter how thirsty she became. The sun was relentless. She slid off the basket, careful to keep her grip on the side so that she didn't drift away, and dunked her head under the water. But the sea was too warm and salty to refresh her. Her throat burned with thirst. Javen helped haul her back onto the basket. It bobbed and dipped beneath her weight as she shifted into place. "You need water," he said.

"So do you."

He smiled down at her, and the corners of his eyes crinkled. "It will be all right."

"Yes."

Javen draped his arm over her and she snuggled closer. "As long as we are together." The burning need for water took her back to the small, sweltering room in Urshanabi's compound. "I have been thirsty like this before. Urshanabi and Ninsun would not let me have any water until I did what they wanted. It broke me. But now, I can endure it. I know that this is not the end, even if it kills us. God is bigger than us, bigger than our lives, bigger than our deaths."

"He gives us ways to endure the unendurable," Javen said. "They say you drift out of your mind before the thirst kills you. You forget the suffering."

Neither spoke for a moment. Milkah licked her dry lips. "We might live yet."

"We might."

But as they looked at the endless sea surrounding them, that seemed impossible. Milkah had never felt so small and insignificant, floating in the emptiness. But God had never felt so big either. Terror nibbled at the edges of her mind. Only the knowledge that the One God was there, in the water alongside her, kept her steady.

"I might be able to find our way when the stars come out," Javen said. They waited for the sun to set as they bobbed in the gentle waves, scanning the horizon for any sign of land. For the first time since she had been at sea, Milkah forgot to search for Leviathan. She realized that she didn't need to anymore. She already had her answer, even though the outcome might not be what she wanted.

They watched with thudding hearts as the sun slid into the sea and plum-colored shadows crept across the sky. The sun turned so bright and golden that Milkah felt she was sinking into another world. She was inside the beauty as deep, silent purple overtook the sky behind her, and streaks of pink and yellow danced across the water. They floated inside the ethereal colors, waiting.

But the stars did not come. The night was overcast. Javen sighed but said nothing. Instead, he just held her closer. They drifted in flat stillness, alone in the endless water. Darkness enveloped them, but Milkah continued to feel an inexplicable calm. The One God's peace spread across the sea with a light she could not see but that was as real as the cold, black water.

As she gazed into the darkness, Milkah pondered how often she had hoped to catch a glimpse of the leviathan. Now the thought sent shivers down her spine. Her feet felt vulnerable and exposed as they dangled in the black water. She remembered stories of bull sharks attacking people upriver. Here, in the depths of the Great Water, there would be bigger monsters. Her toes tingled as she imagined the razor-sharp teeth searching for flesh.

"I wish the blue lights would come back," Milkah said. Surrounded by that mystical glow, she would not fear the creatures of the deep. "But I am sure God sent them when we needed them the most."

Javen chuckled. "It sure does feel like this would be the best time for them."

Something thumped against Milkah's ankle. She screamed before she could stop herself. Javen sucked in his breath and his eyes flew to the water, searching the impossible darkness. "Was that you?" he asked, his voice edged with fear.

"Yes! Was that you?"

They looked at one another as the realization hit them. Both of them erupted in nervous laughter. "It is going to be a long night," Milkah said.

Javen flashed his signature smile. "I hope so. We would not want it to be cut short."

Milkah laughed again. Only Javen could joke like that. Water lapped at their waists as they dangled half in, half out. Milkah kicked her feet a few times. Her body felt tense and tight, waiting for the unseen to strike. "I have heard of a monster with tentacles that are longer than a house and with eyes as big as serving platters. Is it real?"

"Oh, I do not know." He looked away.

"You think it is, you just do not want to tell me."

Javen sighed. "I have heard the stories. I did not believe them until I went to a village where one had washed up."

"You saw it?"

"No. But there were too many witnesses for it to be a lie. There was truth to it, or some truth, at least. Maybe they exaggerated its size. Maybe it did not really have suction cups all over, like an octopus."

"I have heard of the octopus. People eat them, do they not?"

"When they can catch them. They are smart animals, strange as they are."

"So this sea monster is a giant octopus?"

"Not quite, from what the villagers described. But I suppose it's similar, in a way, since it has all those suction cups. I have never heard of anyone seeing this monster alive though, so who can really know? They must live down in the deep. Some people say that they only come up at night." He stopped and frowned. "I am sorry, I should not have said that."

"It is all right. If it is true, it would be true whether you say it or not." But Milkah shivered as she imagined long tentacles reaching up from the dark depths of the sea to suck her under. She pulled her legs up against the basket. "I have always heard that it is a myth, though."

"You are right. It might not be real. It sounds impossible."

Milkah thought for a moment. "Tell that to those villagers."

Javen grunted. "Yeah."

They said nothing for a while after that. But they both kept their feet tucked as close to their bodies as they could.

Milkah awoke with a start. She had not realized that she had been sleeping. "It is all right," Javen said. "I made sure you stayed on the basket. I will not let you slip into the water." She looked up at the sky. It was still as dark and impenetrable as the water. After that, Javen took a turn dozing, and Milkah held her hand over his to make sure that he didn't slide off the side of the basket and sink beneath the sea. But his hand stayed tightly wrapped around the wicker, even in sleep. He murmured and twitched, and she knew that he was not fully at rest.

As Milkah kept watch she began to hear a faint, distant sound. At first, she could not place it. But the noise grew louder and clearer as they drifted closer. She raised herself on one elbow and gazed into the darkness. She saw nothing. But she recognized that sound. It was the crash of waves against something solid. There was land ahead. There had to be.

"Javen," she whispered and nudged his arm. "Wake up."

His eyes flew open and his head jerked up from the basket. "What's wrong?"

"I think we are saved."

He squinted into the darkness.

"Listen," Milkah said.

Javen's expression cleared as the fog of sleep lifted. His face brightened. "Land," he said. It was the most beautiful word that Milkah had ever heard.

They both began to kick. The journey was painfully slow, and fear trickled back into Milkah's heart as the sound of the shore grew louder. They were so close. Now was the time that some disaster would come out of nowhere to rip their final chance away. A rogue wave. Another storm. A shark. The tentacled sea monster. Anything. Anything could go wrong now. She kicked harder, the taste of fear sharp in her mouth, like copper.

They both strained to see, but night stole any view of the beach. They had no idea how close they were, save for the sound of waves, growing louder. Something brushed Milkah's leg and she yelped. She jerked her body away from whatever it was but kept kicking, every muscle in her body screaming to outrun the danger.

"We are close now," Javen said. "There will be fish and seaweed. If something touches you, it is a good sign."

"It does not feel that way." Milkah grimaced and kept kicking.

"It is the last moment before safety that is always the hardest," Javen said.

And then something rough struck Milkah's foot. Then the other. The impact shot up her legs. She straightened them and felt the solid earth beneath her.

"We have made it," Javen said.

They rose from the sea, water dripping from their bodies, and forced their way through the surf. Milkah's steps pounded in time with her heartbeat. They were almost to good, solid land. A wave struck Milkah's back and shoved her down, but Javen pulled her against him to keep her upright. They scrambled toward shore until the water lapped at their calves, then their feet, and then they were out of the sea.

The warm night air felt strange and dry on their wet skin. Milkah dropped to her knees and panted for breath. Javen sank down beside her. They huddled side by side, too breathless and exhausted to speak. The only words they could manage were "Thank You, God."

They crouched on the beach until they caught their breath, and Milkah noticed the faint sounds of life behind them. There was a hint of smoke in the air, tinted with the memory of roasted fish. They turned to look, but the land was shrouded in darkness. Javen pulled Milkah closer to him. She shivered against him, even though the night was warm. "We need to be quiet," he whispered. "We do not know where we are."

They forced themselves up and moved silently along the shore, driven by thirst, until they found fresh water alongside the edge of what must be a village. They both drank deeply and desperately, until their bellies felt too full to hold anymore, and they collapsed to the ground.

Milkah stared into the darkness. A dog barked in the distance and waves drummed the shore. Other than that, silence. Had they survived only to be plunged into a new danger? After all that had happened, she knew that the worst might not be over. The thought was unbearable. All she could do was huddle against Javen, pray to the One God, and wait for the morning light to reveal their fate.

CHAPTER FIFTEEN

Milkah woke up to movement. Javen was pulling himself up from where they had collapsed. He rose to his full height as he scanned the landscape. The eastern horizon glowed with light, though the sun had not yet risen. Milkah looked at his face and her heart constricted. His expression was strange and unreadable. Something was wrong.

"It is not possible," he whispered.

"What is it?" Milkah scrambled up to stand beside him. Her body was stiff and numb. She brushed sand from her arms as she studied Javen's face. Panic licked at the edges of her mind.

Javen just kept staring at the land beyond the beach. The earth was still draped in shadow, but she could make out the silhouettes of palm trees and the cluster of low round houses.

"I cannot believe it," he murmured, more to himself than to her.

"What is it?"

"We are home." The words reached past the thudding in her ears to grip her heart. "What do you mean?"

"This is my village."

"But that cannot be." The fear evaporated like steam rising from a cooking pot. Awe swept through her in its place.

"And yet it is true."

They stared in silence, unable to grasp the wonder of it.

Milkah looked at Javen, not quite able to take it in. "Of all the random things that have happened, of all the coincidences…"

"This one is the most impossible," Javen finished for her.

"None of it was ever random."

"It could not have been." His jaw tightened as the emotion swelled within. "Not when something like this happens. Nothing could have washed us up on this beach but the One God."

"The same God who allowed your father to be swept away," Milkah murmured.

"The same God who allowed the dogs to kill your family," Javen added, his voice a raspy whisper.

"Who can understand His ways?" Milkah was frozen in place, the truth of the moment more than she could comprehend.

"All I know is that He is in control, through the darkest chaos."

"Yes," Milkah whispered. "How can we judge what He does, when He can do a thing like this?"

"Or create the leviathan and set it loose in the waters?"

They stood in silence for a long moment.

Then Javen took Milkah's hand. "Come on." He looked down at her and flashed the most genuine grin that she had ever seen. "I would like for you to meet my mother."

And then they were rushing forward, hand in hand, stumbling over rocks and driftwood, laughing and gasping for breath at the same time. He led her past a row of reed boats and fishing nets laid out to dry overnight. A child cried in the distance.

"The village is waking up," Javen said and picked up his pace. His excitement caught in Milkah's chest. They hurried onto a winding path that cut through the dry brown grass lining the shore. A donkey brayed, and a milling stone clattered.

A tight cluster of houses lay ahead of them. "There," Javen said and nodded to a round structure made of stacked stone with a wood and palm frond roof. There were footprints in the soft earth outside the entrance. "That is my house." They hurried to the low doorway. "Mother," Javen shouted into the dim interior. The smell of heated stone and damp animal fur drifted out to them. There was a rustle and thud, followed by a shout.

"Javen?" A short, plump woman with streaks of gray in her hair rushed outside. She gasped when she saw that it was him, then threw her arms around his neck as she began to cry. "You have made it home to us."

Four girls appeared in the doorway. Two of them were still children, the other two were at the age that comes after childhood but before marriage. "Is that you, Javen?" the youngest girl asked. She tilted her head to the side, studying him. She was skinny and deeply tanned, with disheveled black hair that looked as if she had just woken up.

"Sure is," Javen said and reached out for her. His mother still had not let go, so he pulled his youngest sister against them both with his free arm.

"You look different," the girl said in a voice muffled by Javen's side.

"*You* look different." He grinned and pulled her closer. "You have grown."

"We were afraid that you would not come home this time," one of the older girls said. Then she and the other two girls flung themselves into the group hug, until they were all tangled up together, laughing and crying.

Milkah waited while they celebrated the moment. Her heart turned to her own sisters and mother, who would never greet her again. She thought of her mud-brick home that she would never see again, so different from this round one made of stone. But she was here, alive, with someone who loved her. She ached with grief, relief, and joy all mingled together. She suspected that those emotions would war within her for the rest of her life. Her face felt hot as tears pricked behind her eyes. She quickly wiped them away, overwhelmed by the miraculous welcome and the loss that she still carried within her as a part of her own body.

"Wait, you have to meet Milkah." Javen pulled away from the hug. He was grinning as he looked toward her. His mother stepped back from him and dabbed her eyes with the back of her hand. The red beaded bracelet on her wrist clattered. "Hello, Milkah," she said. "I am Kubaba." Then her daughters introduced themselves one by one. The names were pronounced with a strange accent that rolled off the tongue like a song. "We are far from my home, are we not?" Milkah whispered to Javen.

"Yes. We are far down the coast of the Great Sea, closer to Dilmun than to Ur."

Milkah felt like a stranger among an unknown people, surrounded by fishing boats instead of irrigated barley fields. But then Javen took her hand and held it, warm and secure. "Milkah comes from far away, a good ways upriver from Ur. We have been through a lot together to make it home to you."

His mother's smile crinkled the corners of her eyes, and Milkah knew that it was genuine. She had seen enough smiles to know the difference by now. "Welcome home, Milkah. We are glad to have you."

"Home?" She murmured the word, trying out the feel of it on her lips. This was not her home. These were not her sisters.

Javen looked down at her and his brow creased. He glanced back at his family. "It has been a long journey."

Kubaba's face fell, the joy replaced with fear, as if seeing Javen for the first time. "You look sick, both of you. Something is wrong." She shook her head. "I was too happy to think…" She stepped toward Javen and grabbed his arm. "What has happened?"

"There was a storm. We were lost at sea."

"Go fetch fresh water." She motioned to her oldest daughter. The girl grabbed a clay jar from beside the door and jogged away, her feet stirring a trail of dust behind her.

Javen's mother motioned for Milkah to go inside. "Rest. I will get you something to eat. You must be hungry. You too, Javen."

Javen's youngest sister, Zimu, crept closer and tugged at Milkah's tunic. "I have a new goat to show you. He was born last night, and he's small enough to hold. He does not kick or bite yet."

The girl's hopeful expression reminded Milkah of her own sister. She had always loved animals too. "You will have to show me." Milkah's voice sounded hoarse. She licked her chapped lips. Suddenly she realized how exhausted she was. Every bone in her body ached.

"Let her rest and eat first," Kubaba said. She clapped her hands together in a decisive gesture. "Help me get a meal on, girls." She nodded toward the house. "You two go rest." Then she and her daughters began talking all at once as they headed around the side of the house to a courtyard enclosed by a low stone wall. Kubaba paused at the entrance and turned back around. "Let me look at you one more time." She stared at Javen as more tears welled in her eyes.

"My son, home safe with us," she murmured, before disappearing into the courtyard.

"Are you all right?" Javen asked in a low voice as he led Milkah through the doorway of the stone house. He had to duck to keep from hitting his head.

"Yes. I am fine." The interior was dark and still. Sleeping mats lay against the walls alongside a stack of reed baskets, a clay lamp, and a clay jar.

"Take any of my sisters' mats." Javen picked up one for himself, carried it to the far side of the room, shook it out, and laid it on the floor. "I am right over here if you need me."

Milkah nodded, too tired to get any words out, as she sank onto the closest mat. She laid her head down and felt the throbbing in her temples. Her vision began to blur as she stared at Javen across the room, leaning against the far wall. He was watching her with a concerned expression. "You need to rest too, you know."

"I will. But I want to make sure you are all right first."

"I am."

But his expression was not convinced.

His face was the last thing Milkah saw before darkness overtook her and she sank into a glorious sleep, deeper than she had ever known.

She woke to Kubaba's hand behind her head, gently pushing her up. "You need to drink." Milkah propped herself up on her elbows as Kubaba lifted a clay jar to her lips. She drank deeply. The good, cool water filled her belly, until she felt too full to take another sip. She shook her head and turned away from the jar. Next thing she knew, her head was back on the mat, her eyes were closed, and sleep was closing in on her again.

Occasionally, Milkah felt herself drift back toward the room. She heard low voices, felt a hot ray of sunlight across her face, smelled the scent of grilled fish and fresh-baked bread. But the world slipped away again, and she descended back into the warm darkness of sleep.

When she finally woke up, the sun was low in the sky. The room was empty. She stretched and yawned then pushed herself up from the mat. She felt like a new person. For the first time in weeks, she had slept the deep sleep of someone who knows that they are finally safe. She heard women's voices drifting in the air, followed by Javen's laughter. She padded outside and followed the sound into the courtyard.

"Milkah!" Javen scrambled up from where he was sitting on the floor, gnawing on a piece of roasted fish. "You are awake." A grin overtook his face.

"Come eat," Kubaba said as she motioned for Milkah. A simple feast lay on a wool cloth spread across the courtyard floor.

"We tried to wake you so that you could eat, but we could not get you up. We managed to get you to drink water though."

"It is still morning though, is it not?" Long rays of light slanted across the courtyard from a low sun.

Zimu giggled. "It is evening, not morning."

"Oh." Milkah felt groggy and disoriented but renewed. "I should have known that direction is west. I think I need a moment to wake up."

"You needed your sleep," Kubaba said. "Javen told us what you have been through. A day and a night on the open sea is a terrible ordeal."

"What about you?" Milkah looked at Javen. "Did you sleep?"

"Most of the day." He winked at her. "Just not as much as you, lazy bones." Javen and his family all laughed good-naturedly. It was the first time that Milkah had felt included in a family joke in a long time. She felt the smile come to her lips. Something stirred within her, something that felt right. She dropped to the ground and grabbed a fish with blackened, crispy skin. As she tore into it, the family chatted and laughed. Everyone was glowing with joy at Javen's return.

After the meal, Milkah leaned back onto the palms of her hands and sighed. Javen's sisters passed around a platter of nuts and apples dipped in honey. "I cannot eat another bite," Milkah said, but she took another apple slice anyway. The honey tasted sweet in her mouth. She savored every sticky bite.

After the moon rose in the sky and they had chatted for what must have been hours, Javen's sisters began to clear the clay dishes from the mat. They were still giggling and talking to their brother as they worked. One of the girls poured water into a bowl and stacked the dishes beside it. "Here," Milkah said, "let me help with the washing up." She rose from the mat and stumbled a little.

"No, no," Kubaba shooed her away. "Rest tonight. You are our guest."

Milkah felt strange. Yesterday, she had been a commodity to the people around her. Now, suddenly, she was a person again. Only Javen had seen her worth during the long journey that brought her here. She glanced over and saw him watching her. His face was serious, although the worry lines had disappeared since their arrival. He patted the mat beside him. "Come sit by me?" She smiled and padded over to him, then dropped onto the mat with a sigh.

"Feels good to rest, does it not?" he asked.

Milkah closed her eyes and leaned her head against the stone wall of the courtyard. "It does. I did not realize how much I was carrying until I was able to lay the burden down." They sat side by side in silence for a moment. Milkah listened to his steady, even breath and the clatter of dishes from across the courtyard. She opened her eyes and watched his sisters working beside the light of a clay oil lamp. They chatted in low voices with words that Milkah couldn't make out. Occasionally one of them laughed, and the others joined in. Light danced off their silhouettes and cast moving shadows against the wall behind them.

"You are not yourself here," Javen said.

"What?" Milkah turned to see him studying her. She could make out his features in the moonlight. "It is wonderful to be here."

Javen nodded. "But you are still troubled."

Milkah looked away.

"It is all right. You do not have to talk about it. But I am worried about you. I want you to be happy here. I want you to feel at home."

"But this is not my home," Milkah said.

Silence. Milkah felt her pulse tick in her throat.

"It could be."

His words made Milkah ache with joy and loss at the same time. She couldn't put the conflicting emotions into words so she stared at the ground.

"Do you want to go back to your village? I will get you there safely, if that is what you want."

Milkah looked up and met his eyes. She could see how much the offer had cost him.

"Or you could stay here, with us." He said the words gently, hopefully.

Milkah felt her heart jump, but she could not say the words that swirled within her mind, so she stayed silent.

They didn't speak for a while after that. Milkah watched Javen's sisters bustle in and out of the courtyard to finish the evening chores. Goats bleated from beyond the walls, and the salty scent of the sea drifted through the air to mingle with the smoke from the oil lamps. Zimu, Javen's youngest sister, entered the courtyard wiping her hands on her dress and made a beeline for Milkah. She settled down beside her and snuggled close. "Tell me about where you are from."

"I would not know where to begin," Milkah murmured. Zimu's skin felt warm against hers and the girl's curious expression reminded Milkah of her own sister, who had been about the same age.

"It does not matter where you begin, as long as the story has a good ending."

Milkah laughed and turned her head to look at Javen. Their eyes met over Zimu's head, and a look of understanding passed between them. "She does not know how wise she is," Javen whispered.

"I heard that!" Zimu said. "You are talking about me."

"Only good things," Javen said and pulled her closer.

Milkah leaned in, her shoulder touching Javen's, as his sister cuddled between them.

"I had a sister like you," Milkah began. "And she liked goats too. One time her favorite goat got into the courtyard and ate the bread my mother had just baked for dinner."

"What did your mother do?"

"Fed us dinner without any bread."

Zimu laughed, then lowered her head to rest against Milkah's shoulder. Milkah felt warm inside, but her heart still ached. How could she feel happy and sad at the same time?

"Tell me another story," Zimu murmured.

"She will be asleep soon," Javen said.

"No, I will not. I am going to stay up as late as you."

Javen chuckled. "I will tell you about the giant fish we saw. It swam right under our boat."

"How big was it?"

"Bigger than all the houses in the village put together."

"I do not believe it!" Zimu giggled and shifted to snuggle closer to Javen.

"Some things are real, even though they seem impossible."

Milkah listened as the stars wheeled slowly through the sky and Javen's soft, gentle voice told the rest of the story, until Zimu's breathing evened out and they knew that she was asleep, nestled between them.

But even in that warm, peaceful moment, Milkah could feel the emptiness and distance. There was a family here to love. But they were not her family. They were not her mother or her sisters. Nothing could ever replace what she had lost.

CHAPTER SIXTEEN

The night air was sweltering in the little stone house, so they all slept in the courtyard, where the sea breeze swept up from the shore to whisper against their skin. Milkah awoke to voices on the beach. She startled, afraid that she was locked in Urshanabi's house again, or trapped on a sinking boat. Then she remembered where she was. She heard Kubaba and her daughters shift on their mats and yawn. Across the courtyard, Javen sat up and rubbed his eyes. "Someone has just come back from sea."

There was another shout from the beach. Javen's mother stirred on her sleeping mat. "Your cousin has been trading with that overland caravan from Uz." She pushed herself up and smoothed her hair. "Could be him." She reached for a clay jar, poured water into a bowl, and splashed her face.

The light was still thin and weak, the sun not yet above the horizon. Zimu had wiggled across her sleeping mat in the night to end up against Milkah. The little girl's eyes opened, and she smiled. "Hello!" She threw an arm around Milkah. "I forgot that you were here."

"It sounds like your cousin might be here too."

Zimu's face brightened.

"Let us go down to the beach," Kubaba said. She adjusted her tunic and snapped on an armband. She and the girls hurried to braid and pin their hair, and then they all filed out of the courtyard, groggy but eager. Javen hung back to walk alongside Milkah. "How are you feeling this morning?"

"It felt nice to sleep here last night, with a family again. It was like it used to be, in the house where I grew up."

"It is a good feeling to go to sleep knowing that you are not alone, no matter how dark the night gets."

Milkah smiled. "It is."

"Even though my older sisters snore," Zimu said as she darted past them.

Milkah chuckled. She hadn't realized that the girl was listening. "We do not!" the two young women shouted back to Zimu. Kubaba laughed. "Do not tell lies, now."

Milkah's mind turned back to where her family now slept, beneath the floor of her old home. They would always be together now, through the long dark of sleep. No, that wasn't quite right. Their bodies were there, but she knew that they were actually with the One God now. They were in a place where darkness couldn't reach.

She and Javen made their way down to the beach as the rest of the family hurried ahead. "Maybe he has news of Job," Javen said.

"I hope so. Last we heard he was still suffering."

Milkah turned her attention to the commotion ahead of them. A group of villagers stood around a reed boat on the beach. A man with disheveled hair and damp clothing was gesturing with his hands. Everyone was talking at once. The man caught Javen's eye and waved. "Hello there! I did not expect to see you here."

"I did not expect to be here." Javen jogged the last few paces and hugged his cousin. They slapped one another's backs, then stood back and grinned. "This is Milkah."

"Hello, Milkah. I am Kushim." He elbowed Javen and grinned. "You are with this fellow? I do not know how you put up with him."

Javen and Milkah exchanged an awkward glance. They had not decided their future yet. But Kushim just chuckled and kept going. "You have been down to Dilmun?" he asked.

Javen shook his head. "Did not go as planned." He shrugged and flashed a smile. "Turned out better, actually."

"So you did well with the trading?"

"I have nothing."

Kushim looked confused. "But it went well?"

"Yeah, it did." Javen glanced at Milkah then back to Kushim. "I will tell you later. Tell me about your trip first. You have been up to Ur?"

"Met the overland caravan near there. It was good trading."

"What is the latest news?"

Zimu tugged at Kushim's arm. "Did you bring me something?"

"Maybe." He winked at her. "You will have to wait until we unload to see."

She groaned and scampered away to join the other children clustered around the boat. A handful of boatmen stood among them, greeting their families. One man picked up a toddler and swung her around as she squealed. Another man hugged an elderly woman while a middle-aged woman with a baby in her arms smiled at them both.

"You met the caravan from Uz?"

"Yep. The news is good."

"You have heard the latest about Job?" Javen asked.

Milkah leaned in closer. "Sure did. God has restored him."

Milkah tilted her head. "What do you mean?"

"He is healthy as a horse now. And he has regained his herds and flocks. He might not have as much as he did, but he will soon. His wealth is growing fast. And the best part is that his wife had a healthy child—a beautiful baby girl—and another one is on the way."

"That is good news," Javen said. His face lit up as he glanced at Milkah. Her expression remained solemn.

"Did God speak to him again?" Milkah asked. "Did He explain any of it?" Hearing that Job had been restored was encouraging, but it didn't feel like enough.

"No, God has not appeared to Him again. But He did not need to. It is a good ending. Everything turned out well."

Javen nodded. "I am happy for him. And it makes me feel better, somehow."

Kushim put a hand on Javen's shoulders. "I am glad to hear that." Unspoken words passed between them, and Milkah guessed that Kushim had mourned his uncle along with Javen. The air felt heavy with emotion for a moment. Then Javen broke the solemnity with a grin. "Now, what have you managed to bring back? My sisters will not give you a moment's peace until they get something from Uz."

Milkah watched as the boatmen and their families unloaded the trade goods and passed out trinkets to excited children. She hung back, not quite sure she belonged but happy to see the joy on everyone's faces.

"You are awfully quiet."

Milkah startled and looked over at Javen. "I did not realize you were there. Do you not want to visit with everyone?"

"I would rather spend some time with you."

Milkah smiled and looked down. "I would like that."

He led her down the beach until they reached a tree trunk that lay wedged in the sand. Water had smoothed the wood until it shone like the pebbles in the surf. They sat down, and the trunk shifted beneath their weight. Milkah lost her balance, and Javen caught her around the waist. "Easy now." He laughed and held her tight for a moment longer than he had to before letting her go. "Are you all right?"

"Yes."

"I mean about everything."

"Oh." Milkah didn't speak for a moment. She looked down and studied her hands. In the distance, the villagers stood in clusters, chatting and opening baskets of trade goods. "God has given Job new children, but what about the ones he lost?" Milkah kicked at a clump of sand. "Everyone seems satisfied with how things turned out for Job. But his children are still dead."

Javen waited quietly until she raised her eyes to his. "You are right, nothing will bring back the dead," he said. "But one day, we will see them again, when we go to join them."

A seabird swooped down in a flash of white wings to settle on the water. Javen shifted his gaze to watch as it bobbed in the swells. "Best I can figure, we have to learn how to accept a new life, one we did not imagine or want but one that can still be good."

"I like it here," Milkah said.

Javen's attention shot to her. "You do? I was afraid…"

"It just is not home."

"No." He nodded, eyes still on her. "I understand that."

"I have heard people say things like, 'home is wherever God is.'" She shifted on the tree trunk. "And that is true. But it does not give room for the grief. It does not just go away because we want it to or think that it should."

"You are right about that. All of it."

"You do not think I sound bitter?"

Javen looked surprised. "Bitter? Of course not. You have lost everything. You would be lying to yourself if you suddenly felt happy now, even with this second chance at life."

Milkah nodded. "I am thankful, you know."

"I know you are. And God knows it too. He is big enough to handle all of your emotions. He understands them all. After all, you are made in His image, right? He has these emotions too."

"Hmm." Milkah smiled. "I never thought of that before."

"Does He not grieve and mourn for His people? Does He not get angry at injustice?"

"Yes, of course He does."

"Right. And He is grieving with you, right now. He is not against you or your feelings. He created you to have them. He expects it. Feel all of it, Milkah, even if it seems like the grief will tear you apart. Only then will it start to get better. It will never get better if you pretend that it is not there. The One God does not want you to pretend. Why would He, when he always knows how you really feel?"

The mood in the village was bright with excitement at the return of Javen, Kushim, and the other boatmen. Not everyone returned from sea, so every reunion was cause for celebration. Javen's sisters were quick to smile as they went through their day, and his mother could not stop hugging him. But Milkah was quiet and contemplative as she fetched water, swept the courtyard, and fed the goats. Javen's words had struck deep.

"You are quiet today."

Milkah turned to see Kubaba standing beside her, a water jug balanced on her hip. "Are you feeling all right? Do you need to rest?"

"No, I…"

Kubaba put her free hand on Milkah's arm. "You are homesick."

"Yes, I suppose so. But it is more than that."

Javen's mother nodded. "Javen told me your story."

Milkah hesitated. She set down the basket that she had been carrying. "Do you really want me here? Did you mean it when you invited me to stay?"

Javen's mother looked surprised. "Of course." She glanced at her daughters then back to Milkah. "Has anyone made you feel otherwise?"

"No." Milkah swallowed. "It is just that, back home…"

"They did not want you anymore," Kubaba finished for her.

"You are not afraid that I will bring a curse to your house?"

"Are you afraid that you will be cursed by our presence?"

Milkah flinched. "No, of course not."

Kubaba chuckled and her eyes twinkled. "Then why do you think that you are the problem? Has our family not suffered too?

Has not everyone's, to some degree? Suffering is a part of being in this world."

Milkah wanted to fall into Kubaba's arms. She had not expected to be loved by a stranger. And this understanding that Kubaba offered was certainly love. As if she knew what Milkah was thinking, Kubaba lowered the water jug to the floor and embraced Milkah with both arms. Milkah sank into the hug. Kubaba smelled of woodsmoke and barley flour, the smells of Milkah's mother. She knew that the One God was there, in that hug, in that unquestioning acceptance.

"Now," Kubaba said, Milkah's head still buried in the soft flesh of her shoulder, "I know we cannot replace your family. But we can still be a family to you. A good one, I hope. I do not know what Javen and you have planned for your future, but I believe the One God brought you to me, and I want you to stay."

Milkah drank in the words. They eased the pain like seawater smoothing out the sharp edges of a shell. The grief was still there, but it was softer, more manageable.

"I had another daughter, you know."

Milkah pulled back from the hug to look at Kubaba. "No, I did not."

"I do not suppose Javen would have wanted to bring it up." Javen's mother nodded to a corner of the courtyard, where a fishing net lay spread across the ground. "I will show you how to repair the nets while we talk."

They sat down together, in the shade of the stone wall with the sound of the sea and the other villagers in the distance. "She would have been your age, if she had lived." Javen's mother picked up the net and drew it across her lap. "She was my first girl, and there was something so special about that. We did everything together when she was growing up. Then, when she got older, she became my best friend. We grew even closer after my husband died. She was older than my other girls, and she understood me in ways that they cannot yet." Javen's mother traced the net with a finger, her eyes far away. "She died of a fever. There was no explanation, no reason. She was healthy one day. Two days later, she was gone." Kubaba shrugged. "What you couldn't have known is that I have been struggling with the same feelings as you. You can never replace my daughter, but you can still be a daughter to me."

"Do you really mean that? You barely know me."

Kubaba patted Milkah's hand. "I trust Javen's judgment. And I trust the One God, who washed you up on my beach. That could not have happened by accident. He sent you here, I am sure of it."

"Then why did He let your daughter die in the first place? Why not save her instead of sending a substitute?"

Kubaba shook her head. "I have no answer for that."

One of Javen's sisters strolled past. "They are building a bonfire on the beach. Have you seen Zimu? She will not want to miss it."

"She was milking the goats," Kubaba said.

"Not anymore. I have just been out there."

"She is not in the house," another sister called out from across the courtyard.

"Well, she has gone down to the beach already, then." Kubaba squinted as she studied the net in her hands for broken cords. Then she threw it down. "But let us make sure."

Milkah felt a sense of unease slip into her belly. "I will go with you."

They hurried across the courtyard and past the jumble of stone houses. Milkah's eyes darted across the sturdy walls and palm trees. A girl about Zimu's age walked toward them with a jug balanced on top of her head. "Have you seen Zimu?" Kubaba asked.

"No," the girl answered. "Has she not gone down to the beach? I think everyone else has. I am going as soon as I can."

"All right. Thanks." Kubaba frowned and headed toward the shore.

The unease in Milkah's belly crept up her spine. She tried to swallow it down, but it filled her mouth with the raw, metallic taste of fear. "She has to be here, right?" Milkah asked as she hopped over a ditch with brackish water running through it.

"Oh, I am sure she is." Kubaba smiled, but it did not reach her eyes. "She is probably with her friends."

But when they arrived at the beach, Zimu wasn't there. Milkah and Kubaba scanned the shoreline. A bonfire burned on the beach, and the sparks danced into the sky as the flames crackled. Women crouched around it, roasting fish and goat meat. "There will be a feast tonight," Kubaba said, "to celebrate everyone's safe return." The aroma of roasting meat rose with the smoke to mingle with the scent of salt in the air. A handful of girls helped their mothers clean the fish and turn the goat meat on a spit over the fire. Kubaba trotted over to them. "Have you seen Zimu?" she asked.

"Not for a while," one of the girls said. She stepped back from the spit and pushed a strand of black hair from her eyes. Her cheeks were bright from the heat of the fire. "I think she went to look for driftwood."

"Which way?" Milkah asked.

The girl pointed down the beach. There was nothing there but emptiness and the slow rhythm of waves hitting the shore and receding again.

"Well, she is not there now," Kubaba said.

Milkah's throat felt tight. Everything had been fine a moment ago, but now, suddenly, she couldn't breathe. She stumbled away from the fire. No one could see her like this. Something was wrong with her. She had to get away. She had to escape. No, she had to find Zimu. Fear swirled around her until the edges of her vision blurred. Her heart pounded so hard that it felt like a hammer in her mouth. She took off running.

"Milkah!"

Milkah heard footsteps pounding behind her. But she couldn't slow down, she couldn't stop. She had to find Zimu. She had to stop this panic. She had to stop something terrible from happening.

"Milkah, wait!" Kubaba called out again.

Milkah stumbled and righted herself. Her breath was coming fast. Too fast. Dark spots danced in front of her. Everything felt strange and far away, as if she were wading through water or trapped inside a dream.

A hand caught her arm. "Do not worry, we will find her."

Milkah spun around. She tried to speak, but words didn't come out.

"It is all right. She always wanders off."

"I cannot… What if…" Milkah bent over and braced her hands on her knees. "I cannot breathe."

Kubaba put a warm, steady hand on Milkah's back. "It is all right. You are breathing. It just feels like you are not."

"I think… I think I am dying."

"It is all right. This happens sometimes. Especially after we have been afraid for a long time. Sometimes it happens when we finally know that we are safe and our bodies can let go of all the fear that we have stored inside."

"I am not afraid."

Kubaba rubbed Milkah's back in slow circles. "You sure about that?"

"I just want to make sure that Zimu is all right." Milkah's throat was starting to loosen. Her heart still thundered inside her chest, but she was beginning to catch her breath. "I need to sit down." She dropped onto the sand and pulled her knees beneath her chin. "You think I am overreacting?"

Kubaba crouched down beside her. "I think you are reacting exactly how someone would who has lost everything. I worry about losing the ones I love too. That is why I am out here on the beach right now, even though Zimu is probably fine. But that fear gets me too, sometimes."

"She might not be fine. We cannot know that. How can we ever feel safe again?"

Kubaba sighed. She looked out over the water. "Somehow, we find a way to trust the One God. And then, even if we lose what we love, we know that there is something greater to all of this."

"It all seems so temporary. It can all be gone in an instant."

"This life *is* temporary."

Milkah squeezed her eyes shut. She could see her pulse as a red, throbbing glow behind her eyelids.

"Ah, there they are. See, everything is all right."

Milkah's eyes flew open to see Javen and Zimu traipsing through the seagrass and onto the beach. Her body felt weak with relief. "It is all right for now, you mean."

"Yes." Kubaba looked at her with steady, knowing eyes. "And now is all that we have. Your fears may happen, but they may not. Either way, they are not happening now. Recognize that, or you will never have peace."

Milkah swallowed hard.

"Look at them," Kubaba said. "They do not even know that we were worried."

Javen strolled toward Milkah with one hand in Zimu's, their arms swinging, his steps light with confidence and happiness. He flashed a smile at Milkah. Her heart leaped at the sight of his face, the way his eyes crinkled at the corners, the crooked way his mouth curled up on one side when he grinned. She felt drawn to him in a way that she had never felt drawn to anyone else before.

Kubaba watched Milkah light up at the sight of her son. She smiled softly. "Enjoy what you can in life, while you can. We both know that anything can be taken away."

The thought struck Milkah like the edge of a knife. She realized that she could not imagine life without Javen. And, though she had only known them a short time, she could not imagine life without his family, either. She wished that she had never lost her family. But if she had not, she would never have found Javen. The contradiction made her feel strange inside. It was another mystery that she could not solve. She stood up abruptly, her body tingling with emotion.

"Talk to him," Kubaba said. "You will know what to say."

Milkah looked down at her.

Kubaba nodded. "Go on."

Milkah realized that she had not been able to embrace Javen, not fully. She had not been able to accept all that he offered. And it wasn't just the grief. It was something more. The panic that overtook her had shown her that.

Javen must have seen the warring emotions on Milkah's face, because his smile faded. She hurried to him as he watched her with guarded eyes.

"Are you all right?" he asked.

"Yes," Milkah said, then pulled Zimu into a hug. "We were worried about you."

"Why? Javen and I were looking for driftwood for the fire."

Javen frowned. "I am sorry we worried you. Are you sure that you are all right?"

Milkah nodded.

Javen looked at her as if he knew that she had more to say. "Take a walk with me?"

"I would like that."

Zimu scampered to her mother. Kubaba and Javen exchanged a knowing glance before she led Zimu back to the bonfire.

Milkah tried to find the right words as they strolled the beach in silence. The sounds of the villagers faded behind them, replaced by the soft pounding of the surf. "When we could not find your sister, I felt like I was going to die," Milkah said after a while. "All of a sudden, I could not breathe and I could not think straight. Everything in me screamed that there was about to be another horrible disaster."

"I am so sorry I took her to look—"

"No," Milkah cut him off. "It was not even about that. I thought it was. But really, I was feeling the terror of losing my family all over again. It all came rushing back to me and made me realize that I am afraid it will happen again."

They walked a few paces without speaking. Water washed over their bare feet and receded back again.

"I am afraid of losing you," Milkah said.

Javen jerked his head around to look at her. "You are? I thought, well, I hoped you felt... But you have been so distant... I was not sure."

"Are you saying that you feel the same way about me?" Milkah gave him a teasing grin.

"You know that I do," he said softly.

"Yes." Milkah's expression turned serious. "You were my friend when no one else was. You treated me like a person when no one else saw me as one anymore."

Javen said nothing. He looked down at their feet as they walked.

"I have never had a friend like you."

"And I have never had a friend like you." His voice was soft and hesitant, with an edge of expectation.

"So now I have a friend to lose. What if tragedy strikes again?"

Javen smiled his crooked smile, but his eyes were thoughtful. "What if it does not?"

Milkah slid her hand into his. "Then I would not want to miss out on all the happiness I might have here."

"I think you have a decision to make."

"But it is not quite that simple, is it?"

"No. It is a decision that you will have to make every day, for a long time."

Milkah sighed and leaned her head against Javen's shoulder. She felt the tension in her body ease and wash away with the water that swept over her feet. "It will not be simple or easy."

"Nothing ever is." Javen squeezed her hand. "But we will have each other, and we will have the One God."

"And your family."

"Our family." Javen stopped walking. He took Milkah's other hand and turned to face her. His eyes bore into hers, warm and steady. "Will you stay here with me? Will you marry me? I love you, Milkah, and I want to be with you for as long as the One God wills for us both to live."

Milkah's heart pounded in her chest. But this time, it was not fear. It was excitement at all that lay before her. The adventure of love and a new life, of the unknown future that stretched before them.

"I love you too," she said. "Yes, I will marry you."

Javen grinned and pulled her to him. She could hear his heartbeat against her ear. He was strong and alive, right now. And they were together. This was the life she wanted.

They stood, holding one another, drinking in the joy of the moment, until movement caught Milkah's eye. She moved her head and squinted toward the sea. There was a flash of light, the shine of the sun across a sleek, scaled body. "There is something there."

Javen raised his chin from where it had been resting atop her head. He stared out to sea along with her. The water was flat and calm, empty of movement. Long, orange rays of the evening sun sparkled and danced across the surface.

"It could have been the leviathan," Milkah murmured.

"Sometimes the eye plays tricks on us, especially when sunlight hits the water," Javen said.

"And sometimes the eye sees what is real."

They stared at the sea for a long time. Nothing changed. The smooth surface lay flat as a copper plate. She could not know what she had seen, or if she had seen anything at all.

"It will always be a mystery." Javen held Milkah close as the sea breeze swept over them and rippled the edge of her tunic. "Are you all right with that?"

Milkah waited for the frustration and anger, the longing for answers. It did not come. Instead, she felt the warmth from Javen's hand and from the sun on her back. "Yes," she answered and turned from the sea to look up at him. "I am."

FROM THE AUTHOR

Dear Reader,

I hope you have enjoyed this journey through ancient Mesopotamia. While the setting is a likely time period for Job's life, scholars are not certain of when he endured his trials. Regardless, the wisdom gleaned from Job's story remains as relevant today as whenever it took place, and his questions still echo throughout the ages. Milkah eventually finds peace despite her inability to solve the universal mystery of righteous misfortune. My prayer is that we can all find peace despite the fact that we will never have all the answers that would explain life's sufferings—because our God always will.

Signed,
Virginia Wise

KEEPING THE FAITH

1. Do you see any similarities between ancient Mesopotamian explanations for suffering and our explanations today as Christians? What differences do you see?
2. What struck you the most regarding the ancient Mesopotamian worldview and their understanding of their gods? How does their view compare and contrast with the Christian view of God?
3. What did you think about Milkah's line, "But his children are still dead," when referring to Job's restoration? How does this impact your thoughts on the Book of Job and its meaning?
4. What do you believe is the significance of Leviathan in the Bible?
5. Do you think that Milkah saw Leviathan in the last scene of the book? Why was it important to leave this sighting ambiguous?

LEVIATHAN: A CREATURE WITHOUT FEAR

By Reverend Jane Willan, MS, MDiv

Smoke rose from his nostrils;
consuming fire came from his mouth,
burning coals blazed out of it.

—Psalm 18:8 (NIV)

Leviathan is one of the most fascinating and powerful creatures in the Bible. It represents disorder and evil, and at the same time demonstrates God's control over His creation.

In the Old Testament Leviathan is depicted as a terrifying sea monster. For example, in the book of Job: "Can you pull in Leviathan with a fishhook or tie down its tongue with a rope? Can you put a cord through its nose or pierce its jaw with a hook? Will it keep begging you for mercy? Will it speak to you with gentle words? ... Nothing on earth is its equal—a creature without fear. It looks down on all that are haughty; it is king over all that are proud" (Job 41:1-3, 33-34 NIV).

The Bible uses Leviathan to illustrate God's unmatched, complete power over what He brought into existence. In Psalm 74:13-14,

God's triumph over Leviathan shows His might: "It was You who split open the sea by Your power; You broke the heads of the monster in the waters. It was You who crushed the heads of Leviathan and gave it as food to the creatures of the desert."

This passage proves God's role as the Supreme Creator who can tame and vanquish even Leviathan. The defeat of the sea monster demonstrates the establishment of order from chaos, a theme central to the story of creation. All creation, no matter how powerful or out of control, is subject to God's will.

Leviathan is mentioned throughout the Old Testament, specifically in the books of Job, Psalms, and Isaiah. In the book of Job, Leviathan is introduced as a formidable sea creature embodying the overwhelming forces of nature. The detailed description of Leviathan in Job 41 serves as a powerful metaphor, emphasizing themes of divine power and human humility.

God challenges Job, asking if he can capture or control Leviathan, a creature with impenetrable scales, fearsome teeth, and the ability to churn the sea. This great creature underscores the awe-inspiring power of the divine and reveals human limitations. By emphasizing Leviathan's might over human frailty, God reminds Job of his place in the created order. This encounter marks a pivotal moment where Job's perspective shifts from questioning to humility to reverence.

Psalm 104:26 also speaks of Leviathan: "There the ships go to and fro, and Leviathan, which you formed to frolic there." Here, Leviathan is depicted not as a menacing beast but as a creature of the sea, like any other, swimming in waters created by God. Even chaotic forces are under His control, part of the order of God's rich and diverse creation. Believers are invited to marvel at its intricacies.

Isaiah 27:1, though, presents Leviathan in a more combative light: "In that day, the LORD will punish with His sword—His fierce, great and powerful sword—Leviathan the gliding serpent, Leviathan the coiling serpent; He will slay the monster of the sea." This imagery portrays Leviathan as a force that God, sovereign and all-powerful, will ultimately defeat.

Leviathan is an image that has evolved significantly in both Christian and Jewish traditions. For example, in Jewish tradition, Leviathan represents an adversary God must conquer to establish order in the world. In the Talmud, an ancient Jewish text, Leviathan is described as a gigantic sea creature, so immense that it could envelop the entire world. The Talmud also speaks of a cosmic battle between God and Leviathan, symbolizing the ultimate triumph of good over evil.

During the medieval period, Christian theologians and scholars offered their own interpretations of Leviathan, drawing on the Bible and earlier Jewish commentaries. In these times, Leviathan came to symbolize the forces of evil that oppose God and His creation. This interpretation is evident in the writings of influential theologians such as Thomas Aquinas, who portrayed Leviathan as embodying pride and rebellion against God.

Medieval Christian art also reflected this symbolic understanding of Leviathan. It depicted Leviathan as a horrible dragon or sea serpent, often entwined with fearful imagery. These artistic representations served to reinforce the theological message of Leviathan as a monstrous embodiment of sin and the antithesis of divine order.

The Renaissance and early modern periods saw a continued evolution in the interpretation of Leviathan, influenced by new intellectual currents and artistic developments. Renaissance artists, inspired by classical mythology and an increasing interest in natural history, often depicted Leviathan in more naturalistic and detailed forms. This period also saw a renewed interest in the allegorical and moral dimensions of Leviathan.

In literature, the leviathan metaphor was employed by writers such as John Milton in his epic poem "Paradise Lost." Milton's portrayal of Leviathan draws on both biblical and classical sources, reflecting the era's combination of religious and humanistic thought.

Today, Leviathan continues to be a potent symbol in both religious and secular contexts. Modern Jewish and Christian theologians have revisited the leviathan motif, exploring its implications for ecological and existential themes. The sea monster's representation as a force of chaos has been reinterpreted in light of contemporary concerns about environmental issues and our relationship with nature.

In popular culture, Leviathan has found its way into literature, film, and even video games, often depicted as a colossal and terrifying sea monster. These modern interpretations, while diverging from Christian tradition, underscore Leviathan's enduring relevance as a symbol of the unknown and the uncontrollable.

Over time, the changes in the way Leviathan has been portrayed show how religious beliefs, cultural context, and artistic expression influence each other. By looking at how Leviathan has been interpreted differently throughout history, we can understand how religious symbols are constantly being adapted to reflect the concerns and values of different time periods.

Leviathan reminds us that sometimes the most fascinating and terrifying things in life are the ones we can't fully control or understand. Perhaps the real lesson of Leviathan is that no matter how powerful or frightening the challenges we face may seem, we can find comfort and courage in the knowledge that God's sovereignty reigns supreme over all creation.

VIRGINIA WISE

Virginia Wise is a *Publishers Weekly* bestselling author of Christian romance. A love of history and Plain living inspired her to write her first novel, which takes readers on a journey to an eighteenth-century Amish settlement on the American frontier. The author of nine novels, this is her first work of biblical fiction. When she's not researching or writing, Virginia enjoys painting, spending time with family and friends, and taking long walks in the woods.

REVEREND JANE WILLAN, MS, MDiv

Reverend Jane Willan writes contemporary women's fiction, mystery novels, church newsletters, and a weekly sermon.

Jane loves to set her novels amid church life. She believes that ecclesiology, liturgy, and church lady drama make for twisty plots and quirky characters. When not working at the church or creating new adventures for her characters, Jane relaxes at her favorite local bookstore, enjoying coffee and a variety of carbohydrates with frosting. Otherwise, you might catch her binge-watching a streaming series or hiking through the Connecticut woods with her husband and rescue dog, Ollie.

Jane earned a Bachelor of Arts degree from Hiram College, majoring in Religion and History, a Master of Science degree from Boston University, and a Master of Divinity from Vanderbilt University.

*Read on for a sneak peek of another exciting story
in the Mysteries & Wonders of the Bible series!*

A FLAME OF HOPE:
Abital's Story
BY BETH ADAMS

The servants had been preparing for the banquet for many days. King Ahab had insisted that no cost be spared, and Soraya had been happy to oblige, turning out more roasted meats, platters of cheese, and loaves of fresh bread than could be eaten in weeks. She had ordered honey and spices from the East, and the smells of the roasting birds and of the sweets, layered with nuts and flaky pastry and dripping with sweetness, filled the whole lower level of the palace.

Far from the kitchens, Abital had been kept busy as well, for Queen Jezebel had declared that she must have the finest gown yet for the celebration of the new altar to Baal. Abital had ordered silk from Damascus, this time a deep royal purple shot through with golden threads that would catch the light as the queen moved. She had worked for many weeks, sewing golden trim to the edges and fitting the fabric tightly against the queen's smooth skin.

"Does it look all right?" Jezebel asked as Abital draped the gown around the queen's shoulders. They had finished the final fittings earlier, and now Abital was helping the queen dress for the banquet in her rooms. Even with the doors to the balcony thrown open, the rain outside and the walls hung with dark-colored tapestries made the rooms feel gloomy. The oil lamps set around the chambers did little to brighten the space. The month of Adar was often quite wet, and though the rain brought the flowers back to life, everyone in the palace had grown tired of the rainy season, which never seemed to end.

"It is the most exquisite gown I have ever seen," Abital said soothingly to Jezebel. "And you are the most beautiful queen Israel has ever known. When they see you in this, everyone will admire your good taste and your beauty."

Abital had learned over the years she had served in the household of Queen Jezebel that lavish compliments always pleased the queen, and they also usually made her task easier. Jezebel's moods could be unpredictable, but stroking her vanity nearly always made her more gracious to her seamstress. Jezebel turned as Abital tied the golden cord around the queen's waist.

"You have never been more stunning," added Mara, who stood to the side, by the open archway to the balcony that overlooked the city. Mara was Jezebel's handmaid and served her in her daily tasks. Mara also often bore the brunt of Jezebel's temper and was quick to offer kind words to soothe her queen's fragile ego.

Jezebel studied her image in the polished bronze mirror. She turned to one side, then the other. Jezebel truly was a strikingly beautiful woman, a fact that she knew full well and used often to her advantage. Her smooth olive skin, glossy black hair, fine features, and large wide-set eyes made her hard to look away from, even when she wasn't wearing a gown that cost more than most Israelites would earn in a lifetime. The birth of her daughter, Athalia, last year had not ruined her figure, and she was as young and fresh as the day Abital had arrived at the palace. Jezebel smiled, pleased by her reflection, and turned back to Abital.

"This gown is exquisite," Jezebel said, nodding. "They will be talking about it for years to come."

"Yes, my queen." Abital ducked her head. "It was your design. I only made it happen."

Jezebel came from Phoenicia, a kingdom north of Israel, where it seemed the fashions were more elaborate than was customary in Israel. Abital had learned how to create gowns according to her queen's taste, creating styles that she desired, and that looked nothing like what everyone else in Israel wore.

"Let us put on the necklace the king gave you as well," Abital said.

Jezebel pulled her hair up as Abital fastened the thick gold band, adorned with rubies and sapphires, around her neck. Once the necklace was secure, Jezebel reached for a bottle of sweet perfume, scented with myrrh and balsam, and dabbed the fragrance behind her ears, then let her hair down and gazed at her reflection once more. She nodded. "It is time to go."

"Yes, my queen." Abital understood the cue to step aside.

"You will stay outside the doors, with the others, in case I need you." Jezebel did not wait for Abital to respond. Abital knew her role. She would not attend the banquet but instead stay close to the great hall, hovering just outside with the guards and guests' attendants, in case the queen needed an adjustment to her gown. Abital would smell all the delicious food but could only watch and wait in case she was needed. Mara stepped forward to open the door, and Jezebel walked out, her head high, her shoulders back, humming softly under her breath.

"I will be waiting outside the rear doors." Abital would wait a few moments before she left, so Jezebel would not be seen walking with a servant. Once the queen disappeared down the hallway and was headed toward the banquet hall, the guard Hiram following a few steps behind, Abital turned and smiled at Mara. "I am so glad she was pleased."

"Yes. Well." Mara began straightening her own robes, trying to arrange them neatly. "With fabric as fine as that, it would be hard to mess it up, would it not?"

Abital tried not to let the words sting. She should have known better than to think Mara might commiserate about the difficulty of pleasing the queen. She knew well how Jezebel liked to keep her servants on edge, playing them against one another to jockey for position. Whoever was in Jezebel's good graces had a much easier time of it, and Mara, who spent the most time with the queen, was anxious to be seen as her closest and most trusted servant.

"I know you bear the most responsibility to our queen," Abital said, hoping she sounded placating. She did not wish to get into a power struggle with the maid. "You do a wonderful job."

Mara held her chin up and said nothing as Abital slipped out of the room. Abital had just enough time to return to her own shared quarters to refresh herself before rushing to stand outside the door of the banquet hall. She took off the long, dusty garment she was wearing and replaced it with a newer tunic made of finer linen. Jezebel liked her maids to look presentable, and as the seamstress to the queen, Abital was sometimes given discarded odds and ends that she stitched together to make simple tunics for herself, though she was careful to not make her clothing so fine as to make the other servants jealous. She had once returned to her room to find a new garment ripped in two at the foot of her sleeping mat. None of the maids had ever confessed to the crime, but Abital knew better than to complain, and she had been careful ever since to keep her clothing simple and unadorned.

She smoothed down her fresh tunic, pulled a simple cloak over it, and twisted her hair up, fastening it with a bronze clip. Then she walked through the maze of narrow hallways that threaded through the lower level of the palace. She hurried to the kitchen area, where servants were scurrying, carrying platters loaded with meats and cheeses toward the stairs.

"Can I help?" Abital asked Soraya, the head cook, who was directing servants to take up platters and jugs of wine.

"Can you give Channah a hand?" Soraya smiled gratefully for a moment before turning back to the platters around her.

Abital came up behind Channah, a small girl who was trying to balance a tray loaded down with bowls of dipping oils. Abital reached out to steady the tray, taking one side so they each carried half, and Channah gave her a grateful smile. They emerged onto the main floor of the palace, with its wide hallways and ivory-colored floors. They gave the tray to Adinah, one of the servants clothed in fine linen and silk who would be distributing the food amongst the guests, before Channah turned and scurried back to the kitchen.

"Thank you," Adinah mouthed to Abital, before hoisting the tray and sweeping his way into the great hall.

Abital smiled and then found a spot to stand where she would be out of the way of the servants bringing food up from the kitchen. A few of the king's guards stood nearby as well, wearing the armor emblazoned with the royal crest, ready if the king needed them.

The noise coming from the banquet hall was raucous, and it was not hard to see that the wine had already been flowing for some time. Through the door, which continually swung open, Abital could see that King Ahab was seated at the center of the long wooden table, wearing a richly embroidered vest and a deep purple cloak. Jezebel sat to his right, smiling and laughing as she spoke with the wealthy merchant on her other side who had donated the money for the new altar. Members of the king's family, his closest advisers, dozens of the prophets of Baal, and most of the wealthiest men in Jezreel joined him at the long table, which nearly groaned with the weight of the roasts and pheasants and loaves and freshly baked bread. Decanters of ruby-red wine dotted the table, and goblets were refilled with abandon as the most highly placed men and women in the Northern Kingdom celebrated. The enormous hall, with its soaring ceiling and marble walls and floors, echoed with laughter and conversation and the song of the lute, played by a young boy on the far side of the room.

It seemed as though every person of consequence in Israel had been invited tonight. King Ahab, urged on by Jezebel, had just completed the building of the grandest altar in all of the land, dedicated to the Phoenician god Baal, which Jezebel had worshiped back in her homeland. Dozens of men had died in the construction of the temple, but though the foremen claimed the king was requiring them to work too quickly, leading to accidents, the king had only shortened the deadline for the temple's completion. The lives of the workers, he declared, were nothing compared to the glory that was due to the god Baal. The altar had been unveiled to all of the most important guests earlier that day, and the feast tonight was a celebration in honor of the deity.

Golyat, one of the king's guards, spent much of the evening trying to get Abital to leave her post to go to his rooms with him.

"Baal is the god of fertility, after all," Golyat said, leaning in toward her.

"No thank you," Abital said firmly.

"I can think of no better way to honor the sacrifices of our king." He placed his hand on her arm.

Under Hebrew law, being this close to a man would be forbidden, but it had been many years since King Ahab had governed the nation with a strict adherence to the Hebrew laws.

"No, thank you." She removed his hand.

"Leave her alone," said Elon, one of the older and kindlier guards. Elon had always been considerate to Abital and had known her *imma* when she served at the palace. Golyat listened to the older guard and stepped away, but he kept casting glances her way.

Abital decided that Jezebel seemed content enough, and the kitchen staff needed help as they cleared dirty plates and brought up more jugs of wine, so she stepped away from the guards by the door and took a tray of used dishes from the slight Channah and carried them down to the kitchen once again.

"Bless you," Soraya said as she reached the kitchen. The cook handed Abital two jugs of wine to take up the stairs with her again.

Abital made several trips back and forth to the kitchen before Elon stopped her. "The king is about to speak," he said. "You should probably stay. If the queen has need, it will be now."

Abital thanked Elon, and she returned to her place, waiting, watching as the door swung open repeatedly. Jezebel was still seated at the head table, a placid smile on her face. A few moments later, the king rose, and a hush fell over the room. Once he had the crowd's attention, he began to speak. Elon propped the door open so they could hear.

"I would like to welcome all of our esteemed guests to the palace tonight," King Ahab said. His beard was neatly trimmed and oiled, and the jewels on his fingers and his robe shimmered in the light of the lamps. "It is an honor to celebrate with all of you. This is a great occasion. Today, the largest and finest altar to Baal in the land now stands right here in Jezreel."

A cheer went up from the crowd. "I have no doubt Baal will bless Israel richly for her sacrifice and for this amazing honor." King Ahab's voice boomed through the crowded room. "There are many people to thank for this incredible feat. Among them, of course, is Gershon, whose generous gift made it possible for the marble and gold to be imported and the altar fashioned. Thank you, Gershon, for this generous gift."

Gershon, a round man with a bulbous nose, stood to receive the accolades and cheers from the crowd. A merchant who traded in spices and oils, he was known for his shrewd deals, and Abital had no doubt the recognition he was receiving now made it worth every coin he donated for the statue to be carved.

"But of course, none of this could have been possible without the devotion and urging of my beautiful wife, Jezebel, whose dedication to the god who controls the rain and thunder and fills our land with life is the primary reason we in Israel have the honor of this new altar." The king took Jezebel's arm and gently guided her to her feet, then wrapped an arm around her waist and pulled her close to him. Her gown shimmered and sparkled. She looked stunning.

"Your queen," he said to the crowd, which roared with thunderous applause. King Ahab leaned in and kissed Jezebel, and even when he pulled back, he did not remove his hand from her. Jezebel gazed up at the king with what most probably assumed was devotion. Only those who knew her well, who had spent much time in her presence as Abital had, could see it for what it truly was: triumph. The king desired her, and everyone could see it. He had built the altar for her, and in that moment, Abital understood who the most powerful person in Israel truly was.

"May our sacrifices appease Baal," King Ahab said, and he raised his goblet in a toast. "May our people and our land be fruitful, and may he bless Israel richly."

"May Baal bless Israel," the hundreds in the room repeated, but Ahab had already leaned in to kiss Jezebel again, and the way he positioned his body against hers said he was no longer listening to the crowd of supporters.

Another round of whoops and cheers went up, and just as Abital was beginning to feel uncomfortable, believing the king had truly forgotten hundreds were watching him, a thunderous bang at the end of the room startled them out of their embrace.

Abital saw that the tall golden doors at the far end of the hall had been thrown open, and a man in a ragged cloak and dusty sandals was storming down the aisle between rows of tables directly toward the king. His gray-and-white hair, its wild curls untamed, flew back behind him as he made his way directly to the king.

Elon and Golyat rushed into the room, and guards rushed in through the hall's other doors as well. The guards all raced after him, but the man did not falter or change his course. "King Ahab," the man cried, his hand raised, his finger pointed at the ruler. "The Lord God of Israel has sent me to give you a message."

Somehow—Abital did not see how it could be possible, but it was—the wiry man had eluded the guards and was still storming his way to the head table. From here, Abital could see that his cloak was torn and his feet were caked with dirt. How had he gotten in?

"Is that right?" Instead of anger, Ahab seemed more amused than anything. "And who, may I ask, are you?" He signaled to the guards to hold off, to leave the man be for now. They stopped, one guard on either side of him, Elon directly behind the man.

If the king had thought his attention might put fear into the man, he was wrong, and the man's voice grew louder as he neared the table.

"I am Elijah, the Tishbite, from Tishbe in Gilead, and I come with a message from the Lord." His voice boomed in the hall, which had fallen silent as the crowd waited to watch whatever would unfold.

The king crossed his arms over his chest, apparently unimpressed by this opening.

"Yahweh will not be mocked," the strange man cried. "As the Lord, the God of Israel who I serve, lives, there will be neither dew nor rain in the next few years except at my word."

King Ahab seemed to be waiting for this peculiar man—this man Elijah, from some place called Tishbe—to say more, but he didn't. Instead, Elijah whirled around, nearly knocking into the guards behind him. The guards grabbed him, pulling his arms behind his back and dragging him away, down the aisle that he had stormed up just a moment before.

"Lock him away," King Ahab said.

Abital watched as the oddball man let the guards drag him away. He didn't fight, just went limp as he was pulled toward the door.

Who was he, to burst in here this way, in the middle of a celebration, and to challenge the king? She didn't know what would happen to the man now, but she was sure it wouldn't go well for him.

After the guards had hauled the strange man off, they slammed the doors behind them. And then, after a long moment of uncomfortable silence, King Ahab clapped his hands.

"Let us put that strangeness behind us," he said, taking his wife's hand once again. "Let us remember that this is a celebration." With his other hand, he lifted his chalice. "To Israel, and to Baal."

"To Baal!" echoed the hundreds in the room.

A NOTE FROM THE EDITORS

We hope you enjoyed another exciting volume in the Mysteries & Wonders of the Bible series, published by Guideposts. For over seventy-five years, Guideposts, a nonprofit organization, has been driven by a vision of a world filled with hope. We aspire to be the voice of a trusted friend, a friend who makes you feel more hopeful and connected.

By making a purchase from Guideposts, you join our community in touching millions of lives, inspiring them to believe that all things are possible through faith, hope, and prayer. Your continued support allows us to provide uplifting resources to those in need. Whether through our communities, websites, apps, or publications, we inspire our audiences, bring them together, and comfort, uplift, entertain, and guide them. Visit us at guideposts.org to learn more.

We would love to hear from you. Write us at Guideposts, P.O. Box 5815, Harlan, Iowa 51593 or call us at (800) 932-2145. Did you love *Seeking Leviathan: Milkah's Story*? Leave a review for this product on guideposts.org/shop. Your feedback helps others in our community find relevant products.

Find inspiration, find faith, find Guideposts.
Shop our best sellers and favorites at
guideposts.org/shop
Or scan the QR code to go directly to our Shop

Find more inspiring stories in these best-loved Guideposts fiction series!

Mysteries of Lancaster County

Follow the Classen sisters as they unravel clues and uncover hidden secrets in Mysteries of Lancaster County. As you get to know these women and their friends, you'll see how God brings each of them together for a fresh start in life.

Secrets of Wayfarers Inn

Retired schoolteachers find themselves owners of an old warehouse-turned-inn that is filled with hidden passages, buried secrets, and stunning surprises that will set them on a course to puzzling mysteries from the Underground Railroad.

Tearoom Mysteries Series

Mix one stately Victorian home, a charming lakeside town in Maine, and two adventurous cousins with a passion for tea and hospitality. Add a large scoop of intriguing mystery, and sprinkle generously with faith, family, and friends, and you have the recipe for *Tearoom Mysteries*.

Ordinary Women of the Bible

Richly imagined stories—based on facts from the Bible—have all the plot twists and suspense of a great mystery, while bringing you fascinating insights on what it was like to be a woman living in the ancient world.

To learn more about these books, visit Guideposts.org/Shop

Printed in the United States
by Baker & Taylor Publisher Services